Dream Lover

Suzanne Jenkins

D1715720

2012

1
Cindy

I think I am living a nightmare. I'm frantic because for over a month now, the man I am seeing, I *was* seeing, has not called me. He often drops out of sight for two or three days, but like clockwork, he'll call by the fourth day, always with an excuse. His wife was suspicious; his mother was sick; work was pilling up.

My office is on Wall Street, down about four buildings from Exchange Place where his is located. He has forbidden me to ever set foot there. He told me that his boss has a very, very strict policy on marriage and divorce, morals, stuff like that. He said if anyone suspected he was having an affair, he'd lose his job and then we wouldn't see each other again because he would have to leave the city.

Because our offices are so close, we see each other a lot. He used to escape for a quickie almost every day around eleven. At first, I was a little miffed because I expected him eventually to spend more time with me. We always went to the same place—a public bathroom that is a one-stall closet with a lock on the exterior door on the campus of a university three or four blocks toward the harbor. We'd go in, make love, he'd buy me lunch from a street cart and then we'd say good-bye. He never took time for a real lunch. Rarely, we'd meet for a drink after work. He'd call me at 5 p.m. and say the same thing every time.

"Kiddo, how about a cocktail in ten?" He bought me gifts; bracelets were his favorite. I have bracelets made with every gem known to man. I was getting a little tired of bracelets. Then he switched over to earrings. I have pierced ears. Thanks to him, I have quite a collection of earrings. They are real, too. Not street-vendor jewelry or any junk like that. My sister, Heather, says that the garnet earrings he gave me for Valentine's Day are antiques. Why would he give me a pair of antique earrings? So anyway, we would meet at a dive bar close to the Path Train. He would have time for one drink, two at the most. The bar is very dark. The booths are unpadded, uncomfortable. He always wanted to mess around, so we sat in the back corner where it's private. I was happy to do it because I figured he would be satisfied and then he wouldn't have sex with his wife. Even though he was older—I didn't know his age for certain but guessed he was about forty-five or fifty—he still could do it like twice a day. The bartenders in Manhattan can tell you a thing or two about the sex lives of their clientele.

The first time I saw him I was standing on the corner by my office, buying a hot dog for lunch. He was behind me in line. I paid for my lunch and moved away so I could eat my dog without being in the way of the others in line. He bought a dog and soda, asked for a paper sack, and took it with him. He got into a cab with his lunch. I have never seen a person who could afford to take a cab buy his lunch on the street until that day. After that first time, I watched for him and saw that a couple of days a week he would do the same thing. He'd buy his lunch at the same hot dog stand and then hail a cab. He never looked my way, which was another thing that bugged the heck out of me. I'm young and pretty and have been told I am a "looker." I am a Jersey girl through and through, even though I am originally from Scranton.

Finally, on a Friday about three years ago, he noticed me. He was buying his usual dog and soda and I made sure that I was close behind him. When he turned around to walk away from the cart, he almost smacked me in the face. I looked up at his face with a smile. I had on a tight, low-cut sweater and the highest heels I can walk in. First, he looked me in the eyes, and then I saw his eyes move down. He smiled back. When I finished paying for my hot dog, he was waiting for me.

"Want to eat together?" he said. I nodded yes. "I have to make a quick call," he said. He walked away a few feet and spoke quietly into his phone. "Let's walk to the park, okay?"

We started walking down toward the triangle. He seemed a little nervous, looking around him as if he might be observed. We were just going to eat a hot dog, so I wasn't sure why he minded if someone saw us. He didn't even know my name. We found an empty table and sat down across from each other. He extended his hand.

"Hi there, I'm Jack." He shook my hand and then started opening the bag containing his hot dog. "Thanks for having lunch with me."

"I'm Cindy," I said. "Cindy Thomasini. You work downtown, right?" I asked. "I've seen you around." I bit into the dog, but I was self-conscious. When we talked, I worried that there was food in my teeth, or my breath smelled like mustard. I put it down and drank some soda, trying to swish it around in my mouth as unobtrusively as I could.

"Right over there," he said, pointing to a tall, beautiful building on Exchange Place. "So you're Italian," he said, smiling. "How about you? What do you do?" He was looking intently at me, staring into my eyes. I felt a chill of pleasure because his look said, "I'm interested in you." I told him a little about myself; I'm thirty-one, single, work as a secretary in a pool at the Stock Exchange and live alone in a studio apartment in what was an old slide-rule factory right by the Holland Tunnel in Jersey City. He was interested in my building, the history of it, whether I had a view. I did actually; I could see the top of the Empire State Building. I told him the traffic noise during rush hour going into the tunnel diminished what enjoyment I got from living so close to the city. The only good thing about it was that it was about a hundred yards from the Path Train.

We finished our hot dogs, and then he started to fidget. I mean, he was pulling on his collar and messing around with his tie, everything but looking at his watch. He started to push his chair back to stand up.

"Want to walk a little before we have to go back?" he asked. I was already going to be late; we only got half an hour for lunch. But there was no way I was going to miss one second of time with him. He was an answer to my prayers, a real dreamboat. I smiled and nodded yes. He moved right over to me and took my hand. We walked for several blocks like that. He asked me questions about my family and friends, the people I worked with. I guess he could tell I was lonely; that I was alone. My mom and dad still live in Pennsylvania, near Scranton. I went to school in North Jersey and never went back home. I tried living with girlfriends, but they always got engaged, and then I either had to move out so the boyfriend could move in, or they left and I couldn't afford the rent anymore. Last year, I saved enough to buy the little place I have now and I think I'll probably be there until I find someone to marry, although I didn't tell him that.

Conversation with Jack was so easy. He seemed interested in my life and me. He held my hand, letting go of it and placing his on the small of my back when we crossed the street. Before long, we were on campus, near the public john that became my home away from home. On the first walk, we took didn't end up in the bathroom, but he did seem to gauge the time it would take us to get there and back to Wall Street.

When we got back to the Exchange, we made plans to meet at the vendor the following day. He asked for my office number; he'd call if he were hung up. But he was pretty sure his boss would let him leave right at eleven. He squeezed my hand hard and, looking into my eyes, he thanked me.

"I feel like I had a break from work, from the stress of my office. Thank you."

"What company do you work for?" I asked. He laughed, but shook his head.

"I think I'll keep that private, for now. Okay? Oh, and I'm married. Married with children. My wife has the money in the family and she would sooner kill me than allow me to have lunch with a pretty, young thing like you. So is it still on for tomorrow?" He bent down and looked into my eyes. I involuntarily shuddered. He laughed aloud! I'm such a pushover.

"Yes! Why wouldn't it be?" I smiled back at him. "See you tomorrow! I'm not going to have a job if I don't get back in there." He let go of my hand and we parted; Jack walking backwards, nodding his head in approval while he looked me up and down. The chill went through my spine again. I wish I had run the other way.

The next day, I left my office at 10:58 when I didn't get a call canceling our lunch. I ran down the steps of the Exchange and saw him at the hot dog cart the moment I stepped onto the pavement. That thrill from yesterday—the chill—went down my spine again. He looked just...well, unbelievable. He was like a model. Tall, fabulously built, broad shoulders, narrow through the waist and hips. He had on an expensive suit and was impeccable in every way: crisp shirt, shined shoes, silk tie. His hair was cut to perfection. How in God's name was little Cindy Thomasini from

Scranton able to attract someone who looked like he did? He was aware of our surroundings; I saw him give the area a once over just as I approached him. It must have been safe because he threw his arms around me and lifted me off the ground in a bear hug. It was thrilling!

"You look wonderful!" he said. "I couldn't take my eyes off of you the minute you came out of the building 'Wow!' I said to myself. 'She looks like a movie star!' And you do look like one." He bent down and kissed me right on the mouth. I wasn't expecting it; a public kiss? I had had a boyfriend in high school who, for two years, wouldn't hold my hand in public. I wondered if older men just didn't care how they appeared. He turned to the hot dog vendor and ordered our lunch, asking me what I wanted to drink. We walked to the triangle again and found an empty table. He talked the entire time, asking me questions about my job, if I had a boyfriend, what my plans for the future were.

"No, no boyfriend," I said. "I wouldn't be here having lunch with you if I did." He grinned at me.

"This is just a hot dog! And I'm harmless." He bit into his dog. "I just know that I like a pretty face and you have one. And your figure, ooh-la-la!"

I guess that I must have been suffering from total lack of self-esteem, because no alarm bells went off. Was I becoming desensitized already? A man I had known for thirty minutes comments about my figure and nothing seems wrong about that? I think I was so flattered because he was so gorgeous. I had never dated anyone who wasn't struggling. My last boyfriend worked at a muffler repair place in Hoboken, for God's sake. This guy was like the king. There was an element of unreality about it. I felt like the girl in *Rebecca*. The rich man paid attention to her and swept her off her feet. The only problem was that it wasn't to Manderley that Jack would take me, but to an empty bathroom stall on a college campus.

He was wired all through lunch, paying me compliments, touching my hand, putting his arm around my shoulders. He kissed me passionately after we were done eating. I didn't know if I could move when he suggested that we walk again. He put his arm around me as we went along, and this time—the only time he pretended that we would have a future—he talked about how he would love to take me to the beach sometime. He talked on and on about teaching me to surf. He said the waves broke directly in front of his house; there was a pile of boulders there in the surf left by a glacier a million years ago. He said I was about the size of his daughter and could use her wetsuit, the implication clear and contradictory. I didn't think his wife would appreciate a visit from me. Then we got to the bathroom.

"I have to go," he said, taking his arm off my back. As he walked toward the door, he turned slightly and offered me his hand. "Come in with me," he said softly. "You'll be safe." I guess he could see the confusion on my face. Was I going to walk into my death chamber or just watch him pee? I didn't know him. But something about him was mesmerizing, and I followed him into the bathroom, smiling shyly. I thought he would try to make love to me, but he didn't.

"Being with you has turned me on so badly, but we really don't know each other enough to have sex yet." He was unzipping his pants. He reached into his fly and took out his penis, already erect. "Just stroke it a little, will you Cindy? It won't take much, I promise." So like an idiot, I went over to him and grasped him in my hand. He was right; it didn't take long. He moaned my name over and over and pulled me to him, careful to not get his ejaculate all over our clothes. He snuggled his face into my neck, into my hair, moaning.

"Oh, Cindy, thank you. Thank you." He grabbed paper towels with his free hand while the other arm stayed around me. He was adept at wiping himself off and putting his dick away with one hand. I didn't know what I was feeling then; the flattery was gone. He let me go and I turned to the sink to wash my hands off. I used a lot of the soap; it had a medicinal smell that I would grow to hate. He didn't wash his hands. I could smell his body when he put his hand up to my face to lift my chin so he could kiss me again. He was an expert kisser. I finally gave in and put my arms around his neck and kissed him back. It was a long, deep kiss. He rubbed my back and didn't let his hands go below my waist. I'm not sure if I was grateful or not. I just remember thinking I would have to wash my sweater where he touched it.

"We'd better get you back to the office," he said. I had forgotten completely about my job. What time was it, anyway? We started walking toward Wall

Street and Jack started to talk. He told me about his children, a boy and a girl. His son was looking at colleges and Jack took him from one campus to another, all over the country. He was vague about where he lived; I thought it must be at the Jersey Shore because he talked about the beach. His wife loved the water, so they had moved there from Manhattan soon after he graduated from college. He loved his wife, but she was preoccupied with the lives of their two children and her mother and sisters. He was lonely. He looked at me.

"I'm giving you the opportunity to run from me right now. I'll never leave my wife. My boss is a religious fanatic who will fire me if he finds out I am involved with another woman. Do you understand that? Are you willing to take this on? Er, take me on? Haha!" He didn't say anything about having feelings for me, about being interested in getting to know me better. It was all about what I was willing to put up with.

For some unknown reason, I said yes. I would take him on. That night we met for a drink after work and he asked me to go to a hotel near the Path Train. It was one of the few times we went to a hotel, and he never stayed overnight. It was totally impersonal. Once, last winter, there was a horrible snowstorm. I stayed the night and went into work the next day with the same makeup and clothing on; fortunately, I had a hairbrush. No one seemed to notice.

I don't know why I allowed it, why I chose to waste three years of my life with a man who didn't have one single feeling for me. He used me like an accessory hand. I was a mouth, a vagina, a pair of boobs. When I think about my relationships with other men, there isn't any evidence of self-deprecation, or self-loathing like that I exhibited with Jack. I was raised by loving, caring parents. My father and I have a warm, supportive relationship to this day. Well, until I tell them the news. I'm sure this will throw them both for a loop. My mother won't hear that I am sexually active, even at the age of thirty-one. It is not discussed in our family. I love God and Jesus with all my heart. I know that sounds like a contradiction, after what I've done.

We have had few arguments in our household and they always revolve around religious hypocrisy. My parents are devout Catholics. When I say devout, I mean that they believe the words that come from the pope's mouth are God's words. They take the Bible out of context, choosing just the parts that seem to suit their purpose. An example: My sister went to my parent's home one night last year, shortly before the holidays. I was there for some forgotten reason. Probably for Sunday dinner.

"We won't be coming for dinner Christmas day, Mom." Rather than offer an excuse, she allowed my mother to ask the questions. It was the way things worked at our house. Mom was wiping down dishes as she unloaded the dishwasher. She could never get it through her head that all you needed to do was to let them sit and they would dry on their own. She put the dishcloth down.

"What do you mean you won't be coming for dinner on Christmas? Everyone comes here for Christmas dinner." My mother never considered that one of her seven children would ever not show up for a dinner. We came from far and wide to honor those traditions, no matter how tough it might be to get there. "You'll come."

"Not this year, Mom," Heather stated. "Mark is leaving."

I thought, *So that's the problem*. I'd wondered when it would happen. How long would it take our mother to figure this out? Heather couldn't say, We are getting a divorce.

"Well, you'll come after he goes."

I looked sideways at my mother. Was she being wise? "Mom, Heather and Mark are getting a divorce." There, I'd said it.

My mother picked up her dishcloth again and started wiping. "No one gets a divorce in this family. What are you talking about? Cynthia, you take after my mother-in-law. Your grandmother could take the birth of a baby and turn it into the ugliest story you ever heard."

Heather and Mark could get a divorce; they could both marry other people and start families with them and my mother would never accept it.

"Mom," Heather started, "Cindy is telling you the truth. Mark is leaving me. He doesn't love me anymore." Heather wasn't beyond exaggerating to get my mother to see her point of view. Surely, if the man left, she would have to accept that. "Doesn't it say in the Bible that if he wants to go, you're supposed to let him?"

"Right! That's exactly what it says, Mom," I said. "It says to 'let the unbeliever go,' doesn't it Heather?" She nodded her head yes, but that only fueled the fire. The amazing thing was that my parents hated Mark! He was an atheist Jew who insulted their Christianity at every turn, usually not intentionally. They, in turn, insulted Judaism over and over again. I thought that it might be a blessing that he was going his own way.

"It says in the Bible that God hates divorce! I won't have this kind of talk. No one gets divorced in our family! If the husband acts like a donkey, you lie about it; you don't tell your mother that you aren't coming to Christmas dinner because your husband doesn't love you anymore! Who cares about love! I never heard such talk in my life. You two act like you were raised by a couple of heathens. Wait 'til Daddy hears about this. Just wait." I had the feeling my father would be more understanding, but didn't say so. "I can't believe my own daughter would even entertain the idea of getting a divorce! It's a sin!" she yelled. "You'll go to hell! Why'd we spend every dime we had sending you all to parochial school and then have this kind of sin!" She finally threw down her towel and plunked down in a chair.

My brother, Fred, came into the kitchen and opened the refrigerator. "What's up?" he asked. "I heard yelling."

My mother thought she would get an ally in Fred. "Heather and Mark are getting a divorce! How do you like that?" She hit the table with her open palm for emphasis.

"It isn't such a big deal nowadays. You couldn't stand Mark, anyway. Remember how he kept hanging the baby Jesus by his toes last Christmas?" Mark had insisted on picking the plastic doll out of the manger and swinging him around by his feet, in spite of my mother crying out to him to stop, yelling, "You're making all the blood rush to his head!" Heather had put her head down on the table and pretended she was crying, but she was really hiding laughter from our mother, who was on the verge of storming out of the room. If that happened, it would be weeks before we would get her to talk to us again. This was all blasphemy.

Fred went on. "And what about him dressing up like an apostle for Halloween? A gentile apostle! No, I say good riddance to Mark. Besides, Mother Dear, gluttony is a sin, too, yet I don't hear you yelling at me to stop eating so much." Fred, a three-hundred pounder, had found something good to eat and was taking it back to his room. He was one of three children still living at home. My mother was furious.

"Heather Ann, stop laughing at me this instant. I'm so upset right now. What's keeping your father?" She turned to the telephone and picked it up to see if there was a dial tone. She would call him and make sure he was coming home. Fred had already given him a heads-up. He would calm her down, as only he was able. However, she wasn't finished with us.

"Why'd you ever marry a Jew, anyway? I told you this would happen! He thought he was better than us. He made fun of every celebration we had here." Her arms were crossed over her chest and she had her best

'I told you so' expression on her face. Heather couldn't argue with our mother because she knew it was true. They never should have gotten married. They married for lust. The folks hated him and it filtered down to Heather, who ended up siding with our parents because she had too much to lose if she didn't, forgetting her husband in the process.

"Yes, well hindsight and all that, Mom. I'm sorry I hurt you and Daddy. However, this isn't easy for me. If you're going to yell at me every time I come home, I won't come anymore."

My mother thought about this. "So you'll come for Christmas?" The woman was one-track, there was no arguing that.

"Yes! I'll come! But promise me you won't mention his name!" Mark's name came up once during Christmas weekend that year. My mother mentioned him in a prayer and the entire family moaned. What would my parents say to me when it came time for my unveiling? I'd have to give them some background. Their beloved eldest daughter had had an affair with a married man. Heather and Mark would seem like a gift from heaven after my revelation.

After that first time in the hotel with Jack, I had serious doubts about the future of my relationship with this man. For one thing, the sex was not that great. He wasn't interested in my satisfaction at all. The expression "getting his rocks off" fit Jack to a tee. I kept thinking that a hand job in the bathroom wasn't much different from the hotel experience, and it was cheaper and neater, too. He did ask me to do a few weird things for him. He asked me to pose in my underwear. I was to take my panty hose off (he hated panty hose) and put my shoes back on, and then remove my clothes. Not like a striptease, just like I was normally undressing. He would go nuts. If I wore long pants, he asked me to turn my back to him so he could watch me bend over to take them off. I thought he would pass out from that one.

He liked me to jump on the bed, too. He'd lie next to where I was jumping and laugh and laugh. And then he would tackle me. That was his foreplay. Now that I think of it, I never had an orgasm with Jack in three years. He wasn't interested in it; never asked, "Did you come?" We never discussed sex. I was just to assume that we would do it every single time we were together.

So that was my life for three years. We never had a real date that I remember; just an evening in the hotel. He never took me to a show; we didn't spend a weekend together. It was so textbook. He wouldn't give me a phone number. I did finally find out that his last name was Smith, and when I did, I laughed for at least five minutes. There are over two hundred Jack Smiths in New York, alone. How would I ever find him? It once occurred to me to follow him into his building to try to find out whom he worked for, but he caught me and I didn't see him for a week after that. I learned my lesson.

Another time, we were on the street together and someone with whom he worked saw us. He didn't say who, just that that person had questioned him later in the day about the woman he was lunching with. After that, we didn't stop at our usual vendor for lunch. We ate closer to the campus bathroom. Our love nest.

I got to carrying around one of those metallic blankets that folds up into a tiny, silver dollar-sized bag and we would spread that out on the floor of the bathroom. He would lie down because his knees couldn't take the hard tile. Or he would sit on the toilet and I would sit on him. Only once did someone interrupt us, and Jack just yelled that he was in there, sick. The person wasn't waiting when we came out. For three years, I made my clothing choices to accommodate my lunchtime trysts with Jack. I would go shopping and see something, a dress with a full skirt, or a wraparound skirt, and think, *This would be good for seeing Jack.*

I'd never had many friends, but now I was completely isolated. My sisters didn't question what I was up to.

"I am almost afraid to ask," Heather stated. "I just hope you are safe." Prophetic. Now Heather and Mark are back together with one son and another on the way. Will they ever allow me to touch their children again?

After the first week of Jack's disappearance, I started to get frightened. During the first few days that he didn't show up, I examined each move I had made and word I had said, to try to uncover anything that might have annoyed him. There was nothing. I had become a voiceless, selfless automaton. So that left

the possibility that he had gone on vacation and forgotten to tell me. It had happened before and he wasn't
apologetic when he returned and I confronted him. I
factored nowhere in his life. I was a hand job in the
bathroom during lunch for the price of a hot dog and
soda.

By the tenth day of his absence, I was frantic.
What if he had moved away, or gotten another job?
I had a friend from yoga who worked in the ER at
St. Vincent's; she suggested I check out the obituaries in the *New York Times* when I confided in her. It
took another week and two sick days of searching, but
that's where I finally found him. Jack Edward Smith. I
couldn't read further. It was the correct Jack; this one
was fifty-five, lived at the beach, but on Long Island,
not in New Jersey. I lay down on my bed and pulled the
covers up under my chin. He was dead! His funeral had
come and gone. I needed a calendar to check the dates,
to see where I was and what I was doing when he died.
I got out of bed and brought the calendar back. Somehow, I had to force myself to read the obituary. There
was a related story.

Why would anyone write about Jack? The article
would tell a lot. I was fucking a well-known person!
*Jack Edward Smith, born September 30, 1955, died May 28
in Manhattan. Mr. Smith suffered a massive heart attack
on a train bound for Long Island. He was mugged sometime
before passengers discovered him. He later died in the hospital. His wife, the former Pamela Fabian of Brooklyn, was
unavailable for comment. Mr. Smith was a partner in the
firm Lane, Smith, and Romney. His partner, Peter Romney,*

stated that it was "a sad day for the company. But business will go on." I sat back against my pillows. The story about the boss being a tyrant was a lie. I picked up my laptop and continued reading.

The father of two college students, Mr. Smith was well known in the community for his involvement in the Babylon Athletic League. Generous supporters of the arts in Manhattan, the Smiths rarely missed a performance at Lincoln Center.

He was the son of Bernice Stein Smith and the late Harold Smith of Columbus Circle.

The funeral was held in Babylon the day after Memorial Day. It is estimated that several hundred friends and family from around the country paid homage. The decedent's brother, William Smith, gave a moving tribute to his brother. Burial was private.

I was unable to move. Thinking back three weeks ago, I remembered our dialogue on Thursday, the last day I saw him.

"Have a good holiday. You get a long weekend, correct? The Exchange isn't open on Memorial Day." We were walking back toward Wall Street, but would be parting ways before we reached it. It was the first time I had been with him all week. Was he going to ask to see me over the weekend? During the past eight months or so, he had said he was tied up with a project that required him to be out of the office more and more. He wouldn't always be downtown at lunchtime. "So what are you going to do with yourself?" he asked. And then he did the unforgiveable: He looked at his watch.

I should have suspected something, because the previous autumn he stopped seeing me for the rare nighttime rendezvous . We were limited to one or two half-hour screws a week and we rarely met on the street anymore. I would have to walk to the campus bathroom. I was sure he either was seeing someone else who might run into us or his boss was getting suspicious. It was starting to bother me enough that I was building the courage to say something to him, and then he had to go and die. I couldn't even stop seeing him on my own.

I decided I would sell the jewelry he gave me; it meant nothing to me now. And I couldn't pass that hot dog cart again without feeling like crap. I certainly wouldn't be making any farewell visits to the bathroom. I gathered everything he had given to me and took it to a jeweler I knew in Journal Square. He offered me almost eight thousand dollars for it. But before I took the check, I thought of something else. I wanted to have something to prove we had been together, and the only thing I had was the jewelry. He never called me, so I had no cell phone records, and he always paid for the hotel, so I didn't have a receipt. There were no ticket stubs, no mementos of any kind, except for fifteen or sixteen pieces of jewelry. The guy in Journal Square thought the garnet earrings might have been estate pieces. I had wondered if they were stolen. Having read that he was a partner in a Wall Street firm of some kind, I hadn't researched that yet. He was probably rich, too. His parents were from Columbus Circle. That fact said a ton. I left without selling the jewelry.

I needed a plan. The first thing I could do was go to his office. I wanted to see where he worked. He hadn't said much about anything; the only person I knew anything about was his boss, the religious fanatic. Now that I knew he was a partner, all of the boss talk was a lie. At lunch, I decided to make my visit. The obit had said his company was Lane, Smith and Romney. I went in the front entrance and walked to the directory hanging by the elevators. His office was on thirty-five. I got on the elevator, my heart pounding so hard I wondered if my clothes were moving. What did I have to be afraid of? He was dead. He wouldn't get angry with me. The worst that could happen was that I would be escorted out. I wouldn't cause a scene. I just needed to be validated.

The elevator opened directly into the reception area. It was gorgeous. There was a gleaming desk made of some light, modern wood, with a giant brass sign bearing the partners' names. The lighting was perfect, soft area lighting and direct work lights over the receptionist. She was young and attractive and smiled a big, toothy smile.

"May I help you?" she asked.

"I'm here for Mr. Smith," I lied. That would get their attention. The receptionist frowned and asked me to have a seat. She picked up her phone and keyed in some numbers, speaking softly into the receiver.

"Someone will be right out," she said. In less than a minute, a tall, beautiful young woman walked in. She extended her hand.

"I'm Sandra Benson," she said. "Did you say you had an appointment with Mr. Smith?"

I didn't speak for a minute, unsure what to say next.

"Not an appointment. I'm just here to see him."

Sandra Benson spent a few seconds thinking and then said, "Come with me, won't you?" And she smiled down at me. When I stood up, I realized she was several inches taller than I was. Although I was sure she was younger, I felt silly and immature next to her. It was stupid to come here, but now that I had risked it, I needed to find out more about him. What was he? I was examining why I had allowed him to treat me so badly and I wanted to know why he did it. Who was Jack Smith? I followed her down a long, low-ceilinged, narrow passageway. When I entered her office, I was surprised at its size, the height of the ceilings, the view of the harbor, and the loveliness of the art she had chosen to hang. I would later come to find out that Jack himself had bought the oil painting of vividly colored flower gardens that hung on the wall behind her desk.

"Sit down, won't you?" She pointed to a chair positioned in front of her desk as she walked around to sit behind it. I felt as though I was at a job interview, and in a few moments, this person would be asking me why I felt that I was suited for the job. "Now what can I do for you?" she asked. She had a pleasant smile but I could sense a tension behind her eyes, as though she had been through this before. She waited patiently for me to start talking, but as soon as I opened my mouth, the tears started. I was disgusted with myself.

"I was seeing a man who worked here, and I haven't heard from him for a few weeks. I was just wondering if he was okay. I don't mean to cause any trouble." She pushed a box of tissues toward me but remained silent. Her facial expression had barely changed, but it was discernible: I was correct; she had been through this before. I wasn't the first one. Then she smiled at me.

"Why don't you tell me about it? Jack is a well-loved man. Have you been seeing him long?" I couldn't read Sandra Benson. Was she really concerned? Or digging? I decided I didn't care. I needed validation.

"We have been together for three years." When the words were out, I realized how ludicrous it sounded. We weren't really together, but I would not tell her that. I could see that the news was not welcome. She stood up and began walking around her desk. I was thinking she might show me the door but instead, she went over and shut it, turning the lock.

"That's a long time. But I am confused, so please forgive me if I ask too many questions. First of all, I think I need to tell you that Jack passed away. Memorial Day weekend. He had a heart attack on the train." Although I knew it, hearing it for real made me cry again. She didn't know that I had come there aware he was dead. I wanted information from her, so I stayed in character: the shocked and grieving girlfriend. I put my head down in my hands and had a good ball. She didn't move to comfort me or say anything to try to make me feel better. She actually looked a little pissed but was doing her best to hide it. I found myself wondering if she had been fucking him, too.

"Were you a client of his?" The young woman looked like she was in a position of authority in the company; her office alone said "important" and was not one that your average secretary would occupy. Surely, she would know who was a client and who wasn't. I was not going to lie.

"No, not a client." I felt silly after that. What did I hope to accomplish? Why did I bring a purse full of jewelry with me? Was I hoping to extort money from his business? What power did I have? So what if he screwed me? Millions of men did the same thing every day and never suffered a consequence. I guess I simply wanted some acknowledgment that I existed, that what I had with him was worth something. But what? I didn't have anything of value with him at all. I could have gone on and had another relationship that meant something and it wouldn't have mattered to him at all. I suddenly knew that I had loved him. I had kept hoping each time we were together that he would love me. But it wasn't possible. He may not have been capable of loving if he could use someone as he used me. A free whore. I started to stand up, to leave. "I'm sorry to have bothered you. I don't really know why I came here after all, but I am sorry he is dead," I said.

She spoke up finally. "No, don't go. I can see that Jack meant something to you. Do you want to talk about it?" She started to walk around her desk again.

She had a look of concern on her face, but there was something about her eyes that alarmed me. They were cold and hard. She had to have been involved with him, too, in some manner. A casual business associate wouldn't have been so intrigued, would she have? "Let's go get a cup of coffee. I'm ready to get out in the air for a little walk. How about you?"

"Okay. I apologize for interrupting your day. I need to call my office first, though. I shouldn't have gone to work today. I'm going to tell them that I'm ill."

She leaned forward and pushed her desk phone toward me. "Go ahead and use my phone. The number is blocked; they won't know where you are calling from. We don't always get great cell phone reception on this side of the building." She walked to the door and unlocked it, letting herself out and giving me privacy. I called and explained that I had gotten ill while out for lunch and would not be back for the rest of the day. Of course, that meant sneaking around. She came back in to retrieve her purse.

"Is everything alright?" she asked. I said it was. "We can take a cab north and you won't have to worry about anyone seeing you. There is a little coffee shop right by the bridge that I like. Is that okay?" Sandra was being so kind; I had forgotten that she might be a competitor for the affections of Jack Smith. But that wasn't possible now, was it? He was dead.

We walked side by side along the corridor and stepped into the elevator. We didn't speak. Once outside, I felt the rush of air leave my lungs; I had been holding my breath. What was I waiting for? This woman, a colleague of Jack's, someone possibly in love with him, was interested in me because of him. Was she operating out of curiosity? What would make a work associate interested enough to take time away from her job to cross-examine me? My women's intuition was boiling over. I thought I would allow her to continue being the dominant female and do the questioning. I would listen carefully for anything that might shed some light on her relationship with Jack. I watched her step off the curb and raise her arm for a cab. One came right away. She was dressed in a summer-weight suit that didn't look high end, with a silk blouse underneath it, and very expensive shoes. She saw me looking at her feet and laughed.

"No matter what, all women love shoes," she said. "They weren't as expensive as you'd think. I got them on eBay!"

"No way!" I exclaimed stupidly. "How did you know they were real?"

"I've dealt with the seller before." She turned her foot so I could see the sides and back.

"Stunning!" I exclaimed. I never bought shoes anywhere but at Marshall's in Newport Center. My salary precluded designer shoes. "It might be dangerous for someone with my budget to start looking on eBay for a bargain."

She looked at me curiously. "What do you do?"

"I'm a secretary at the Exchange. I have a degree in math, but couldn't find a job and didn't want to teach. My family is disgusted. I have already been there for nine years and in twenty, I can retire. I think

I'll stay. If I don't get fired first." Why did I say that? After the first few months of escaping every day for a forty-five minute rendezvous with Jack, I never gave it another thought and no one chastised me for taking long lunches. It occurred to me just then that maybe he'd had a hand in it. Maybe he knew someone at the Exchange. "Let Cindy take longer lunches so I can have sex with her." I wondered if that was why I was still employed.

"There is a lot of energy in that place!" she said. "It must be fun!"

"Not really," I replied. "I'm in the pool. I don't work for one individual, so there isn't any camaraderie at all. Maybe that's why I am still there. No gossip, no dynamics between people. Very rarely, there is a romance and then boy oh boy! You should see the magpies hopping around, trying to spread the gossip or get another story. Fortunately, I am usually too busy to take note of what's going on. And I am always the last to know. Always." I wondered why that was. No one was interested in me and I really wasn't interested in anyone. Maybe that was why I was alone. I didn't care about anyone with whom I worked. I didn't care about anyone, period. Jack had been the first man to capture my attention in a long time. How shallow was I that I would suffer the shame and humiliation of being used by someone just because he was gorgeous? We arrived at the coffee shop. I got out of the cab first and then waited on the sidewalk while Sandra paid the driver. It was her idea, after all. I didn't have the money to be taking cabs all over town. She led the way and I followed her. We sat at a table in front of a grimy window. The Brooklyn Bridge was right over us. I could sit there for hours and watch the cars file up the ramp. It was cool and dark in the coffee shop, an old diner car that had lasted through several neighborhood gentrifications. It was on the decline at the present time.

"So, what shall we talk about?" I asked Sandra. And then without prompting, forgetting my previous decision to allow her to lead, I went full-steam ahead. "I didn't know Jack that well. I certainly didn't know he owned the company. Let's see if I can repeat this correctly. He told me that his boss was a tyrant, a religious fanatic." I stopped myself in the nick of time, but she was wise to me. I almost let it slip that he lied so he'd have an excuse not to be seen in public with me. She was looking at me uncertainly; I could tell I had confused her. I had to keep the upper hand now and maybe confusion was a good way to do it.

"What circumstances led to him lying to you?" she asked.

Oh no, you don't, I thought to myself. "I would rather not say," was the way I answered that one. She could dig a little more if she wanted information from me. "In what capacity do you work there at Jack's place? If I may ask."

"I'm a partner," she replied. She looked uncomfortable. Good, I thought. Tit for tat. It figured she was a partner, although she seemed a little young. I didn't inquire further because I didn't really care. I wanted to know why she was so interested in me and asked her.

"Why do you care so much about what I have to say? It's not like it will affect anything Jack had or did." I had an interior giggle at that; it was just enough of an allusion to make her think otherwise. She looked out the window. I was still having a difficult time getting a read on her. But something told me that she had been in his bed, and not just as a screw. Then I thought I would take a chance. She could just say no, or mind your own business, or fuck off. "You are his girlfriend."

"Was his girlfriend. Remember, he's dead." She looked me right in the eye. "I have my reasons to want his reputation to stay intact. That and the fact that his widow and I are good friends now." I don't know why I found that difficult to believe. Would she invite me into the fold? I remembered the wife's name: Pamela. Pamela, Sandra, and Cynthia...the three women of Jack Smith.

"Trust me; I am not going to expose him in any way. I can promise you that. Although truthfully, he doesn't deserve it. He deserves my wrath. But I guess that I am to blame for all of it because I allowed it." I had said it. *I had allowed it.* It was the most difficult admission I had made. Jack used me because he could. He never forced me. I came willingly, eagerly. "Wow, I think I just had a breakthrough. Thirty-one isn't too late to save oneself from being an asshole, is it?" I asked her.

Surprisingly, Sandra Benson laughed. "No, no it isn't. I hope I can do it by that age! Anyway, I don't think you are an asshole at all. If what you just did was to make an admission of guilt, then let me reassure you. You are not alone."

She didn't say anything more, but my feeling was that perhaps Jack had had more than one victim. We drank our coffee in silence. She hadn't said much, but Sandra Benson had given me the validation I sought.

If I were able, I would keep going. One foot in front of the other. If my life were so empty that a silly sexual relationship with a married man was the only thing I had to look forward to, and then I had better make some changes, maybe even look for a new job.

It's not too late, I thought at the time. But it was. It was too late for me.

*

Sandra Benson left the young woman at the coffee shop and went back to her office. She looked out the dirty windows of the cab, wondering how her day could have gotten worse when just a few hours before, she was sure it was as bad as was possible. She'd have to do some serious thinking before she made one more move.

2

Organic Bonanza in Babylon was packed with women doing their grocery shopping. Many were in tennis or golf attire, some were in gym clothes, and a few wore bathing suit cover-ups. Usually, it was the tourists who wore bathing suits in public. It was an unspoken rule that locals dressed appropriately in town—except for a few younger wives who had the bodies for bathing suits and were, therefore, forgiven and teenagers, who could wear whatever they wanted.

Pam Smith loved the grocery store. When Jack was alive, she could be seen there at least four times a week. Now that he was gone, she was usually there twice, once to pick up food for her and her mother, and the next time to get food for her weekend guests. Always pleasant with a smile on her face, the clerks loved seeing her, and made sure all of her grocery needs were met. The guy in the meat department specially butchered steaks for her back when Jack was alive, and when Jack had started to watch his weight, he trimmed them extra lean for her without her having to ask more than once. Almost every employee was there to serve the public and in spite of the astronomical prices and the big chain store just two blocks inland, the women in town patronized Bonanza because they didn't want it to go out of business.

She pushed the grocery cart up and down the aisles, wandering over to the deli counter and looking over the case, thinking about what she would fix for lunches for the next couple of days. She wasn't making a big deal about food the way she did when Jack was alive. But with company coming for the weekend, Pam had a reason to shop again. There were no other customers at the counter, but she took a number anyway. The two young clerks were whispering to each other and ignoring Pam. When the click of the number dispenser didn't alert the girls that a customer was waiting, Pam decided to forgo cold cuts and find something else for lunch rather than disturbing them. She moved away from the counter. One of the women looked out of the corner of her eye to see Pam leave.

"She's gone," Marion whispered to her coworker, Jean. "Thank God I didn't have to look her in the eye. I'm telling you, it creeps me out big time, just her being in the store." They turned around to look out on the expanse of the store.

"Keep your voice down! I never should have told you about it. If she finds out, my sister is going to kill me. You have to promise not to say a thing to anyone. She had to take some kind of oath to work in the hospital that she wouldn't squeal about anyone's personal business. She shouldn't have told me, either." Jean was worried now; why'd she ever say anything about Mrs. Smith to big-mouthed Marion?

"Why *did* your sister say anything to you if it is such a big secret? Shit that goes on in the hospital isn't supposed to be dinnertime conversation, you know."

Marion hated Jean's sister; jealous that she got into nursing school in the first place and now made decent money while Marion was stuck at Organic Bonanza on minimum wage. "Anyway, I've hated Mr. Smith ever since I was in girl's T-ball," Marion said. "He would drool all over Alice Mackenzie. Remember her? She was a skinny-assed blonde even when she was eight. His precious angel of a daughter got the attention of the other coach. The big girls like me were ignored or yelled at or both. He never let me play once we got up to Little League." Memories of the way she was treated as a child boiled over into her present thinking about Pam Smith. "I'm not surprised that haughty bitch has AIDS. She probably got it from that prick of a husband of hers."

Jean gasped. "Keep your voice down!" she repeated. Their boss, the head of the deli department, came up to them and told them to get busy; there had been a complaint that the deli department wasn't manned. What had they been doing all morning?

Pam went through checkout and took her groceries to the car. She was getting her hair done in twenty minutes, so she had just enough time to unload the bags and ask her mother to put the cold stuff in the refrigerator. She'd do it if Nelda wasn't up to it. But her mother was ready, dressed in her heels and stockings, to go into the city for the weekend. Pam's mother-in-law, Bernice Smith, loved having Pam and Nelda stay with her at her brownstone mansion in the heart of the Upper West Side of Manhattan. At first, she resisted the idea of the two of them "infringing on her privacy."

After the second day of a trial visit, she loved it. Having other women in the house with her was like having a big slumber party twenty-four hours a day. And since Pam was paying for the upkeep of the house, it was only fair that she and her mother be welcome there. When winter arrived in a few months, Pam would travel back and forth between the beach and the city. Nelda could do whatever she liked. At seventy-seven, both Nelda and Bernice were capable of taking care of themselves. But having someone around to assist them if necessary was becoming more than just a luxury. Pam had made a deal with the staff to stay on full time, but she had to hire an additional person to be Bernice's assistant—a combination companion and nurse's aide. Bernice had to be reminded on a daily basis that Candy was not her personal maid.

While Pam was at the store, her sister Marie called the house. Marie was Nelda's youngest daughter. She wouldn't be coming to the beach for the weekend after all because she didn't feel well enough to make the trip, or at least that was what she told her mother.

"I'm going into the city to stay with Bernice. I'll come downtown and look after you," Nelda said.

There was no way in hell, Marie thought. If she needed her mother, the woman would make every excuse under the sun not to come. *What was with her?* "No Mom, that's not necessary. I just need some rest. Having you here, I would feel like I needed to entertain you. Stay uptown."

Nelda gave in. She didn't really want to go take care of her daughter anyway. At forty-five, Marie was old enough to take care of herself. After they said good-bye, Marie curled up next to her sleeping lover and closed her eyes.

As soon as Pam walked through the door, Nelda told her about Marie. Pam didn't say anything in return; afraid her anger at Marie would be obvious. Pam's patience with her sister had grown thin. Sure that Marie wasn't sick at all; she was probably making an excuse to stay home so that she could do something that Pam wouldn't approve of, or why the secrecy? Anyhow, the last thing they needed was their mother second-guessing why Marie wasn't coming.

"I wonder if Sandra is on her way," Pam said. She decided to call her. If no one was coming to the beach this weekend, she would be free to spend the time with her children and their friends. Sandra picked up on the first ring. Something had come up at the last minute and she wouldn't be coming either. Pam's anger grew. *Those two are so selfish!* she thought, conflicted over needing to see them in spite of not being able to depend on them. She shook her head in exasperation, picked up her purse and left the house again.

3

Delores Frank was an intake coordinator at the New York State Department of Health, Manhattan Office. For the past twenty years, she monitored AIDS cases in the city for the state of New York. Every case that crossed her desk was cross-referenced with cases throughout the city. On Monday, she had received a file that made her blood boil. She read through it once, and then called an emergency meeting with her boss, Ron Peterson, and two interviewers. She arranged for lunch to be brought in at her expense. She wanted her colleagues to be relaxed while she talked to them, not looking at their watches, or hearing their stomachs growling. They arrived right on time and crowded around the sandwich tray, fixing plates of food.

"I'm starving! Thank you for getting lunch, Dee," Maggie Daniel said as she piled veggies on her plate.

"I am, too," Betty James said. "I didn't think I would have any time to eat today; we've been so busy. Did everyone in Manhattan just suddenly decide to contract HIV? I hate to think of what the rest of the week is going to bring."

Dee Frank hated to add fuel to the fire. "It did just get worse," she said. "I feel badly about what I am going to dump on all of you. Let's sit down and I'll fill you in."

"I knew I should have called out sick today," Ron Peterson said. "I'm going to jail if I don't close some of the files that are already on my desk." He pulled out a chair in the midst of his favorite women. "So dump away, Dee Frank." He bit into his gigantic sandwich and moaned with his eyes closed. "Better than sex."

The women groaned. "Oh yuck. Thanks for ruining lunch for me, Ron," Betty scolded. "Get it over with, Dee."

"Well, to start with, evidently someone dropped the ball over at Saint Paul. They had a fellow, a man named Jack Smith, come through the Trauma Department at the end of May. He had a heart attack on the train, and the ER tech drew blood and sent it off, according to protocol. The problem is that no one followed up when he died the same night up in the CCU.

"An ER nurse-manager was cleaning out some files and she came across the printout of his ELISA and it was positive. No follow-up testing was done because he died and as I said, the ball was dropped. We don't know why blood wasn't sent during the autopsy.

"Now here is the clinker. When I got this report, I called his wife. Are you ready for this? She just found out she's got AIDs. And, evidently, she is in contact with two of her late husband's sexual partners. One has AIDs and the other is HIV positive. Their names were already in the system but we just haven't gotten to their paperwork yet. I think we have a real mess on our hands," Delores said.

"The wife gave me the names of the two other women. One, a Miss Sandra Benson, is pregnant with Jack Smith's baby. I then called Miss Benson. She gave me the names of two possible contacts—a William Smith, Jack Smith's brother who is at Riker's and has admitted to being a sexual partner; and his wife, Anne Smith, in city jail." Dee stopped talking. And then she remembered the second partner. "There is the other woman who has AIDS, Miss Marie Fabian. She is Mrs. Smith's sister. Jack Smith has two college-age children that Mrs. Smith has agreed to question." Dee took a long breath and let it out slowly. She felt sick to her stomach. Her three colleagues looked at her, shocked. This man evidently was a whoremonger and an adulterer of the worst type; he didn't care whom he slept with. He was dead; how would they find his victims?

"We are going to have to advertise, I'm afraid," Betty said. "If you all agree, I'll get a court order going. If and when it's instated, we can start with the underground publications. I'm not ready to expose his family in the *Times*." All but Maggie shook their heads in agreement. This policy, although tricky to pull off legally, had worked for them in the past. Betty had a standard ad that she took out with the decedent's name in small type.

Friends and Friends of Friends
You may have information that is desperately needed.
If you are a friend, or a friend of a friend of Jack Smith,
please contact Helen Davenport at
718-555-1212
immediately.

Helen Davenport was their pseudonym for the Health Department.

"What is going to work for us in this case is that he was mugged on the train after his heart attack. That fact was advertised in the *New York Times* in a story that accompanied his obituary. To anyone who knew Jack Smith—but not about his proclivity for sexual promiscuity, not that I am judging him—it might appear that we are looking for information about the mugging. They won't be tipped off so easily," Dee said.

"Oh, I don't know," Maggie argued. "He was a family man, correct? Don't we have some obligation to protect his children, at the very least, from slander? I mean, even if you only place those ads in the most obscure papers, the court order will still be part of public record. Good luck trying to get those documents sealed."

"Good point. What's the alternative?" Ron asked.

"The problem is that if we wait, his victims may be having unprotected sex. It is no guarantee that anyone will come forward, anyway. But at least we will have done what we are supposed to do legally," Dee said.

No one else said anything.

Finally, Betty spoke up. "How's this for a compromise? Let's wait until Thursday to file the order. It will give us through the holiday weekend for someone to come forward. In the meantime, let's interview the five known contacts. Does that sound like a plan?"

"I think so," Maggie agreed. "Hopefully, we can determine right away if there is a need to go public. Why'd I ever go into this field?"

"The same thing just crossed my mind," Dee said. She finished her lunch and got up to start the mountain of forms each interviewer would need. Ron Peterson walked back to Dee's office with her.

"I'm not convinced that waiting until Thursday to file is a smart move," he said. "I have to countermand your plan. We don't know anything about Jack Smith right now. I know we are not supposed to form opinions based on behavior. But what we can do is to project possible outcomes based on past behavior. The scary part is that I recognize his name. His family is Columbus Circle, Central Park West, the whole nine yards. That scares me. Rich people think they can get away with murder. No, I think I'll give it day and if we don't uncover anything by closing tomorrow, you better file with the court."

"Ah, why didn't you say anything when we were all together?" Dee asked. Then she added, "Sir."

Ron smiled. "Because you work for me and I want you to tell them." He walked into his office, dismissing her, and closed his door.

"What an asshole," she whispered to herself. So she went back to the conference room where Betty and Maggie were having a final cup of coffee.

"Ron wants to file by tomorrow afternoon unless we can convince him that this was isolated behavior on Smith's part. Sorry, Betty. I thought it was a good plan, but he's the boss." Dee went to the food tray and started cleaning up their lunch mess. "I'll take one of the interviews and that will speed things up. Why don't you two head out to Long Island and talk to the wife this afternoon if she is available. I'll head downtown and start with the girlfriend."

"He's probably right," Betty replied. "The longer we wait, the more difficult it will be for contacts to come forward. I just feel sorry for the family. Did he say anything about the media we chose?"

Dee shook her head. "I'll help you decide where to place the ad when the time comes," she said. "Maggie, would you get copies of his credit card statements?"

Dee went to her office and closed the door. She looked through her notes and found Sandra Benson's contact information. She sat down at her desk and pulled the phone closer, keying the numbers in. A generic "hello," followed by a chipper "Lane, Smith and Romney! How may I help you?"

Dee asked for Sandra Benson. Another ring. Another hello.

"Miss Benson?" Dee gave the woman a chance to confirm it was she before she went any further. "This is Delores Frank from the Department of Health here in Manhattan. How are you today?" They always asked that question to allow the client time to absorb the Department of Health shocker.

"I'm okay," Sandra answered hesitantly. "I'm nervous about this call."

"Yes, I understand that, truly Miss Benson. Can we meet somewhere to talk privately? I understand you are at your place of business. I can tell you that I am a Public Health representative. Everything we discuss will be confidential." *Expect public humiliation for your boyfriend*, Dee added silently.

"Where and when?" Sandra asked. "I'm available now, if that will help. My office is downtown."

"I'm in Chelsea, Miss Benson. You tell me where to meet you and I'll be there," Dee said.

"I can come to you. As a matter of fact, I would rather come to you. My office may not be as private as I think it is and I don't want to take any chances," Sandra confessed. They arranged to meet in half an hour at Dee's office. There was a little-used, comfortable, and private interviewing area with an unmarked door accessible from Twenty-eighth Street. The locals weren't even aware of its tenant.

Sandra knew the purpose of the meeting. That it should take place so soon after Cindy Thomasini's visit was unsettling. There was a timeliness to these things that brought terror to Sandra rather than peace. Slowly, what she thought she knew to be true about her life was being destroyed.

4

Betty James picked Marie Fabian to interview after the meeting with Pamela Smith was completed. She and Maggie left the Smith house in Babylon with sadness and compassion, but, strangely, also with admiration. Pam Smith was a woman who, only a month or so into grieving the loss of her beloved husband, had discovered shocking information about the man. Not only was he a philanderer who left a pregnant mistress behind, he had sexually abused his wife's sister from the time she was fifteen years old. And to make matters worse, all three women had positive Western blocs, confirming that they had HIV or AIDS.

When Betty and Maggie had pulled up to the front of the Smith house, they both sighed. It was such a picturesque house; white clapboards with green shutters and a cedar shake roof. From the street, it appeared to be a modest Cape Cod with a large, three-car carriage house in the front. The garden was lovely; salt-tolerant perennials grew in colorful clumps along a split rock path to the front door. As they walked the path, the true size of the house became evident. It was a trick to the eye. The door was eight feet tall and wide enough for two adults to go through side by side, yet from the curb, it had looked like a gnome's door.

46

Pam greeted them both warmly and led them into a wide hallway. But it was what lay beyond the low-ceilinged hallway that took the women's breath away; a large set of sliding glass doors opened up to a vast veranda right out of *House Beautiful*. And then, the vista of the sea. The dunes rose just high enough to obscure the beach. The only thing one could see from that vantage point was the very tips of the beach umbrellas and the vast blue of the Atlantic Ocean. The doors were open and the sounds of gulls calling, of the surf hitting the sand, and of children's laughter made Betty and Maggie want to take their shoes off and run to join them. They immediately relaxed, staring at the water and saying nothing.

Pam laughed aloud. "It's the magic of the sea," she said. "Enjoy it while you are here." She stood in the doorway and swept her hand toward the veranda. "Come and sit, won't you? I have a light snack for you." She would struggle to stay in character no matter what these interlopers threw at her. Faking peace had gotten her this far.

The women moved forward, mesmerized. Later, Betty said she didn't remember even arriving at the house. It was as though they went from the car to sitting on the veranda in one movement. Betty pulled her chair out without taking her eyes off the water. Maggie couldn't stop looking around.

"Check out that rock garden. I might have to take a picture later," she whispered, reaching into her briefcase to pull out the paperwork she had on Pamela Smith. It was the law that hospitals and laboratories send the names of new HIV-positive cases to the Department of Health for surveillance data. She also had Partner Notification forms, which were not mandatory in the state of New York. It was ethical and moral to tell the interviewers who your sex partners were, but it was not illegal if you chose not to do so.

In the case of a dead person, what the team had planned on doing by taking out a cryptic ad was considered illegal by some factions, but could be supported if the behavior of the decedent was so promiscuous that many lives were endangered. Also, if a person known to be HIV-positive infected many partners in a wanton manner, which may be the case here, a court order would absolve the team from criminal charges if the family found out and sued. There was always the risk that a citizen who became infected with AIDS by a person known to the Department of Health could sue if he or she had not been notified by the department. There were so many angles. The staff always tread lightly. The women wanted to err on the side of conservatism, but their boss was quicker to act. It was his head that would be on the chopping block.

Pam Smith was a known HIV case because her physician had contacted the health department and sent in the required paperwork. She had been on the list of people to interview. When her husband's blood tests were found, she moved to the front of the list. No one wanted to disturb the peace of another human being, but it had to be done. As though she were entertaining long-lost friends, Pam returned with a tray of iced tea and cake. But the illusion would not last for long.

"Mrs. Smith, do you understand why we are here?" Betty asked. Pam acknowledged that she did, gritting her teeth. "We want you to know that everything we say here is confidential. Also, that some of the questions we ask may be painful for you to answer. You are under no legal obligation to reveal anything to us. If you feel like we are coercing you at any time, please say something right away. Is that clear to you?"

Yes," Pam replied. *Get on with it, will you?* she thought. *I hate you, Jack.*

"Okay, we can get started. Have you had unprotected sex, which includes anal, vaginal, or oral with another partner? Unprotected means without the use of a condom or rubber dam."

"No," Pam answered, shivering involuntarily. She clenched and unclenched her fists, resolving to stay calm no matter how gruesome and depraved this meeting became.

"Have you shared needles to inject intravenous drugs with anyone?"

"No!" Pam exclaimed. *What the hell did they think she was?* The interview continued for several more minutes with the same questions being answered different ways. Pam was quickly losing patience until the last question was asked.

"Do you know of any other partner your late husband may have had sex with, or shared intravenous injected drugs with?"

Pam stared at Maggie with an unreadable emotion; either contempt or stubbornness or complete disgust. But she answered. "Yes. He slept with my sister, Marie Fabian, and with Sandra Benson. I can provide telephone numbers for both women if you don't already have them. However, I gave Miss Frank this information."

"Do you suspect there were others?" Maggie asked as gently as was possible.

Pam looked out to the sea. She thought of the attractive young women who had shown up at Jack's funeral—there had been at least twenty of them, and they had come alone—and thought she might have an answer. She remembered an odd young woman who had come to Bernice's seventieth birthday party a few years ago, and then materialized again at the funeral; of the gorgeous model type who had just happened to run into Jack on the beach, right in front of the house, but claimed not to have known that the Smiths lived there. What would disclosure mean to her family? It was all hearsay. No one had any proof until someone stepped forward. What difference did it make? Would saying yes mean they would search further into his life? Truly, she wanted to know. Having her head stuck in the sand, as she evidently had done for most of her adult life, had not worked for her.

"Yes," she answered. "But having said that, I must ask that you divulge what information you are able to gather to me. I won't ask names, but I must know the truth." And then she thought of her mother-in-law. She remembered reading Jack's accusation in a legal brief found after his death, that his father had sexually abused him and his brother, Bill for most of their childhood. *Could Jack have gotten HIV from his father?* Then there was a risk that his mother was infected, too. *Oh, my God.* "I just thought of something," she said looking at Maggie. "My mother-in-law may be infected." She didn't need to say another word. Betty James nodded her head. She reached out a hand to Pam.

"Please accept our deepest apologies for having put you through this. I wish there were another way to gather information. As for your request, we will stay in touch with you. That's all I can say right now." Betty looked over at Maggie for confirmation.

"Anything you need from us, you only have to ask," Maggie said. "We will do what we can to help you through this, okay Mrs. Smith?" They stood up together to end the questioning. But Maggie wasn't ready to leave. "Can I just walk down your path here? I am dying to see the water. It will probably be the only time this summer that I get to the beach."

"Me too," Betty said. "Every year, we say we are going to go to the beach for a picnic and then we end up in Philadelphia with my husband's brother." The three women walked down the wooden path to the beach. It was a gorgeous day for sunning and swimming, but not for them. They didn't speak for several minutes. Finally, Maggie said it was time to go; they had to get back to the city by four. She was reluctant to move from that spot on the boardwalk. "But I don't want to leave!" she whined.

The women laughed together, and Betty tugged at her colleague's hand. "Let's go," Betty said. They gathered up their papers and stuffed them away. Pam, always the gracious hostess, waited patiently while the intruders prolonged their departure. Finally, they were gone and she was alone. *Yet another humiliation at the hands of Jack. One more slap in the face. Thank you, Jack! Great work! I wonder how we will escape public scrutiny this time. How much more can my pride take?* Her mind was running rampant as she cleaned up the cake mess from entertaining the public health pests. Her usual compassionate resolution wasn't working. It wasn't their fault that she was embarrassed by their questions, she reasoned. It really didn't make any difference at all if the whole world knew what a scoundrel her late husband had been. The painful fact was that soon she was going to be forced to tell her children about the AIDS. Maybe once that task was over with, she would return to being her usual, content, optimistic self. But for now, she chose to wallow in self-pity, not caring where it took her. For once, she was giving in to something negative and painful without giving herself the usual pep talk. There was nothing she could say this time that would help.

5
Melissa

Something is happening to my body and it is really scaring me. If this keeps up, I will have to go to the doctor, which I hate. I hate how the nurses look at me as if I'm a freak when I walk in. No one in that clinic asks any questions to me directly. They start every inquiry with "I wonder" or "I guess."

"I wonder if this could be related to your tattoos." Or my favorite, "I guess this could be a residual effect of drug use." No one has ever treated me for drug addiction, or tested me for it, that I know of. Their treatment of me comes from the way I look. And that pisses me off. One nurse in there is so goddamned fat that she has to walk down the hall sideways, her pannus swaying back and forth, yet she treats me like a pariah. A few years ago, she even had the nerve to comment aloud about a little weight I had gained…six pounds in a year. I went from a whopping 112 pounds sopping wet to 118. I am five foot six. I attributed the gain directly to Jack. That man couldn't stand to be around me unless he had fed me first. We went out to dinner all the time.

Of course, when he started to see Sandra, that stopped. I understood. Jack and I were possibly better friends than we were lovers. As lovers, we were wild, depraved, sadistic. As friends, you couldn't ask for a better man. He made sure that I was taken care of, I can tell you that. He knew he was going to die. I don't know how he knew it, but he did. I read the paper, so I saw the obit right off. I was devastated. He had given me an envelope with twenty thousand in cash about six weeks before he died.

"Take this, doll, and get it in a safe place. I don't care where you put it. You can use a bank but only for part of it, a little each month, or they start asking questions. That house you are in is safe enough." He got me a real safe and installed it in my bathroom closet. He used a hand drill so my housemates wouldn't hear the noise, and stuck it way in back, on the floor. That thing isn't budging; no one will be able to get it out.

Over the years, he gave me money and I have a nice little nest egg, thanks to Jack. Until he died, he was giving me two thousand a month. I don't have to touch what is banked. Twenty thousand will last me a long time. It doesn't take much to live the kind of life I live. He bought my house for me. I live in the Bronx. I love it up here. I teach anthropology at the community college. My house is within walking distance of the school and only during the worst winter snow does it feel as though it's too far. Jack also loved the Bronx. He told me his father once had an office there. He and his father had a great relationship and Jack was devastated when he died. It almost destroyed him. I saw a big change in Jack at that time. He lost a lot of his zest for living.

I am a New Yorker through and through. My parents lived in Bronxville until 9/11. That ruined the city for them. They couldn't stand it anymore and moved to Florida. I thought that was passive aggressive. I'm almost an albino, for Christ's sake! How can I go to Florida? Unless I become one of those women you see who wear the long-sleeved shirts with long skirts and big hats with veils. Or a nun. I could wear a habit. Or a burka.

When I saw that he died and where the funeral was, I got my friend Todd to drive me out to Babylon. I have a terrible sense of direction and never, ever, if I can help it, leave the city. But I had to go to Jack's funeral. I had seen his wife before. A couple of years ago, she came to a birthday party at his mother's mansion. He invited me and of course, I went. Jack knew he could trust me. I clean up nice, too; don't stand out the way I do when I am in my regular clothes. I wear long sleeves and long pants and remove the jewelry from the most outlandish piercings. My hair is so blonde that it's almost white, and it's natural, too. My body hair is pure white, almost nonexistent. I have pale blue eyes. It set me apart all of my childhood. The best thing about having such pale skin is that tattoo artists love inking me. I have never paid for a tatt. Jack loved my tattoos. He often went with me to the Village studios; he liked watching them work on me. He had a fantasy that he was a tattoo artist. Once, we got fine-tipped felt pens and I let him go to town drawing on my body! Ha! I had marker on parts of me that I couldn't even see. It was very erotic.

At the funeral, I tried to make contact with his wife. I felt certain it would be something that Jack would have wanted. But no matter how hard I tried, she would not acknowledge me. She knew. That was why. She looked at me with a stare that burned through me. Her face was expressionless, but I felt her hatred of me. I was glad then that Jack wasn't there to experience it. I found myself curious about their relationship. It couldn't have been much because he was so busy with his sexual conquests. He chose to stay with his wife and children, to have a life that everyone who knew them envied. But I knew better. And I wasn't the only one.

During the years we were lovers and friends, Jack had many women, too many for me to count. I lost track of who he was seeing as a self-preservation tactic; it was too painful to be aware of him sleeping with someone I knew, or seeing him on the street with another woman. Once, about two years ago, while I was lecturing on the history of language and its relation to culture, I saw him out my window talking to a woman. I totally lost my train of thought as I walked over to look out at him. My students followed me and soon we were all standing at the window, looking at Jack. *Why is he even on campus?* I thought.

"Who are we looking at?" one of my students asked.

"That man there, the one in the suit talking to the redhead," I replied. "I wonder why he's here?"

"Ah, teach, that should be obvious!" Jack was taking the woman in his arms for a kiss. "What's his name?" At that moment, they knocked on the window trying to get his attention, yelling and laughing. It worked, because he looked up and saw us. He made eye contact with me—even from a distance, I'm difficult to miss—and I waved at him.

That marked the end of our physical relationship, but we remained good friends, still seeing each other weekly or more often, and Jack still taking care of me financially. He had said that he never gave any other women money, not that it would matter to me. I didn't ask for it. Jack was funny about people; he didn't shy away from speaking his mind, but he also had a soft heart. I think because of my coloring, he felt sorry for me. I was different, but not grotesque, at least in his eyes. By giving me money, I was his own, personal charity and he didn't have to get his hands dirty.

And then he started to see Sandra. He still called me every day, and came up at least once a week to take me grocery shopping or out to lunch. But the dinners and the shows and movies stopped. He explained right away that he thought he was in love. It was someone he had known for a while, someone from his office. To say that I wasn't hurt would be a lie. I may have hoped down deep inside that he would return to me someday and that I would be the one who would change him, who could drive him to monogamy.

Sandra may have been the first woman he dated whom he took his time getting to know before seducing. They were friends for a long time before they dated. And he was "normal" with Sandra, if Jack was capable of normalcy. Jack thrived on kinky, almost masochistic sex. I didn't see him having a long relationship without something depraved on the side. I mean, his marriage was the same thing. He may have been planning to replace Pam with Sandra. I was glad I didn't have to be in on that fiasco. Of course, his death ended the threat.

Life without Jack is boring. Men who are interested in me are generally creepy middle-aged pedophiles who like a woman to look like a ten-year-old; or teenage boys who think I am cool because I look like a ghost with tattoos all over its body. So I am alone and will probably be alone for a while. I'm still grieving. No one has ever cared about me the way he did. He completely accepted me for who I am and embraced all my strangeness. I wish I could be friends with his wife; there are things I know he felt for her that she should know. But I doubt if that will happen because I don't have any respect for her. Today I have to get the courage to make an appointment with a doctor. I am really frightened by what he will find.

6

Sandra got a cab to go the four or so miles to meet with Dee from the health department. Her afternoon thoughts had been dominated by how her relationship with the wealthy, upper-class Jack Smith had totally destroyed her life. She had hurt his wife, who was a kind and generous woman; contracted a deadly disease; put her unborn baby's life at risk; and now was going to suffer through the humiliation of providing a survey of her sexual escapades to a stranger from the public health sector. All she thought about during the ride was how glad she was that she had not slept with her only male contact since Jack; a cop by the name of Tom Adams. He had entered her life like a whirlwind and exited it just as quickly. She imagined having to call him to tell him that he would be getting a visit from the Department of Health and it made her physically ill.

The cab stopped on the corner of Twenty-eighth and Broadway and she got out there. The door to the interview room was unobtrusive. She knocked. It was opened right away by a woman who could look Sandra in the eye. She rarely encountered another woman as tall as she was. Dee closed the door after Sandra passed through and then offered her hand.

"Thank you for coming. I'm Dee Frank," she said. "And you are?" You just couldn't be too careful when dealing with people's lives; she wanted to hear who this was from Sandra's own mouth before they moved on. Sandra identified herself. Dee led her to a pair of chairs with a small round table between them. She had several papers spread out. "Have a seat," she said. Sandra sat down and Dee sat opposite her.

"I received notification of your blood test results, Miss Benson. You were named as a possible partner of Jack Smith. Could you verify that?"

"That's correct." Sandra would later add this to her list of things for which she had Jack to thank.

"Now, here are the questions that I must apologize to you in advance for asking. Have you had unprotected sex, which includes anal, vaginal, or oral with another partner? Unprotected means without the use of a condom or rubber dam."

"No!" Sandra exclaimed, repulsed.

"Have you shared intravenous needles with anyone?"

"No."

When Dee asked the final question, Sandra thought for a few moments about whether she should mention Cindy Thomasini's name.

"Do you know of any other partner Jack Smith may have had sex with, or shared intravenous injected drugs with?" Dee looked at her intently. Sandra was looking back at Dee with equal intensity. Finally, she made up her mind. She couldn't lie. If it made Jack look bad, he brought it on himself.

"Yes, I met another woman that he was having sex with just a few hours ago. That you would call me within minutes of leaving her is unnerving. I keep trying to understand the purpose for all of this." Sandra opened her purse and took out the sheet of paper on which she had written information about Cindy and handed it over to Dee Frank. "She is thirty-one. She was in a relationship with Jack for three years." Sandra had not yet had the time to think too deeply about what Cindy had told her. Jack was screwing her while he was sleeping with Sandra. Only a few times a week, Cindy had said! *Oh, my God.*

Dee thanked her for the information and they concluded the interview. Sandra left the office without saying good-bye. She was worried that if she opened her mouth, yodeling screams would emerge that nothing could stifle.

She couldn't get a cab, which just pissed her off even more. She decided not to go back to the office; by the time she got downtown she would have to turn around and leave anyway. There was a subway entrance on Twenty-eighth Street and she would get on the train there and get home. She just wanted to be home with the doors locked. Her apartment was on the Upper West Side. It was in a genteel neighborhood. She didn't want to think about AIDS and mistresses and shared needles. Several times in the hot subway car, she felt faint. The man next to her smelled bad—body odor and cigarettes. *If I have to barf, I'll just face him and do it in his lap. Don't adults know that bathing is not optional?* An image of her late parents shimmered in front of her face. *Relax, you'll be fine.* She could hear her mother's voice. *You make me so proud! You are proof of my worthiness.* Her mother used to tell her that repeatedly. Finally, Sandra gave in. She couldn't control the tears. Thank God her parents had died. She couldn't imagine having to tell them she was HIV-positive, let alone unmarried and pregnant by a married man.

Fortunately, no one on a subway train cared if she cried. She just let the tears flow. When her stop came up, she got off the train and dried her tears as she walked up the stairs to Broadway. She'd had a stomachache all day, probably because she was constipated. There were so many lovely manifestations of pregnancy that are never talked about and she had almost every one of them. She would stop in the grocery store and pick up something to eat for dinner and get an enema, too. Eating was so boring that she had to remind herself constantly to do it. At her last visit to the obstetrician, she was shocked to learn that she had lost four pounds that week. The doctor warned her to either reverse the trend or go into the hospital where he could monitor her nutrition.

She strolled up and down the aisles looking for something that would grab her interest. Nothing looked appetizing. Finally, she saw pizza bread. The crust was shiny with olive oil and the fat from the pepperoni that had melted out when it was in the oven. She grabbed a loaf. A few more things looked promising and she was ready to check out. She placed her items on the counter along with her enema. The man behind her was looking at her strange selection of purchases.

"Glad you aren't eating dinner at my house tonight?" she asked him.

The walk home was only four blocks but it felt like miles. The day had gotten away from her and she realized that she hadn't heard from Pam. She wouldn't say anything to her about Cindy Thomasini. It was irrelevant. Sandra would protect Pam from any more horrendous news about her husband. About Jack. She realized that after what she had done to Pam, she had deserved to hear from Cindy about her affair with Jack. *Revenge is mine, sayeth the Lord*. She felt separated from God. But wasn't that when faith played a major role? The tiniest faith was all it took. *Faith the size of a tiny mustard seed*. She needed that right now. Needed to believe that the baby would be safe, that she wouldn't die young and leave the baby an orphan and that Pam would continue to be her friend.

Her front door loomed ahead and it seemed to take forever to get there. She didn't notice the car parked in front of her building where no parking was allowed until the door opened and a tall, handsome police officer unfolded himself out of it. Her heart did a little summersault. Tom Adams.

"Don't scream," he said and walked up to her.

"Get lost," Sandra said. "I have nothing to say to you." She kept walking toward the front door.

"Just give me a minute, will you please?" Tom Adams had long legs but was having to skip along beside her to keep up. "I'm sorry!"

"Don't you have some parking tickets to write?" She reached her door and struggled with the key, shaking him off when he attempted to help her unlock the door.

"If you'd wait a minute, I can get it for you," he said.

"Go to hell!" she yelled. "Go back to Brooklyn or wherever it is you live. You are the last person on earth that I want to hear anything from right now, do you understand me?"

Without another word, he took the bag of groceries from her and pulled her against his body with his free arm. She allowed the intrusion.

"I don't believe that for a minute," Tom said.

"Believe it, jerk," she said. And then she started crying. "And I hate you!"

She let the tears flow down her cheeks, wetting his shoulder. She gave him the key and he opened the door for her. When they got into the apartment, they didn't speak as they put the groceries away. She forgot about the enema until it was too late. He picked it up and read the label aloud. They laughed.

"It's not that funny," she said.

"Yes it is," Tom replied.

He filled the teakettle while she got the new coffee pot out from under the counter; she hadn't thought she would ever need it again. He prepared tea for her while she made coffee for him, neither saying a word. Then he followed her down the stairs to the back patio; they would sit in the shade of the surrounding buildings and drink their beverages. They still hadn't spoken more than a few words beyond the bickering. She thought about the note he had left her the last time they were together, just a week or so before. In it, he told her he didn't think he could handle her past and knew that it was ridiculous to expect her to pretend that it didn't exist. So he was bowing out of her life. She remembered the way it had affected her; *what else could happen?* she had thought. *Good riddance.* But now that he was here, now that she felt him and could see him, she realized that if he did that to her a second time, it would leave a mark. She looked at him intently.

"Don't ever do that to me again," was all she said.

"I won't. I promise. Forgive me?"

"Yes, I think I will. And not just because you are so damn cute. I need you, unfortunately. In case you haven't noticed, I'm not the most desirable woman around right now." She had nothing to lose by being self-deprecating. If he couldn't tolerate it, the sooner he left again, the better. "You're the only one who will put up with me."

He squeezed her hand. "I love you, Sandra." There, he had said it. Once he had said it, he couldn't take it back. He was almost thirty years old and he had never said 'I love you.' He had never felt love for a woman before. He was willing to face the wrath of his family, to lose their respect, even their love, for this woman. He would give everything up for her. He wouldn't lie; before, he could only imagine a life with Sandra and her baby if he was able to claim the baby as his own. Now, he knew that he would raise another man's baby with as much love as if he had provided the sperm himself. This was his wife. This woman was the one that his mother said she had been praying for since the day he was born.

While they sat outside, listening to the sounds of traffic dying down as rush hour came to an end, Tom thought about the prayer and how hypocritical it was of him to think he could ask for anything when he wasn't being honest with Sandra or himself. Despite the fact they'd only been together for a short time, they felt passionately about each other. Yet they had already allowed several pink elephants into their lives. For one thing, Tom realized that he was lying to himself and to her when he said that the baby's parentage wasn't important. He had said he didn't care what everyone would think about him and Sandra, but he did care. He expected Sandra to end her relationship with Pam. He wasn't jealous of a dead man, but he thought that every time the two women would get together, they would talk about Jack and try to keep him alive for the child's sake.

Sandra realized that her relationship with Pam might be a temporary thing. She felt it. Even though they needed each other now, it was part of the grieving process. At the beginning, she and Pam were free to share stories about Jack with each other, things that no one else would know. The telling grew very one-sided as the women discovered that only Pam had stories that were validated by her marriage to Jack. The ones Sandra wanted to share were too painful for Pam to hear. They emphasized the emptiness of Pam's marriage, and nothing more. If Pam and Sandra were going to live in a vacuum for the rest of their lives, making their lives a shrine to Jack would be fine. But they weren't going to do that. They were going to try to move on.

Tom and Sandra had spent an afternoon last weekend with Pam and her sister, Marie, in Babylon, and it was an eye-opener. He hadn't thought he was a prude, but was he? After about an hour in the company of their chef that night, Jeff Babcock who was Pam's neighbor, Tom realized that his tolerance for the man was near zero. And it wasn't because he was gay; Tom was not a homophobe. No, it was because Jeff Babcock was a bore. And Marie? Being in her presence on two occasions was two too many. She was a nut case. Tom was only surprised that he had never encountered her before in police matters because her kind made up the bulk of his arrests. Pam reminded him of all the wealthy matrons he had met who had empty, frivolous lives.

Tom fought the temptation to investigate Jack Smith because if Sandra found out, it would definitely mean the end of them as a couple. But his police intuition smelled a rat; worse than an AIDS-infected rat. He needed to get up and move; these thoughts were making him nervous.

"Do you want to walk down to the river?" Tom asked. "We can sit in the park and watch the sun go down." They went back into the house, putting their cups in the kitchen. Sandra got a light sweater even though it was warm. Into her purse she put a bottle of water and a small package of tissues. She went into the bathroom and got bug-repellant wipes out of her beach bag, just in case. Tom watched her with curiosity.

"We're just going down to the park, not taking a trip to Coney Island," he joked.

"You laugh, but I'm ready for anything." *Not pregnancy or sexually transmitted diseases,* she thought. But if they could avoid talking about that every single time they were together, they might learn a thing or two about each other, so she kept those thoughts to herself. There were other interesting topics to cover.

"I can see that," Tom said. And she was right; it was cool down by the water, the mosquitoes were terrible, and he got thirsty and asked for the water. "I never get thirsty! I'm a guy!"

Tom talked about his sisters. Sandra told him she was frightened to meet his family. The idea that they were in Brooklyn and she had lived in Manhattan all her life was scary enough. They would have nothing in common

"My sisters will love you!" he said. Was that the truth? He wondered. They would probably hate her. His sisters were critical snobs. He couldn't see them with Sandra at all, but he wasn't going to say that. He would protect her from reality for as long as he could.

"The truth is that you don't need to meet them until you are ready. Eventually, I will tell them the truth about not being the baby's father. If they can't accept that and be respectful, they don't have to see the baby. This brings us to the next issue. Do you want to have more? Because I want kids. A lot of them," Tom stated.

"I never thought about having children! This baby was a huge surprise. But I want it so badly; I guess I must want children." Sandra was feeling very protective of her unborn baby at that point. Did she want competition for him or her? Possibly someone who would take all of his father's love away? Jack and his real father suddenly entered her thoughts; Harold was Jack's stepfather, a secret discovered after his death in documents stored in Jack's desk. A chill went through her. History was repeating itself, only this baby's life would have a better outcome than Jack's did.

She thought of the HIV. Would her doctor dissuade her from getting pregnant again? It was something she hadn't thought of. She didn't bring it up because once again, she didn't want to ruin the mood.

At dusk, they started walking back to Sandra's apartment. Although they were silent, Tom held on firmly to Sandra's hand, looking at her and smiling from time to time.

They arrived at her apartment. "I'm going to pull my car around back. Want to come with me?"

Sandra felt the flush move through her body as if she were on a rollercoaster ride. He was going to spend the night.

7
Blythe

I'm having a bad financial month. When Jack was alive, I got used to the money he gave me. Two thousand dollars in cash every month. It was enough to cover my rent, electric bill, and food. He told me to save it but I never did. Now I have to pay all my bills with the paltry money I make from my job, which is next to nothing when you have to start living on it. I am a bartender at Prestige. It's not prestigious, however. It's a dive. Jack lived a block from Prestige. Just one block over from the opulent Madison Avenue lifestyle is a filthy alleyway and Prestige is right off the alley. Jack came in every night for a drink.

I've been working there for a long time. I'm a career barmaid. It isn't what I had planned on doing with my life. I graduated from college. The job was supposed to be for just the summer. In the fall, I was going to start teaching in Smithtown. But that never happened because I met Jack. The first time he saw me, he hit on me. "Boy, you sure are pretty," he said. I thought, *You've got to be kidding me! What a corny line.* So I decided to keep it corny and answered, "I bet you say that to all the girls." We started talking. He came in the next night and we talked. He made the night go by quickly. He didn't waste any time letting me in on what he wanted from me.

I found out later that he lived in the neighborhood and that he lived alone. That was all I was able to learn about him. I still lived in Brooklyn at the time, but Jack wanted me to move into Manhattan. There was no way I could afford it. He never asked me to his place. "I don't take girls up there," was all he said. He refused to discuss it. The first time we slept together, he got a room for us down the street. It was a crappy hotel, but not exactly a fleabag. He didn't stay the night, but told me to, and gave me money to get breakfast in the morning. It was great not having to go back to Brooklyn in the middle of the night. For months, we went to that hotel a couple of times a week. I know why he got sick of the hotel. He found me a studio apartment in Midtown so he could take our "love life" a little farther onto the dark-side.

"It's time for you to move here," he said. "There are things I want to do to you that I can't do in a hotel room." He laughed, coming to me and "pretend" biting my neck. Then he gave me some money. "Don't spend all of this on your rent. If you can't afford to live here, you should stay in Brooklyn. Do you understand me? I want you to save some of this each month."

At first, I did set some aside, but then I would see a dress or a pair of shoes and have to buy them. I have always been terrible with money.

I found out quickly that if I demanded anything of Jack, I wouldn't see him. He would stop coming to the bar, stop calling me. There'd be nothing for days.

I never had his cell phone number, either. "I'll see you almost every night during the week. I'll call you daily. If that is not enough, tell me and we'll stop this right now." I thought I could do it. I thought seeing him that often would be enough. Sometimes it was, sometimes it wasn't. I slowly got used to our life together. He'd come into the bar shortly before closing at two in the morning and have a drink or two and then he would walk home with me. He'd stay for an hour or so and go back to his own place. He never, ever spent the night.

Weekends sucked. I hated being in that neighborhood on the weekends because it was completely dead. My windows faced the windows of an apartment next door. It was like a closet, dark and closed in. I didn't know who lived in my building and didn't want to know. I survived by working every weekend. I had to; there was nothing else for me to do. I didn't have many friends in the city. All of my family was in Brooklyn and the few friends I used to have there had moved on. Jack never called me on the weekends. I didn't know where his apartment was or what he did that couldn't include me. In the early years, I would walk up and down Madison Avenue for hours at all times of the day and night, hoping to catch a glimpse of him.

Then out of nowhere, I guess it was about 1999, I was forced to go to the ballet with my family because my sister's brother-in-law had a small role in the production. As we were waiting in a long line to go in, I looked up just as Jack, in a tux, was helping a rather plain woman not much older than I was out of a limousine. He offered her his arm and she took it, smiling into his eyes. They walked ahead of all of us who were waiting to get into the nosebleed section; a photographer's flash going off in their direction. I couldn't take my eyes off them. For a fleeting moment, I had the impulse to run up to him and demand that he acknowledge me, but then I chickened out. What would he do if I embarrassed him in public? Was he famous? I thought his name was a pseudonym. Jack Smith? It just sounded fake. I didn't have a computer but on the rare occasions I went home to Brooklyn, my sister would allow me access to hers for quick searches. I did find out that he was really Jack Smith. There on the Internet was a picture of him with a pretty, blonde woman at someone's high school graduation. And then another of Jack and the young woman with whom I saw him at Lincoln Center, but this photo was taken at the Met at an art opening. In another photo, Jack stood with a man. The article was about some building project on the Lower East Side that would save the neighborhood. The neighbors were up in arms, calling Jack and this man "destroyers of New York" who were trying to convert the colorful area into one in which rich people just like Jack would be comfortable living. Of course, it was too late, the Jewish deli had already left the area and a taco stand had taken its place. Jack had waited too long.

Although I learned little bits about him, he would continue to be a mystery to me until I saw his obituary. Actually, I missed it, but one of the other bartenders who saw me leave with Jack night after night for years

and years saw it and saved it for me, waiting until closing time Monday night. Jack hadn't shown up and I
would have been wondering about him for weeks. He
had done that in the past with no explanation, or a
meager one if I pressed him. I figured out that he took
vacations from time to time. The article that accompanied the obituary said he lived in Babylon. I thought
of all those weekends wasted marching up and down
Madison. He wasn't even there in his apartment. But
Babylon? Wasn't it a quaint little village? Why would
Jack live there? Wild Jack, sadistic Jack, secretive Jack?
His antics would not have gone over well in Babylon.

But I couldn't stop from wondering what was
there. Well, I would never know unless I spent some
time digging around. I had nothing more to do. I had
wasted over fifteen years of my life waiting for Jack. I
was thirty-seven years old. I couldn't afford to pay my
rent because I was suddenly two grand a month poor-
er. I couldn't do anything but tend bar. Could I?

And then I had a thought. Jack had been a great
teacher; he had shown me the tricks of a dominatrix.
He kept his collection of devices and magazines in my
dark little studio apartment. They were his legacy to
me. I could place an ad in one of those magazines; he
had used services from those classifieds often enough.
I think I just figured out how I will make my rent this
month.

8

Betty and Maggie left Pam's after the interview. Pam kept thinking of the albino girl. Over the years, she had seen her at several family functions, Little League fund-raisers, and the funeral. Pam couldn't get her out of her mind. She went through the basket of sympathy cards sent after Jack died and found one she was sure was from the young woman; Melissa McMann. Pam wanted to search online for her phone number but the only computer in the house was Jacks, and it had not been used since the kids left after July 4th. She picked up the mouse and turned the computer on. After a little research, she found out that Melissa didn't have a landline. *Maybe the number is in Jack's cell phone.* Pam's heart did a little beat skipping. She opened the drawer of his desk and got out his cell phone. She had never done that before, never looked at his phone contacts, maybe because she was afraid of what she would find. Up popped a couple of hundred names; most appeared to be women. Feeling sick to her stomach, she scrolled through the alphabet to the M's and found Melissa's number. It was a Bronx exchange; seven-one-eight.

It's was late, after eight-thirty at night. As heat spread through her body, Pam decided to call Melissa because she'd never get any sleep if she didn't confront her right then. Using Jack's cell phone, Pam keyed in the number and it was answered right away by a shocked, "Hello, Hello! Who is this?"

Melissa sounded younger than Pam remembered.

"Melissa, it's Jack's wife. Please don't hang up on me, I'm not angry, I'm not calling to admonish you," Pam said, having forgotten that Jack's phone number would show up on Melissa's Caller ID.

"Oh, God! I saw his number! I think I might throw up," Melissa cried. She had been at the funeral. She had seen his body in the casket, but there was his number. *Oh, God.*

"Dear, I am sorry to upset you. We need to talk, okay? I want to meet you. I want to know about you. I want to know what Jack meant to you. But we need to talk about other things, too. Can you meet with me?" Pam asked.

"Yes, but you're scaring me!" Melissa yelled.

"Well, I'm sorry; I don't know any other way to do it. I would rather not come into the city. Do you think you could come here to me?"

"I don't drive," Melissa said.

"You live in the Bronx, correct?" Pam asked.

"How'd you know that?" Melissa countered.

"I recognized the exchange. But I have your address from funeral flowers. Did you get my thank-you card?" There was silence. "You can take the train to Long Island."

"I do remember. The card, I mean. I guess I could take the train."

Pam told her what train to take and she agreed to come.

"I have a class in the morning," Melissa said, and Pam's heart sank. *He'd been sleeping with students?*

"What year are you in?" Pam asked.

"I teach at the community college up here," Melissa answered and Pam tried not to sigh audibly with relief. They hung up. Although she felt ill, sick to her stomach, her bowels rumbling Pam knew she was doing the right thing. She'd tell Melissa and then she'd let the Department of Health know; they could question her about with whom she had been sleeping. It wasn't Pam's business.

Pam started thinking about the cell phone and the contacts. She made herself a cup of tea. She sat at the counter in her perfect kitchen and started to scroll through the names, hundreds of them, all female. There were six Melissas. She put the phone down and looked up at the ceiling, laughing. *Where the hell was I?* And then she thought, *He had Monday through Friday, every day, year after year after year, and evidently, while she was at home primping, he was with as many other women as he could pack in. How many did he have a day, and were they all sexual relationships?* She decided she was going to call every one of those women. She'd call Maggie Daniel and tell her. She'd give her the contact information after she was done with it. But as Jack's wife, she wanted to do the calling. It was her responsibility.

<hr>

Melissa's brownstone in the Bronx was not what her friends expected when they went to see it for the first time. Thinking they would find a rundown, hippie hangout that smelled of incense and mold, reality was a shocker. Jack had bought her a large, restored Victorian. The interior was light-filled and modern, with subtle paint colors and spare but comfortable furniture. The bathrooms were huge marble-and-porcelain originals that craftsmen had taken the time to bring back to their former beauty. Across the back of the house was the large kitchen, a dream kitchen for a future cook. Although she knew she wouldn't use it much, it raised the resale potential of the house.

She had two housemates and their financial contribution made it possible for her to refrain from dipping into the money that Jack had given to her. For now.

The next morning, she taught her class and when she was done for the day, left for Grand Central for a two-hour train ride. The car wasn't crowded because it was the middle of the day. When she got to the station in Babylon, she called Pam as she had been asked to do. But Pam was waiting for her, sitting in the parking lot. Pam recognized Melissa right away. Against her will, she envisioned Jack and the tattooed woman naked together. A sneer of scorn went through the muscles in Pam's face. Shocked, she pulled the rearview mirror down and rearranged her expression to the usual one of concern. She got out of the car and went to Melissa. Melissa saw her walking toward her and didn't know what to expect. Pam put out her hand to shake Melissa's, smiling. She hid well her surprise at the girl's appearance. All of those tattoos had been covered up somehow at the funeral.

Back to her usual welcoming self, Pam led Melissa to the car. She unlocked the doors and they got in.

"Thank you for coming," Pam said. "Do you want to go to the house? Or do you want to talk in the car?"

"I'd like to see the house. I feel like I know it in my head. I want to see the ocean," Melissa replied.

Waiting for the pain, for the flush of heat, Pam realized she was over it, that Jack couldn't hurt her anymore. Somehow, in a few short months, she had come to this place of peace—*or was it emotional death?* They pulled up in front of the house and Melissa had the same reaction everyone did: she loved the beauty of the house and its setting. She was thinking, *I can't picture Jack here. It's too removed from the action.* "I can't picture Jack here." Melissa stated, repeating her thoughts. "I can't believe he was ever comfortable here."

Nix not being hurt by Jack anymore, Pam thought.

Melissa's expression challenged Pam to argue. But Pam was intrigued and said as much. This young woman might be the counter-irritant that would make all the positive ass-kissers she had encountered since Jack's death ring false. All she had heard from others was how much Jack had loved her and how he couldn't wait to get to the beach. Now, maybe she would hear the truth and it would do so much to help her understand how her life with had ended up the way it did. If he had wanted to be at the beach, he would have been at the beach. Not in the city; not with other women. Other men in their community commuted into Manhattan every day and came home at night to be with their families. Jack didn't want to be there. Melissa was right.

"Come sit on the veranda. I'll get us something to drink. I am anxious to hear why you think he wouldn't be comfortable here." Pam showed Melissa the way to the veranda and then went back into the house to get refreshments. While she was preparing their drinks, Pam decided that her approach regarding the AIDS matter would be to blame everything on the health department. She arranged a tray of ice-filled glasses, a pitcher of lemonade, and a plate of cookies: a civilized snack for an odd couple.

"You don't have to tell me anything about you and Jack," Pam said, hoping just the opposite. "I am just making an assumption because I remember you being at different functions. I don't know if Jack always included his girlfriends in our family functions, but I remember you. I remember you at the funeral. Something told me I needed to contact you," Pam said.

"Yesterday I was visited by interviewers from the Department of Health and they informed me that when Jack died, blood was drawn and they tested him for HIV. He tested positive." Pam was watching Melissa, who was sitting up very straight, looking at Pam. She had decided not to reveal anything about her own health. She assumed Jack told his girlfriends that he didn't sleep with Pam anymore, so she would hold on to that little bit of dignity if she was able. "That is all I want to say to you. If you did sleep with him, get tested for HIV."

Melissa thought of her fear of being ill lately, her concern that she needed to see a doctor. But HIV? "I stopped sleeping with him two years ago. And we stopped having any kind of sex when he started to see Sandra."

She knew about Sandra? Once again Pam asked herself, *Where the hell was I?* Pam felt her heart continue to beat in spite of the pain. She was glad that the young woman could tell her the truth; it was satisfying some of her curiosity. She didn't want to say or do anything negative because she didn't want Melissa to stop that train of thought. She wanted her to keep being honest.

"It looks like he might have been infected for a long time. You should get yourself tested." Pam reached over and patted her hand.

Melissa couldn't believe it, and she finally said so. "I can't believe Jack had AIDS and he slept with me without warning me. I can't believe it."

Pam was looking out at the ocean. "I feel the same way. I don't expect you to say anything to me. I just wanted you to know. I have that responsibility because I remembered you and that you came to Jack's funeral. I wasn't aware of his affairs then, but recently, when I found out about his HIV status, I became suspicious that he'd had an affair with you. Knowing that, I had the responsibility to tell you. I didn't want you to get that kind of news cold turkey from the health department. It's evident that you meant something to him. Because of that, because he cared about you, I have that responsibility to you. I don't even know what that means yet, but I feel something toward you."

Melissa looked away from Pam and looked out at the water. "You don't owe me anything. You don't have any responsibility at all. I don't feel anything for you. I'm going to leave now. Will you take me back to the train?" Melissa's response stunned Pam. *I stepped out of my comfort zone to contact one of Jack's sexual partners and this was all she had to say in return?* Feeling her blood pressure rising, Pam wanted to reach forward and slap the young woman across her face. No wonder she had allowed an affair with a married man old enough to be her father!

They got up from the veranda and Pam got her purse and keys. On the way out to the car, Pam ignored her intuition to leave Melissa alone and decided to expose a little more. "Sandra got to the hospital before I did when Jack died. She was called first. I met her in the hospital. Because of that, she and I have ties. Because of Jack, we are almost related. We can talk about Jack together, things no one else would know. We can talk about the way he made us feel, like there was no one else in the world as important. If you ever feel like you need to connect in that way, you can call anytime."

Melissa couldn't believe Pam was saying this because she knew she would never need to talk to her again. "Don't you realize your husband couldn't have loved you? Loved you yet treated you like that? Fucking other women? Not just me. Not just Sandra. I don't want to go into what I know about Jack. I feel no responsibility to those other women. They brought it on themselves. You and Sandra getting together to talk about how special Jack made you feel is a laugh! Oh, Jesus Christ! Are you kidding me?"

Pam let her guard down and started laughing along with Melissa. Melissa was shocked. She expected the woman to haul off and smack her silly. Instead, she was agreeing with her.

"It does seem that way, doesn't it? But I know that he loved me. As much as he was capable of loving, he loved me. He might have loved Sandra, and he might have loved you and how many other women. Maybe he just had a huge capacity for love. Until he loved Sandra—and I never told her this—I never felt a lack in our relationship. I knew he wasn't giving me everything that he could. My sister says that my head is in the clouds. 'Get your head out of the clouds.' And you know what? She was right. I had my head in the clouds." She pulled up to the train and was happy the conversation had come to an end. She may have revealed too much.

"Do you have it?" Melissa asked as they pulled into the station parking lot.

"I thought your impression was that Jack didn't have sex with me," Pam said "That we didn't sleep together anymore. Anyway, I just found out he had it yesterday, remember?"

"I guess that answers my question." Melissa got out of the car without saying good-bye.

But Pam wanted to say one more thing to her. She rolled down her window and called after Melissa. The young woman walked back to the car. She was on the verge of tears. "Will you let me know what happens?" Pam asked.

"Why? What's the point?" Melissa was suspicious of Jack's wife, but more fearful of slipping into the realm of needing her. She didn't want to need her.

"Why?" Pam repeated. "Because I care about you. Tell me I'm an ass, that you understand why a man like Jack would be unfaithful to someone like me. I am an ass! But I'm a caring one."

Melissa tried to squelch laughter, but it was too strong. She laughed aloud. "Well then, I am an ass, too. Jack made asses of all of us." She leaned in on the car door, sticking her arm through the window opening to shake Pam's hand. "Actually, the truth is that he was an ass, and we were just normal women wanting love." She laughed again. "I read that in a book by Dr. Phil."

Pam smiled at her, a pleasant, empty smile. They said good-bye and Pam pulled away from the train station entrance. Mentally and emotionally exhausted, Pam had tried to engage Melissa in ways that she'd never with Sandra and Marie. But she hadn't gained much information. She was sorry Melissa hadn't said more about her relationship with Jack. Pam had figured out that Jack had many women, and Melissa had confirmed it. But more details than she really wanted to know would come later, much later.

9

Betty James and Maggie Daniel parted ways when they returned to the office from their interview with Pam Smith in Babylon. Dee gave Cindy Thomasini's phone number to Betty and Maggie left to meet with Marie Fabian, Pam Smith's sister, at her apartment in Hell's Kitchen. Maggie would then take the ferry home to New Jersey. It would be a perfect way to end the day.

Marie left work early to get home and straighten up her apartment. She was a wreck. It was okay to meet with the health department, but now she feared that she would get into trouble if she divulged the name of the man with whom she was sleeping currently. She wanted to tell him first, let him hear it from her. They'd had unprotected sex a few times. Did that guarantee that he would get it?

Why did she screw him when she knew she was sick? She really liked the man and he was bound to be pissed off at her. Oh Lord, why'd she do it? She wanted to go on as if nothing was wrong, as if she hadn't done anything bad. She decided to lie, then. She would tell the health department that she hadn't slept with anyone, that she didn't know anyone who had slept with Jack. She would exercise her right to privacy. They couldn't do anything to her, could they?

When Maggie got there, Marie didn't offer her a seat. They stood by the door that opened into the living room, which offered a view of the Hudson River and the city of Weehawken beyond. Maggie gasped when she saw the view. *What did this woman, who was nearly her age, do for a living to afford a place with a view like this?*

"I just have a few questions to ask you. Can we sit down somewhere?" Maggie saw Marie glance at the dining area, as if contemplating whether she should invite her to sit, when she sensed a change in Marie.

"You know, I really don't have anything to say. If my doctor has notified you that I have HIV, then so be it. I have it. But that is all I want to say. There is nothing else to tell." Marie walked to the door and removed the chain. "Sorry you came all this way for nothing."

Maggie thanked her and left, not feeling hostile or angry; her ferry was right down the street at the river's edge and she would be home in less than a half an hour. She was worried about the woman's truthfulness. But there was nothing she could do or say about it. She started walking down the hill, headed for her ride home.

Marie's hands were shaking. She couldn't base a relationship with Steve Marks on lies. Jack had done it, and had been successful at it, but look what happened to him. What was happening to her? She had been on a collision course; having unprotected sex was only one thing. She hadn't taken her meds, was drinking to excess, and had quit eating. She knew she was going down a steep path of self-destruction. But her death wouldn't be the only outcome; she had Steve Marks's mortality to worry about.

Marie was going to lie and tell him that the health department had just notified her, but she thought through the scenario. If he called them, he'd find out that she had lied. She struggled with this all night. By omitting the truth, by exposing him to HIV, she had done the unforgivable. And the thing that really backfired on her was that she liked him! After he had stalked her and bugged her at work, it turned out there was a ton of chemistry between them.

She called him after work the next evening after avoiding him all day. She had decided not to make excuses. She was crazy, he had pursued her, and she had not thought of the consequences. The Department of Health had visited to question her about her partners and she thought of him, knowing that she owed him the information so he could get tested right away. There was silence. And then, the unexpected. He started screaming at her like a crazy man.

"You stupid cunt!" he yelled into the phone. "What the fuck did you do? Did you give me AIDS? You goddamned bitch, I should have known! If I have it, if you gave it to me, you're dead! You realize that, right? I'll fucking kill you!" He hung up.

She stood in her bedroom with the phone still at her ear for several minutes, waiting to move until her heart rate slowed down enough that she wasn't in the stroke zone. What was she going to do? She thought she had better leave town; time to flee to Babylon! She threw some clothes into a bag, grabbed her wallet and keys, and left five minutes after he'd hung up. Even if he'd been at the bar up the street when she'd called, it would take him longer than that to reach her. She drove out of the garage and onto Thirty-fourth Street like a demon possessed, frightened that Steve would do as he said and kill her. She found herself chanting, "Don't let him have HIV, don't let him have HIV," faster and faster until it sounded like "Doughn lettem av H ivy." By the time she got to the bridge, she was laughing!

"Yeah, God, doughn lettem!" she yelled. *"Oh fuck!"* And then she made the mistake of looking in her rearview mirror and there was Steve Marks, tailgating her Honda, riding the bumper and going for the kill. She could see his watery blue eyes, bugged out of their sockets, and his purple face. She decided at the last minute that getting on the bridge and being stuck on the expressway with a maniac trying to run her off the road was not smart. She pulled off the ramp, into the coffee shop parking lot. She made sure her doors were locked and then she called 911. When the dispatcher answered, she screamed, "He's going to kill me! I'm in the parking lot of the coffee shop under the bridge! Help me!" Suddenly, Steve was at her window with a rock in his hand, slamming it against the glass, screaming, "Get out of the goddamned car! You're dead meat!" He must have said that ten times, jumping up on the hood and flinging himself at her. Finally, strangers from the coffee shop came to her rescue and pulled him off her car. She looked around at the men struggling with him and said, "Fuck it, I'm outta here,"

and gunned the engine, squealing tires kicking dust and gravel into the faces of her rescuers, and she got back on the bridge ramp, heading toward Long Island. She'd make Pam call Andy, the cop, and see if he could help her in some way. Andy had tried to date Pam but it was too soon after Jack died. He still stayed in touch with her. Marie knew that she would not be staying in Manhattan for a while, at least until Steve Marks calmed down.

Betty went to her office to call Cindy Thomasini and set up an appointment for her surveillance interview. The home phone number was a Hudson County, New Jersey exchange. It wasn't their responsibility to notify partners who weren't living in New York. Betty got out the appropriate forms and placed Cindy in the hands of the New Jersey bureaucrats.

10
Cindy

I was a good Catholic girl. My parents were strict about the oddest things when we were growing up. I wasn't even allowed to watch the movie our school sponsored that explained the process of menstruation to the girls in fourth grade.

"Why do you want to fill your head with that garbage?" my mother said. "You have your whole life to suffer with monthlies; they don't need to spend my tuition money forcing it down your throat. Anything my girls need to know, I will tell them. Anything the boys need, their dad will provide." When the time finally came, she made a public spectacle of me. I went into the bathroom to pee one morning after I had just turned thirteen. I pulled down my underpants and there it was, a bright red, bloody crotch. I had a hot flash. Fear spread through my body. Did I have to tell my mother? I shared a room with Gayle and Carrie, but they were already up and gone for the day. They had boxes of pads in the closet. I went back to our room and fished around until I found what I needed. I would tell them later. I managed to get through the day, worried the flow would go through to the back of my ugly, navy blue pleated skirt. All day I kept my back to the lockers when I walked the halls to class.

When I finally got to the bathroom, there was only a dot of blood. I had spent the whole day being a nervous wreck for nothing. I told my sisters that night and it was Gayle who insisted I tell our mother.

"She'll be dragging you to the doctor's to find out why you didn't start. No, we have to tell her. I'll go with you. Just buck it up. We are all tortured by her when we go through it; you're not alone." So Gayle dragged me to confess to my mother, who looked like she had performed a miracle by giving birth to a female who was growing up.

At dinnertime that night, we were almost done with dessert and I thought to myself, *Ah, you escaped exposure.* But I couldn't be that lucky. My mother stood up at her end of the table and produced a big box of Kotex with a ribbon around it.

"Everybody, before you leave the table, listen up! Stand up, Cynthia." She gave me a look that said, *Get up kid, you can't get out of this humiliation.* "Cynthia got her monthly visitor today!" She placed the box in front of me and started clapping like a crazy woman. My sisters covered their faces and my brothers started laughing, almost falling off their chairs. Father sat at his end of the table, a huge smile plastered across his face. "You are lucky to be a girl in this day and age," my mother continued. "You can be a mother *and* have a life! You don't have to be chained to your family like I am!" Later, she whispered to me that I'd better make sure that period showed up each month, or else!

My mother also wouldn't buy me a bra, so that by the time I was twelve, I was the only girl in gym class who wore an undershirt. Granted my "boobs didn't pop out" until I was fifteen and then I thought my mother would have a cow when she noticed. I'll never forget coming downstairs to the breakfast table on a Saturday morning in my flannel nightgown; my seven brothers and sisters already there before me, my father at the head of the table reading the paper, and my mother standing behind him with a frying pan full of scrambled eggs in her hand.

"Lord forgive us," she said, looking at me as I came into the room. Everyone looked up. My brother Jeff was reading the funny pages and he was the only one who ignored me. "Cynthia Margaret Thomasini, what in heaven's name do you have stuffed in your nightgown?" I could feel my face start to burn. The color had started at my navel and made the trip up my body in seconds, reaching my face in time for my sister Heather to get up from her chair. She took me by the shoulders and gently turned me around, whispering, "Let's go up and get dressed." She shot the look of death at my mother before we left the room, but it was too late. The rest of the kids were laughing at me. It would be remembered as the day my boobs popped out. My mother would bring that up at every family get-together after that until, finally, two years ago, we all moaned and my brother Fred said, "Ma, give it a rest, will ya?" I told her that I would never come for another Sunday dinner if she were going to bring up that story again. Our reward for such disrespectful behavior was a two-month reprieve during which my mother refused to come out of her room when we went to visit.

My father and Fred would cook the Sunday meal and we had the best time without her.

She was miserable most of her life. She had a family of well-behaved, intelligent, employed children and none of us could do a thing correctly. It was a constant contradiction; she insisted that everyone come for dinner once a week, but then would complain about how much work it took to feed us. She especially took exception to everything I did. My brothers and sisters said it was because I was the baby. She'd had too many hopes for me. I was supposed to accomplish everything that the others hadn't.

I finally made up my mind when I was newly out of college that I wasn't going to strive anymore. I watched my sisters kill themselves getting master's degrees and doctorates and then spend the next years raising their families, too tired to enjoy them. I know I copped out, taking that silly secretary job, and then getting involved with a married man. But it was so easy! I didn't have to do anything taxing to please Jack. My house didn't have to be clean, I didn't have to buy him gifts, or remember his birthday, or figure out something different to cook for him every night. After a while, I don't think he even noticed what I was wearing or listened to what I said. I didn't even have to shave my legs. All I had to do was pull down my underpants and sit on him. Half the time, I didn't even face him. It was impersonal, boring. Then last year, (now I know that he was dating Sandra by then) each time I saw him I wondered why I was bothering. But I had gotten myself into such a rut that I guess I was afraid of what would happen if I broke it off. I would be so alone.

Yesterday, a caseworker from the New Jersey Department of Health and Senior Services called me. I had been exposed to HIV. They don't tell you who the infected person is in New Jersey, but I started laughing because there is only one person who could have exposed me and that was Jack Smith. The Jack Smith of Babylon, Long Island. The dead Jack Smith. I don't even have the satisfaction of slapping his face. There is nothing I can do. I went to the lab after work today and had a blood test. They have a rapid test now, so I don't have to wait for six days like they used to in the olden days, the caseworker told me. The early days of HIV. It's not as bad now, she said. I wonder why they are allowed to say that. But the damage has been done. You will never tell my parents that a person can live a normal life with AIDS. I keep thinking how my mother will react when she hears what I have to tell her this time.

II
Maryanne

I'm past the age where I can examine my life and make changes. I will have regrets about the way I lived for the time I have left and I probably will die unhappy. I should be able to retire without worrying about keeping a roof over my head. But it's too late. When I first laid eyes on Jack, I knew he would be trouble. Why didn't I run in the opposite direction? Where was my self-respect? My goal was to set a good example for my daughter, and what did I do? I brought a disease-ridden pervert into our house. All I could see was a handsome gentleman who made me feel like I was the most precious thing in the world.

I guess I am what you call a career waitress. For the past twenty years, I have waited tables at what was Gwen's Counter. Gwen's went out of business about two weeks ago, a month or so after I read that Jack had died. So in one fell swoop, I lost my boyfriend of almost twenty years and my livelihood. Now this latest news. It's enough to cripple a person; to make you want to stay in bed and pull the covers up over your head.

Jack brought his mom into Gwen's for lunch the first Wednesday I worked there. He didn't say anything to me at that time, but I noticed him watching me out of the corner of his eye. It was a new job, but I had waited on tables in the past. Before I was married, I waitressed for a short time. I didn't work while I was married, but then when my husband, Paul died I discovered that he had lost all of our money gambling in Atlantic City. I never even knew that he had left the state! And all along, he was taking the bus down there every Wednesday, losing his paycheck. We were living on credit and I didn't know it until he died. Jack came in alone for breakfast the next day and teased me about getting his order wrong.

"I wanted wheat toast with roasted peppers and this is roasted rye with black pepper. Are you new here?" My husband had died less than a year before, so what I was new at was flirting. Jack was born to be flirted with, however. Even though his order was perfect, I reached over for his plate, getting just close enough so he could smell my perfume.

"Oh I am sorry! Let me change that for you," I said.

He grabbed my arm. "I'm just kidding! You didn't answer me. Are you new here?"

He was so handsome that I started to shake a little and could feel the sweat forming in my armpits. *How attractive!*

"Yes. I'm new here." I looked over to the counter, hoping someone needed me. No luck.

"Have coffee with me," he asked. "The boss won't mind."

"No, sorry, it's against the rules." I turned to walk away from him. There was a sick feeling in the pit of my stomach, like I got caught doing something illegal.

"Wait! Meet me after work, then." He was persistent. I continued walking away from him.

Then curiosity got the best of me. I turned around and walked back to the table. I looked him in the eye to see if he was kidding me again, but there was a simmer going on behind those dark eyes. *Don't answer him,* the still-small Voice said. But I was sucked in, so I ignored it. My women's intuition was always right on target, and for some reason, I allowed my yearning for attention get the best of me that day. To make matters worse, he was younger than I was. Not by much, but just enough that it made me self-conscious. It made me feel like a charity case. And for years, that would define us as a couple; me, the older widow with a special-needs child, and Jack, the knight in shining armor come to save us. I conveyed the delusion that he was helping us to my daughter, Katherine. All through her teen years, she would wait for him as if she was waiting for a date. "Is Jack coming today?" she'd ask, pulling the blinds apart to look down on the street.

He'd usually tell me in the morning if he would be able to stop by. Every day, he came into Gwen's for breakfast, and on Wednesday, he'd come with his mother for lunch. I knew he was married, so I had to keep quiet about us in front of her. It wasn't easy, even after all that time. I was so hungry for information about him. When I got older, I knew I should be making plans for my future. Jack put money in trust for Katherine's care after I was gone, and that was a huge worry off my mind. But what about me? My ego was so damaged for some reason that I didn't figure into the equation. I didn't allow myself to think about what would happen when I could no longer wait tables, or when Jack retired and left the city for good, moving to Long Island with his wife. I chose to live in the moment.

That day has come. Jack is gone. I went into work as usual that Monday morning. Evelyn, the manager, handed me an obituary she'd cut out of the *New York Times* on Sunday. I read the paper, but I didn't read the obituaries—hadn't since Paul died. I saw Jack's name, his full name. Seeing it in print with the names of his wife and children made me physically ill. I needed to throw up. Evelyn knew about Jack and me; I had waited tables there for half my life, practically. She saw the relationship develop, and she facilitated it, letting me sit with him in the morning if it was quiet, or leave early with him if he came by to take me home.

I knew Jack was seeing a younger woman, another person who lived way up town. She lived near the colleges; I was closer to Washington Heights. They were just friends, he said, friends who slept together. When he started to see Sandra, he saw less of that other woman. I didn't know if Sandra knew about me or the other woman. I doubt it. She seemed like someone who would expect fidelity, who would demand respect. Jack and I didn't talk about it much; when we were together, we only had eyes for each other. He didn't see me any less frequently after he told me that he thought he was in love with Sandra. He still needed something that Katherine and I provided for him, some grounding or lack of strife. I am totally without pretension.

Everything about my life is honest and real. Except for betraying Jack's wife. I believe Jack "de-stressed" when he was with us.

With Jack, sex was just sex. He needed the release. He made sure I was satisfied, and that was kind of him. My husband never did know where my clitoris was. On rare occasions, Jack would visit me after Katherine was asleep and we would go to bed. But most of his visits were in the early evening, right after I got off work. He enjoyed sitting around my old kitchen table, drinking coffee with Katherine and me. He did puzzles with her all the time—the most boring, childish, jigsaw puzzles that I didn't like doing. But Jack could really relate to her. We would have a laugh or two; he would stretch and yawn, and then get up like his back was killing him. Katherine got hysterical when he did that.

"You're not that old!" she would protest. He would make a show of walking to the door hunched over, holding his lower back, while we laughed at him. He'd turn and wave to her and she would come up to him for a hug.

"I'll see you in the morning," he'd say, and then give me a kiss good-bye. That was it. He watched my daughter grow up into a young woman who would never get married, never hold down a job, just barely able to dress herself. I think he loved her. Katherine had a beautiful wardrobe. I never expected any gifts from him, but for her they arrived weekly. Huge boxes from Macy's on Thirty-fourth Street were delivered to my shabby house. Or from the teen shop at the World

Trade Center—I think it was called Dots—and when she got older, designer things from the fancy shops on Fifth Avenue. Always for Katherine. Jack would call in the afternoon when she was due home.

"Was the stuff for Katherine delivered yet? What'd she say?" He was as excited as if he were the schoolgirl getting gifts. He just liked doing things like that for her. Katherine would greet him with a big slobbery kiss when he would get to the house. If I was still at work, he would pick me up and we would drive up together. I never worried about Katherine coming home before I did. From the time she was little, I always had good childcare for her, thanks to Jack.

The woman I worked for, Evelyn, used to shake her head. "It doesn't make any sense for that man to pay for those fancy agencies. Why doesn't he just pay you to stay home with your kid instead of working in this dump?" I knew Jack felt that people should work. His wife never did, to my knowledge, but that wasn't my business. Everyone else in his family did. He could have afforded to support us all, but we went to work every day. Katherine had the best healthcare, the most trustworthy childcare, physical and speech therapy— you name it.

When we first met, I told him that I had a child. "I can't meet you for coffee," I said. "I have a child with brain damage." He looked shocked. I don't think Jack had ever been exposed to anyone who wasn't perfect. It was like he was visiting a Third World country. "My sitter will only watch her for the hours I work, so I have to get right home." I was clearing his breakfast dishes that morning so long ago.

"I'll come to your house, then. I want to meet your child. It's a girl, correct? You said 'she'." He seemed suddenly emotional. I was torn between compromising the safety of my house by allowing this man to see where I lived and shaking him up by allowing him to meet my daughter. Katherine, who was only two, had a rare, genetic, birth defect that made her face appear almost as though it were two separate halves. Her eyes were far apart, and she had a cleft palate which, although it had been repaired, made talking come slowly for her. Other than that, she had a normal body. Her hair was flaming red, gorgeously thick and curly. I decided to let him come. It might drive him away to see someone who wasn't born absolutely perfect. Jack surely wouldn't allow imperfection in his life. But I was wrong. He was taken with Katherine. He came into my house, which by his standards was probably modest to the extreme, and the sitter was holding Katherine. She broke into a huge misshapen grin when she saw Jack for the first time, reaching out for him.

"Da! Da!" she hollered. I laughed and took her from the sitter. She was struggling to get at him.

"Can I hold her?" he asked. I could see he was choked up, really having a difficult time holding it together. She had that effect on people, Katherine did. She was so innocent, so loving, that you were able to overlook her unfortunate face and see something deeper, something ethereal. I nodded my head to him and he reached out for her. If toddlers could fly, she almost did into his arms. She put her little arms around his neck and repeated her odd sounding *Da Da*. He turned his back to me while I paid the sitter. He patted her head and was humming something, some rock song, something from the eighties, totally inappropriate for a child, but she loved it. She would not be taken from him, either. Every time I reached for her, she screamed bloody murder. I fixed the three of us dinner and he didn't mind holding her. She sat on his lap while he fed her, making a mess of his expensive suit until I thought of placing a towel around him, although by that time it was too late.

We would remember the next time, though. He would come again and again to see Katherine. He slowly fell in love with her. I saw Jack cry over her when she had another surgery to correct some of her oral anomalies. She was in pain and he couldn't stand it. Rather than running, as my husband had done, Jack insisted on talking to the doctor. Katherine was never in pain again if they could help it. She always had a private room and private-duty nursing care when she was hospitalized.

Then Friday would come and we wouldn't see him for the weekend. That was difficult. I knew he was going home. I appreciated it that Jack told me that he went to his beach house on the weekends. But not being able to contact him, even in an emergency for Katherine, helped me to keep my perspective about the importance of us in his life. We were only important as long as it didn't interfere with his real family.

He never, ever mentioned his perfect children or wife; it was only after his death that I came to understand something of what his family was—wealthy, successful, beautiful—and of Jack's ego. Of course, it was a smokescreen. We know that now.

⌖

I spent last night tossing and turning, unable to come to terms with my own stupidity, my own inability to see my worth. When he first started coming around here, I should have demanded to get what we needed. He probably never would have come back. What I learned about Jack in the past weeks is that he might have been generous with things he could buy, but with his time, he only had so much because he was spread so thinly. How he managed to see so many women and still make the load of cash he made is a mystery. The only one of us who knows more of the story is Melissa. She's giving me the dirt because I think she feels sorry for Katherine. Maybe if I know the truth, I'll be able to keep going because I won't blame myself for everything that has happened.

The middle of the night is not a good time to make plans. For one thing, pain is magnified—tripled and quadrupled in the darkness. *Weeping may endure into the night, but joy commeth in the morning;* a psalm from my childhood Bible reading. I lay in bed for hours, determined to find a way to get restitution for the years I put into the relationship. I don't want to be acknowledged, but I do want to be taken care of as he promised. There is no way I can survive without help, from either his family or his estate. I saw a lawyer about being paid from Katherine's trust, and that is not going to happen. It is only there for her after I die. I am worth more to her dead. It is almost as if Jack did that on purpose so I would keep working. I'm almost sixty years old! I am tired of working, tired of juggling Katherine's care and a job. It's true that millions of people do it every day, but I can't find a job now! I just don't qualify for anything.

I'm going to Babylon. I just decided it. I'm going to confront Jack's wife. She needs to know that her highly thought-of husband had what is, for all intents and purposes, another family—a family that he visited several time a week for years, albeit only an hour at a time. Still, it was no easy trip up here.

Melissa called me yesterday morning and wanted to come over. She wanted to talk. I thought it would be great to have someone to talk to who knew him, with whom I could be honest. It's so hard to grieve alone. And then, her real purpose was revealed to me as she sat in the same chair Jack sat in, the chair no one else had sat in for almost twenty years. From that chair, I heard the words from Melissa, "Jack was HIV positive. You better get tested."

HIV. Human immunodeficiency virus. Does his wife know? I asked Melissa. "She was the one who told me," Melissa replied.

Pam Smith had called this tattooed freak of nature on the phone and invited her to the Most Holy of Holies, and told her she had been exposed to HIV by her late husband, Jack. Those exact words had gone from Pam's mouth to Melissa's ear.

12
Melissa

I've made arrangements to go to Maryanne's house. Maryanne was with Jack longer than anyone was, almost as long as he was with Pam. Jack had two perfect kids and a perfect wife, and when he met Maryanne, he discovered that not everyone has a perfect life. Some people struggle, some people are poor, some people are born differently. I decided that Maryanne was the only one whom I cared a goddamn about and only then because of her kid. Jack loved that kid. By the time I met him and started dating him, or whatever it was called that we did, she was a teenager. The other women I knew about, well I would think about warning them. Right now, I could only deal with Maryanne. She was the redhead my students and I saw Jack with on campus, the one on whom I had based my decision to stop seeing him romantically. Out of respect for her and for myself, I did that. So we had that connection, too.

Maryanne's house was a shock. I thought of my wonderful brownstone and wondered why I deserved it when he had allowed someone who he had been with for almost half of his life to live like a pig? The cab turned onto her street and all I could think was, *Please God, don't let that dump be my destination.* And of course, the cab stopped right in front of it. She had the lower floor of a dilapidated brick brownstone, a rarity on that gentrified street. The owners hadn't repointed the brick, or replaced the windows, or taken care of the granite stoop and the wrought iron, so that you took your life in your hands walking up and down the steps. There was trash all over the little front garden, the fencing long gone. I could smell ancient cooking odors when I opened the door to the hallway.

Maryanne's door was the first one on the right. A staircase led up to the second floor. So she would have the sound of walking above her, on top of everything else. The street was quiet enough; the only positive in a sea of negative. She answered the door right away. I could smell pine oil cleaner, thank God. At least she was clean. The room was narrow but long; a kitchen table and chairs from the 1940s was in the bay window. There was a bookcase on the wall opposite the door, and I could see stacks of jigsaw puzzles and a couple of sets of old books; the complete Dickens and an even older set of Goethe. I found myself wondering who this waitress from the Bronx was.

That may have been a glimmer of what attracted Jack. Because it sure wasn't her appearance. I had only seen her from a distance that one time, and she had looked lovely then—bright red hair and a willowy build. But now she was haggard and skeletal with an inch of gray roots showing, and horrid red-orange lipstick. So this was Maryanne. She seemed surprised by my appearance, too. I had on a wife-beater and my tattooed body was on display. I almost didn't get a cab because of it. I had my hair in the usual braid down my back, although I had been considering getting it cut boy-short. I don't like the androgynous look, though. It isn't the way I feel about myself at all. I put out my hand to shake hers.

"I'm Melissa. I have seen you once; I doubt if Jack told you about that," I said to her. She looked at me, surprised again.

"I don't remember meeting you," she said, but she did take my hand. "I may have been having a rough day, so please forgive me."

"No, we didn't meet. I teach at the community college and I saw you and Jack together on the campus." Her eyes glazed over as she was attempting to remember being on the campus.

"How long ago? I must be in a fog." She hadn't let go of my hand yet and the heat from her was starting to make me uncomfortable. I gently extricated myself from her grasp and walked over to the shelves, pretending to look at the puzzles.

"It must have been about two years go," I told her. "It's no big deal."

"I can't believe I forgot meeting Jack somewhere else besides Gwen's. Katherine went to a summer program there one year, maybe three years ago. That could have been when you saw me. He would meet me from time to time for lunch when I was off during the week. I wonder why he met me there."

The poor woman was clearly confused, while I saw the situation with crystal clarity. Jack had wanted me to see him with another woman. It was too much of a coincidence that he chose to embrace her within view of my classroom window. I hoped it was so I would stop being intimate with him for my own good. I would never know. I was free to imagine whatever I wanted to about any situation, so I chose to develop scenarios that were only beneficial to me.

"Have a seat," she said, pulling out the chair closest to the door. I had a feeling it was a special chair because it had a new seat cushion on it. "This was Jack's chair," she said, answering my question. "He sat here every time he visited—for the past twenty years. Well, almost twenty. I am confused about dates right now. Please forgive me." She turned to the stove to get a freshly made pitcher of tea. "Want some tea?" she asked. Her voice had changed, it was softer, almost disconnected. I thought I might have hurt her, which I didn't want to do. The hurt was yet to come.

"Okay. No sugar, please." She opened the top door of the old refrigerator and got out a metal ice tray. I saw a similar one at a flea market downtown once. She popped the handle and the ice cubes came out easily. The glasses that she pulled out of the cabinet matched the tea pitcher. They were covered with painted slices of oranges and lemons. "I like your tea set," I told her, trying to bring her back to earth, to engage her. "Are you okay? I mean, apart from Jack dying."

She gave me that blank stare again. "No, actually I am not. I lost my job and am having a devil of a time trying to pull myself together. If Jack was alive, I know he would help me out."

She had said it simply, as though it were factual. I thought that maybe he wouldn't have helped her by giving her money; he would have known to whom to go for unemployment, or for another job. But a handout? No. I think it was then that I realized why he was so generous with me and not with Maryanne. And I only say this in the most apologetic way, not judging her at all, only as a way to explain the slanted view that was Jack's. Because I had worked so hard putting myself through college and was working, and continued to go to school to get a Ph.D., I think he may have felt I was worthy of his help, or his gifts or charity, whatever you call it.

"I hardly know what to do next. I'm just paralyzed with fear," she continued. "Jack put money in a trust for Katherine's care after I die, but I can't touch it."

I got confirmation then that I was correct. Jack could be a taskmaster. He had dangled money in front of Maryanne, teasing her, tempting her. I was not going to save this woman, but my curiosity was getting the best of me. "Did he help you out while he was alive?" I asked.

She looked thoughtful for a moment. "He did, but I always needed to spend it for something."

I thought of that book collection.

"He also gave Katherine lavish gifts. She has a wardrobe that takes up the entire extra bedroom. Would you like to see it?"

I nodded yes. She led the way to the back of the house and opened a door that led to a staircase off a small den or office. The bedrooms were on the upper floor. I was so turned around by the apartment's configuration I felt like I needed to put breadcrumbs down so we would find our way back. Maryanne was just confused enough to scare me.

"Is this part of your apartment, too?" I asked, thinking, *No, dumb ass. We are going into the neighbor's house to see the clothes.*

"I have three bedrooms up here. It's nice sleeping at the back of the house." We got to the spare room and she made a grand sweeping gesture as she opened the door. "After you," she said. I was almost afraid to enter before her in case she was a lunatic and was preparing to lock me in. What was wrong with me? Anyway, the clothes were impressive. I have seen vintage shops that had less inventory.

"Does she wear all of this stuff?" I asked, thinking, *Maybe it's a source of income.* This was Manhattan, after all.

"No," she answered, "but I could never sell any of it, if that is what you are getting at. Jack bought these things for my daughter. He had them delivered to the house so she would be surprised when she came home from school. They aren't mine to sell."

So that was that. I wanted to speak my piece and get out of there. "Can we go back down now? I really have to leave in a few minutes."

She waited for me to walk out and then closed the door. We went back into the kitchen. Maryanne sat down across from me. She folded her hands on the table. I wasn't sure how to approach this, but decided to take a cue from my sister-wife Pam and blame it on someone else. She had used the department of health; I would use her.

"Pam called me this week," I said and then put the glass of iced tea up to my lips. It was weak and cold, refreshing. "She had news from the New York State AIDS Surveillance Task Force that blood drawn during Jack's autopsy was positive for HIV." There, I had said it. What she did with that information was entirely up to her. But I did want to warn her. "I have had the test. I am going to report to the caseworker that I told you. Other than that, there is nothing more that I can do for you."

Maryanne sat there, pale white skin against her mousy faded hair, hands folded in front of her. "Tell me that you understand what I said to you, Maryanne, because I am leaving now."

So quickly that it caught me off guard and scared the hell out of me, she jumped up and started screaming bloody murder. She held her hands in front of her face in a half-assed attempt to muffle herself and jumped around the kitchen, screaming. I got up and backed up against the wall in case she came at me.

She began pounding the table. "No! No! No!" she screamed. "I don't believe it! You're lying! Get out! Get out! Get out!"

Well, to say I left quickly is an understatement. I had even checked out the windows in case I had to jump. I backed to the door, opened it without trouble, and fled that stinking hallway, relieved that the noise hadn't attracted any attention. People would think I was beating her up. That certainly didn't go the way I expected. But there was no other way to get the news to her without having an impersonal and horrific visit from the health department. It was something I could do for Jack.

I ended up having to walk for a mile to get to the 181st Street subway entrance. Even though I was doubtful, I hoped I would get a chance to connect with Maryanne again someday, at least to meet her daughter. I wanted to tell her how much Jack had loved her.

13

Pam was having a good day. They were becoming more common, the days that she almost forgot the situation she had found herself in since Jack's death. She was sitting on the veranda with a new book, completely absorbed in it. Now that Labor Day had come and gone, the beach was empty except for a few stray sunbathers. It was certainly hot enough to be out there, but school was back in session. Summer was officially over. Nelda was settled in the mansion at Columbus Circle, ready with a deck of cards and fifth of gin. After a week of shopping and going to the theater, she and Bernice had the weekend planned: brunch at The Village Green, gossip, and cards. Ben would spend all day driving the limousine around town.

Fortunately for Pam, the first auction of Bernice's art and treasures was wildly successful, yielding enough money to keep her in the lifestyle to which she had grown accustomed for at least five years. Pam had her on a strict budget, but she was keeping the car and driver because the ladies really needed him there. Ben did a lot more than just drive; he did repairs of every kind, including plumbing, electrical, and some carpentry. He had his apartment above the carriage house, so there was always someone in residence to make sure the ladies were safe. Alice, the cook; Mildred, the maid; and Candy came and went every day, but the weekends were staff-free. Only Ben was there to do driving if absolutely necessary. A part-time cook who had worked as Alice's assistant in better days came in to prepare meals if needed. But when Nelda was there, she liked to do the cooking. And they loved going out. Bernice had a restaurant budget and she was strict about adhering to it.

Pam was amazed that after so much resistance, she had come around. Bernice was back to being the loving grandmother that her children knew. So with her mother safely ensconced in the mansion, and her two children on their way back to school, Pam was free to be alone. No one was hounding her to get out, do something, live! Oh, Lord, if she heard her mother say that one more time, she was afraid she would have to walk into the ocean and drown herself.

"When your father died, I didn't spend one minute moping around like you do," she said.

"Mother, that is not exactly the way I remember it," she replied gently. She wasn't going to argue with her anyway. In the few months they had lived together, Pam had developed the skill of blocking her mother out. She did it with respect though; her children would do it to her soon enough.

And Marie had shown up unexpectedly. She seemed a little frazzled, but didn't offer any explanation outside of needing to get out of town for a few days. *Was it okay if she camped out there?* she asked. Marie had escaped to the beach with a cooler and a book. Pam didn't think she would see her anytime soon.

So for the first time in a few weeks, she was alone. And she planned to enjoy it. Having the children home for Labor Day had been wonderful. They were growing into such superb human beings. It made her sad to think that Jack would miss it, but the truth was, he'd had very little to do with their upbringing. She alone had dealt with the day-to-day ups and downs of having two small children who grew into active, demanding teenagers. She had a huge capacity for sharing and she would do that for Jack, keep his memory alive for their children and treat it with respect. The impact that Jack's upbringing had had on him was becoming clearer to her with each disclosure. Thankfully, the constant revelations seemed to have ended. The past few days actually had been boring. Pam guessed there might be a danger in the continuous drama; a sort of sister to Munchhausen's syndrome maybe? She had read about people who thrived on this kind of life, who became addicted to tragedy. Having a few days without any new developments in the life and death of Jack Smith was welcome.

However, it was ending. There was a knock on the door, just barely discernible from the veranda. Pam put her book down and pushed away from the table. She looked out the side light and didn't recognize the woman standing there. Unlocking the door, she said hello and smiled. The woman stood there staring at her, mouth open, and Pam knew immediately. Something in her gut said, *here's another one*. The woman was worn out. Pam could feel her discomfort, her hesitancy. She was staring at Pam, checking her out, thinking; *Jack never mentioned how attractive his wife was.*

"Can I help you?" Pam asked gently. She opened the door completely, thinking that standing behind the door, being afraid to open it all of the way, was making the woman ill at ease. And then she did something that took the woman aback. Pam held out her hand to the stranger. "Come in, won't you? I believe you might be a friend of Jack's."

The woman could hardly believe her ears. She had come to threaten Pam, to demand she be given money, to confront her about the years that Pam chose to look the other way while she wasted her life with Jack. Now, in the presence of the real Pam, the woman lost her purpose, and began to cry. She had walked through life in a daze, suffering through one disappointment after another. She had been guilty of the same thing she accused Pam of: looking the other way. Only in her case, she had averted her eyes while her husband gambled their life away.

Pam reached out to her to take her arm and Maryanne stumbled over the threshold. Pam held her until her shaking body began to calm down. The ride to Long Island; the sleepless night; the worry about her blood test; and now the kindness of someone who should have hated her, compounded by her regret that she had come to the woman's door unannounced, made Maryanne feel like a total loser. Pam was a gentlewoman, a person of dignity, and Maryanne was an adulterer who continued to make mistakes and not take responsibility for them.

"Please, please forgive me! I don't know what I was thinking! I came to ask you for money, to harass you. That's not me!"

Pam gave her a tissue and she blew her nose. "I'm just at my wits end. I am so sorry!"

Pam led Maryanne toward the veranda. "Let's sit out here, shall we? I don't know why, but I get all the bad news on the veranda and it still is the best place to be in the house." They walked through the sliders. Pam pulled out a chair for her, one facing the water. "I'll get you something to drink, okay? Have you eaten today?"

She was standing next to Maryanne's chair, bending over in a stance of compassion. It said to Maryanne, *I'll take care of you. Sit here and rest awhile. Everything will be okay. It's not as bleak as it seems.* "No, I haven't eaten. I don't even know what day it is."

Pam patted her on the back. "I'll be right back with something. Stare out at the ocean for a moment; it has magical properties in the worst of times." She went back into the house and Maryanne sat at Jack's table, in his house, on his veranda, waiting for his wife to bring her refreshments guaranteed to make everything alright. Maryanne wondered if Pam was medicated.

Pam was back in a few minutes with a tray of iced tea and cake. She had smiled to herself and thought, *I'm delusional. I actually thought I was going to have a peaceful day.* But there was something about the sad creature who had appeared on her doorstep that stirred compassion. She might as well get used to it, she had decided a while ago. Who knew how many women would appear for an audience? Melissa had said there were others. They should have no control over how she felt about herself. It was Jack's doing, not hers; just as Jack had no control over her destiny. He might have given her AIDS, but there his influence stopped. She poured the tea into glasses and garnished them with lime and mint. She cut cake that her mother had made, light yellow with fluffy frosting, putting a piece on a pretty china plate and placing it front of Maryanne. She sat down across from her.

"I'm Pam. What's your name?"

Maryanne was dumbfounded. She was sure that when Pam had let her in, she knew who she was. "Don't you know me?"

Pam shook her head.

"I thought because of the way you greeted me that you must know about me, or know of me."

Pam shook her head again. "Before I say anything more, I need to explain to you that what I do know is that my perception of Jack's life will be different than yours. Can I say that without hurting you further?"

"I guess so," Maryanne replied. *What difference does it make?*

"I believed my life to be one way, and now I've learned that it was another. So I know you are hurting and confused because I have been there myself. I don't think I can be hurt anymore but that may be tested and revealed to be incorrect." Pam laughed at the idea that something worse could be exposed. "So I am assuming that because you came to my door, you had been involved with my husband in some way. I would like to hear your story, if you want to tell me. Truly, it can't be worse—or shall I say, more dramatic—than several I have already heard."

Pam had a penetrating gaze. Maryanne was quickly losing her nerve. What could she say that would make any difference if everything Pam had just told her were true? "I wonder if my story is worthwhile telling, then," she said.

"Absolutely! I want to know about you. You had something that Jack needed, evidently. By knowing what it was, I am finding out more about myself. You can imagine how much change I must be facing, trying to understand the woman I was. Why am I revealing so much to you, for instance? Honestly, I think your age has something to do with it. So far, I have only learned or heard about young women. I'm happy that he was with someone my age, to tell you the truth."

Maryanne turned the facts over in her head, trying to decide how to start. Did Pam want a narrative about Jack's life with Katherine and herself? She'd start with Katherine. "I have a handicapped daughter. Her name is Katherine. She has rare genetic defect that affected her face. It's called Apert Syndrome. But she also had a cleft palate and some brain injury." Maryanne stopped there and looked at Pam. She was going to reveal the length of the relationship now, and she knew it would be shocking to Pam. "Jack loved her. He met her when she was just two years old and she's in her early twenties now."

Pam was trying to keep it together, but hearing that Jack had had a long-term relationship with someone, and she never, ever came across any evidence of it, was yet another reason that self-examination at this juncture of life was crucial. She decided she had nothing to lose by admitting shock. It might even validate the woman somehow. "Well, there you go! Just when I didn't think he could do anything more to hurt me, bingo! I'm totally surprised."

Maryanne felt terrible again and sniffed back the tears. "I'm sorry, okay? I used bad judgment, and was selfish, and honestly, stupid. I want to tell you the negative crap, too, but don't want to hurt you anymore, if that's possible."

Pam told her to go on.

"He ate breakfast every morning where I worked." Maryanne told the whole story to Pam.

Finally, Pam asked, nervously, "Did my mother-in-law know about the two of you?"

"No, never. I wasn't allowed to speak to him when they were in the restaurant together." She was drained. She hoped that Pam would ask questions. Giving a lengthy talk about Jack was taking its toll. She didn't say anything else.

"Did you love each other?" Pam was looking intently at her, but with kindness again.

"I loved him, and he loved Katherine, but I don't think Jack loved me. He felt sorry for me. He came to my house way up in Washington Heights every week to see Katherine. Very rarely—and I think this was purely for my benefit—he would wait and come at night. When I say rarely, I mean a few times a year. He was never that interested in it, if I can say that frankly."

Pam thought for a while of the impact of what she had just heard. Jack had driven from his office downtown all the way up to Washington Heights. That was at least a half-hour ride, but in rush hour, maybe longer. She felt so sad for her children. They were competing for his affection as much as she was. And no one was aware of it.

"Tell me about your daughter," Pam said. She wanted to try to understand what was so compelling about this child that would pull Jack in. "You said she had a birth defect."

"It's a genetic defect. Her face was affected. I hate to say deformed. Her eyes are so far apart that they don't work in unison. She had a bilateral cleft palate. Jack saw her after the surgeries to correct the cleft palates, but she still had to have several more. He was there for her, paid most of her expenses so that she would have a private nurse while I went to work."

As Maryanne continued with the story of Jack's goodness to them, Pam floated back and forth between disgust and compassion. It wasn't the little girl's fault that that schmuck had been drawn to her. Pam had fear in the back of her brain that the child had been molested, too, but she didn't voice it. If nothing had been said or noticed, then that was good enough for her.

Besides her coworker, Evelyn from Gwen's, no other woman knew the whole Jack story that Maryanne was unloading on his widow. Once she started talking about it, she couldn't stop.

Pam felt herself slipping into despair again, but she was able to pull out of it each time the feeling came over her. *Where in the hell was I when he was sitting in the child's hospital room? Or driving an hour up north to see her instead of coming east? What was so appealing about a deformed child and her mother when he had two toddlers and a wife at home waiting for him? She tried to do the math; had they even moved to Babylon yet? Was he doing this when his family still lived in the city? No, it couldn't be. Could it?* Pam had wanted to do a timeline of Jack's escapades at one time; she wanted to print out a giant calendar that covered all the years of their marriage and fill in the boxes with the names of the women he had fucked at the appropriate times. But she didn't do it because it would mean spending too much time on worthless information.

Pam looked at Maryanne closely while she was talking, and Pam's heart went out to her. She was so thin; Pam could tell she must have stopped eating. Her gray roots were inches long; Pam guessed she had stopped coloring her hair when Jack died. She found herself wondering how she'd found out about his death. Did she read it in the paper the way Melissa had? Or Cindy, about whom Pam knew very little, who'd searched the internet obituaries when Jack disappeared? She found the courage to ask and was saddened to find out that Maryanne's boss had cut the obituary out for her; she hadn't read the obituaries since her own husband had died twenty-two years earlier.

"I'm sorry about you losing your husband. You have suffered many losses," Pam said. *What else could I say? Losing your husband didn't give you the right to mess with mine?* But Maryanne was just a drop in the bucket of Jack's messes, just one of many women. "So what can I do for you, Maryanne?"

"Do you really want to help me?" Maryanne asked, making eye contact with Pam for the first time in a while, having recited her story while looking out to sea. She sat at Jack's table, but had trouble placing him there. Did he like the beach house? He rarely had spoken of his life. Maryanne believed that he was trying to prevent her from knowing enough to be able to infiltrate his personal space. The danger that he might forget where he was and whom he was talking to would increase if he allowed that to happen. His secretiveness wasn't only so that the women wouldn't be able to find him.

Pam nodded. Yes, she did want to help. "I'll do whatever it is you need to move forward." She was prepared to do anything at this point. Jack would have wanted her to, although what he wanted was becoming less and less important.

"I need money, first of all. I lost my job when Gwen's went out of business last month. I'd like to stay in touch with you, if it's possible. I miss a connection with Jack so badly. He didn't mean to, but having him in my life monopolized it so that I have no friends to speak of." Pam completely understood; it had done the same thing to her. The money thing was tougher.

Where would it end? Did she owe something to Mary-anne?

"Can I think about what you are asking? I don't want to make any rash decisions here, Maryanne. If Jack owes you something, you deserve to have it. Was he giving you money regularly?"

Maryanne felt that she needed to be totally honest from the onset. If she ever decided to sue his estate, lies could come back to haunt her. Then she thought, *Sue? Who had ever mentioned a lawsuit?*

14

The end of summer can be a melancholy time or one filled with fun and adventure. Marie's life that week vacillated between hysterical fright and intense fabulousness. Jeff Babcock knew how to party. When he had a few drinks in him and had to act straight for the benefit of his family, he was wonderful! By the time Marie got to Pam's house on the day of the confession to Steve Marks, Jeff was there. He had come to talk to Pam about being his date for a graduation party his brother Ted was having for his twin girls, who had finished their studies at Union College. Marie walked through the door from the beach as Jeff headed to the veranda, Pam at his side. He looked crestfallen when he saw Marie, but she had to hand it to him, he pulled right out of it in a matter of seconds and even acted pleased that she had come from the city even though it was obvious that he would rather have Pam as his beard for the party.

"Your timing is perfect, my friend!" Jeff said to Marie. Pam swiveled her head around. *Friend?* Pam thought. *Yuck.* Then she remembered that he had come out to Marie. She played dumb. Marie kissed her and went off to the veranda with Jeff, leaving Pam with her thoughts.

Pam was exhausted anyway. She hadn't said anything to her children when they were at home after all, about AIDS or about Sandra's baby; anything that was unpleasant was left out of the conversation. She felt a distance growing between herself and Sandra and thought that it was okay. She would miss Sandra. She would think about the baby, but she had done a complete turnaround regarding the baby's importance in the lives of her children. She would tell them someday when she was ready, but not now.

In the meantime, that young police officer, Detective Adams, had come back to Sandra and asked for forgiveness. Tom realized that he couldn't live without her. He would have to force himself to make a compromise and tolerate Pam and Marie when Sandra realized she could more easily live without Pam than she could without Tom. She would give up her friendship with Jack's family if that was what it took to keep Tom around. No one told any of this to Bernice, who would probably forget about the baby in time.

Pam wanted to be alone to think about Maryanne. What was she going to do? She had to see a lawyer; that was clear. The woman was so sad and she really needed some help. The emotional toll of taking care of her daughter alone would be horrendous. Add to that the death of the boyfriend and the loss of a job. Pam realized how lucky she was that she had enough money to live without worry. Was it worth the tradeoff of the garbage Jack left behind? Probably not. But she had no control over what he had done. She could only control her own actions. And she felt badly for

Maryanne. Jack had given Pam enough to make life pleasant, and if it worked out, she would share some of it with Maryanne.

The following day, Pam called her attorney for some advice. She learned that she had no legal obligation to help Maryanne and Katherine, and they had no grounds for a lawsuit, if that was a concern. Although her lawyer didn't think she should do it, Pam could give Maryanne money if she felt that it was something she had to do, and it wouldn't obligate her in the future. But because Katherine wasn't Jack's daughter, she and Maryanne had no rights to anything that had formerly been his. Pam felt saddened and empowered at the same time. She could do what she felt was morally responsible without setting a precedent that would be obligating.

15
Frieda

Jack told me once that I was the only married woman he had ever slept with, besides his wife. I'm not proud of having had an affair. My husband is a busy man, always involved with another woman somewhere in the world, but that should not have influenced my decision to remain faithful or to be unfaithful. Jack was simply irresistible. I met him at a business function and the next thing I knew, we were in bed together like two wild animals. Of course, I thought it was a mutual need, a symbiotic attraction. Then Jack felt like he could confide in me and that entire allusion was blown. Jack was insane. He truly was crazy. A lunatic. How did he managed to run a company, raise two normal children, have several lovely homes, and the respect and admiration of the community, and yet no one discovered him? Jesus Christ, my faith took a beating on that one.

My office is Midtown, Third Avenue between Forty-second and Forty-third. To get to Jack in the worst traffic, all I had to do was walk up to Grand Central, take the Five Six train downtown and get off at Wall Street. Twenty minutes, tops. I am ashamed to admit that we often had sex in his office. He would shut the door and we would go at it. I bathed my rear end in his private bathroom many, many times.

Like I said, we were introduced at a business meeting. I don't even remember the purpose of the meeting, but it involved lunch and we were lucky enough to sit next to each other. Peter Romney, his business partner, is my brother-in-law. I met Peter's brother Benjamin, whom I later married, in Argentina, my home. He was there on business and there was instant attraction between us. I thought the name Benjamin Romney sounded like such a sturdy, honest name. My father and mother instantly liked him. We dated for about three weeks and then he had to go back to New York, so I went back with him. For the first five years, I modeled for a living. Then I got pregnant. I got my real estate license because I didn't have the energy to get my pre-baby body back, and I was getting older.

I needed a workup done on a historic property in Queens. The buyers wanted to remodel, but they were in the historic district and there were all sorts of parameters that needed to be observed. I wasn't sure what Pete's business was at the time, but Ben said that was what Peter's company did. So I took the information to Peter and he agreed to do the project. He told Jack right in front of me, "Don't fuck my sister-in-law." Exploding with laughter, Jack assured him that no such thing would happen, but of course, it already had. Now I had an excuse to be in his office. I saw Jack several times. He was always all-business, as he should be, and pleasant, as well. Jack was a real people person.

You never know for sure if he is being sincere or blowing smoke up your ass.

Sometime before Fredericka was born, Ben and I got married. We had a lavish New York wedding. Jack and Pam Smith came, or were invited, I should say. He brought his sister-in-law instead. I don't remember her name. She is one of those ageless women who, depending on the light, can look anywhere from twenty-five to sixty years of age. She was definitely on the older end of the scale when I met her. I was disappointed that Pam didn't come, but later, I was glad. I don't think I could have slept with her husband if I had met her. It's not my style.

After Fredericka's birth, I saw a big difference in Ben. I don't really think he wanted a family. Now Peter, he would have loved it, yet has never been married and doesn't even have a girlfriend. He isn't gay!

Ben is never home. I mean *never*. He doesn't seem happy when he is home, and has no interest in me or our daughter. She will be five in October. I'm thinking about moving back to Argentina. There is nothing left for me here, nothing. With Jack dead, I will only have work and taking care of my daughter. My husband is in China right now. He was home for six weeks this summer; we had a brief rekindling of our romantic relationship, but then he got antsy again and left. I was crushed. When we were making love, I could only think of Jack and how selfless he was in bed. He only wanted to satisfy me. The result is that I will never be satisfied with anyone else.

16
Maryanne

Pam Smith called last night. She asked to meet me at Jack's mother's house on the Upper West Side for coffee this morning. "It will save you from having to come back to Babylon," she said. She never mentioned coming up here to my house. She just wanted to talk, to touch base again. She said she enjoyed hearing about Jack and his affection for Katherine; he was caring and interested in another human being. She was sorry that she didn't see that side of him, which I thought was a bunch of crap. Anyway, I agreed to meet her. I took the train down, and then walked up Broadway. When I got to the address, I was stunned. So this is the Columbus Circle mansion. I have seen pictures of it in magazines over the years. I knew his mother still lived there. The owner of Gwen's was in awe of Mrs. Smith, fawning over her when she came in on Wednesdays with Jack. She hoped Mrs. Smith would tell all of her fancy uptown friends about the coffee shop. But Mrs. Smith didn't want anyone to know about it. It was her special place to have a meal with her son.

I was nervous about approaching the house; it has a brick wall around the property with huge iron gates at the entrance to the path up to the door. There was the sound of water splashing. The gate squeaked so loudly it hurt my ears. And then I saw the source of the water: a beautiful fountain in the center of a magnificent garden. It was one of those secret places you read about in the Sunday *Times*. I couldn't imagine having such a thing right in my own yard.

I wondered if everyone in the household was looking out the windows at me. I knocked on the door. A uniformed maid opened it and stepped aside so I could come in. She showed me to a small, comfortably furnished room to the left off the hallway. Down farther, on the right, I saw light spilling out of a large doorway and heard the sounds of female voices and laughter. I sat down and looked around, taking it all in. There was very little in the way of clutter, no antiques or bric-a-brac, and no art hanging on the walls. It sort of looked like they were getting ready to move and had packed up everything but the furniture. After I'd been sitting there for about a minute, the maid returned with a coffee pot on a tray. She asked me how I took it as Pam walked in.

"I'll pour, Millie, thank you very much. Good morning, Maryanne," she said turning to me. "Thank you for coming." She didn't seem to expect me to reply because she kept on talking as she poured coffee for us. "How do you take your coffee? Or are you a tea drinker? I have both here." I told her I'd take coffee. "Millie just can't serve drinks without something fattening. I'll put two of these on your plate." She placed a cream-filled pastry of some kind next to a crispy-looking cookie. It was too much sugar so early in the day, but I'd eat it to be polite.

"The reason I asked you to meet me today is because I want to help you with your finances. I'm going to be very upfront with you about everything, okay?"

I nodded my head yes.

"Here's a check for ten thousand dollars. I realize that won't last forever, but it should help you stay afloat until you can apply for unemployment or get another job." The check was drawn on a bank in Babylon, and had Jack's name on it as well. Seeing his name there in the corner made me sad. I didn't feel anything else; no gratitude or relief. Just pulsating sadness.

Sitting there with Pam in that fabulous mansion and taking what probably amounted to her grocery money for the month pissed me off. I thought it was smart not to open my mouth. I did wonder if she was going to make this a one-time gift or if more would be coming. As long as I had something to eat or drink to occupy me while I sat there, I was safe. I felt anger building. Who did she think she was? Was this a buy out? I remembered the kind way she had acknowledged me as someone who knew Jack when I went around to her house unannounced. Why was I being such a bitch?

"It costs so much to run a household nowadays, I imagine you are petrified about doing it without any money coming in. If Jack were alive, he would know what to tell you. He would have ideas that would help you overcome this. All I can do is write a check. I haven't worked in almost twenty-five years. I know that must seem silly to you. 'What does this woman do with her time?' you must be asking yourself. I often wonder how I stayed so busy, myself. What was I doing that was so important? It's just the way one lives one's life. I never felt like I was wasting time. Of course, with all of these stories coming out about Jack now, I realize that I have nothing to show for my life outside of my two children. You feel the same way about your daughter, don't you? She gave you purpose. So what do we do now?"

Pam looked at me. I could feel her despair. I realized my disappointment in the way my life had turned out was nothing compared to what she has gone through. Here was someone who was completely taken by surprise after her husband died, learning of his secret life. Now I was adding extra burden to her. I was suddenly ashamed. "I can't take this check. I don't deserve it." I handed it back to her.

She smiled at me, but shook her head. "No, I want you to take it. Truthfully, I was interested in see-ing what your response would be, if you would take it and ask when the next one was coming, or refuse it. I'm glad you refused it, because it will make it easier for me to help you again in the future. Gosh, I feel so good right now!" She reached over from her chair to hug me.

I had sort of a creepy feeling. Was I her charity case for the day? A good deed, a slight overlooked? Or a payoff for the shitty way her husband treated me? Why couldn't I just accept the check as a gift and get the hell out of there? I decided to go for it. I submitted to her hug and when enough time had passed, I stood up and told my first lie to her.

"I need to get back uptown. Katherine is due home soon; she had a half-day today. Thanks so much for the check. I will apply for unemployment. Don't know why I haven't done that already." I picked up my purse and started walking toward the door. Pam stood by the coffee tray, gathering up our cups. I wondered if she would walk me to the door. She bent over to pick up the tray and was carrying it as she followed me out of the room to the front door. I opened the door and turned to her to say good-bye.

"Can you see yourself out?" I detected a note of something in her voice, but I couldn't place it. Relief?

"Yes, and thank you again. Good-bye."

She turned and walked away with the tray, toward the back of the house. I wouldn't gain admittance again. And she trusted me not to come back and harass her mother-in-law. I wondered why I thought so little of myself, but then I remembered that I had shown up at the beach without an invitation. Maybe I wasn't to be trusted after all.

17
Ashton

Our circle of friends knew all about Jack's accident on the train. News spreads fast in our community. He was on the train, going home to his wife, and he had a heart attack after having a fight with his brother. Those two had been at each other's throats for the past two years. It was a tragedy, because they'd been so close as kids, rooting for each other and protecting each other from their maniac dad.

I grew up with Jack. We played softball together in Central Park every Saturday of our lives until he left for Long Island. I knew why he did it, why he moved Pamela and the kids out there. He wanted to be free to be himself. He couldn't do that with a wife and family over on the next block. He didn't worry about his mother because she was a closet drunk; you could pull the wool over her eyes and she was never, ever the wiser.

We used to have the most raucous lovemaking in the morning after his father left for the office. He and his brother Bill had bedrooms on the third floor of that hideous monstrosity of a house on Columbus Circle. That is another story. I am a designer, and let me tell you, what was done to that place in the name of restoration was a travesty. Anyway, every Friday night, a big group of us would have a pizza party at Jack's. His father was a queer from way back, but he managed to stay out of site. He may have had hidden cameras set up, for all I know. But he had too much to lose to try anything with any of his son's friends. I was one of the few people who knew that the old man beat up on the boys pretty good. It's a fact of life among rich people that perverse crap is allowed to go on because no one would believe it.

Jack wasn't just bisexual. Jack loved all sex, all of the time. When we were young, Jack tried everything that came his way. If a girl was willing, he took her on. I knew I was gay as a kid and I loved Jack as a friend, so when the time came for us to couple, it was thrilling. It was the wildest sex I had as a young person. He was crazy! Jack had a violent side, too, and I may have been the one to introduce him to the S&M community. It is a safe place for people to go who want that lifestyle. He eventually hooked up with a bartender Midtown, a woman who was into it, so he had an outlet for that aspect of his life. He didn't have to risk public exposure by practicing in a large group. It was never my thing, thank God. I am a gardener, for Christ's sake; that's as dirty as I want to get.

Jack was sick. I don't think anyone realized *how* sick until he died. People whispered while he was still alive, but the real talk began after the funeral. Fortunately, everyone loved Jack, so there would be no blackmail. No one was going to go to his wife and try to get money from her or threaten her with exposure of him. I think for the most part, our circle was afraid to go to Pam, even to offer comfort.

Pam had a formidable reputation in Manhattan. Everyone knew Jack and knew what he was into, how wild and depraved he could be. But his wife, well he put her up on a pedestal. Pam may have been the only person on earth of whom he was in awe. He told me once that she wasn't capable of having a negative thought or speaking a cruel word. He would purposely bait her to try to get her to say something hateful and she couldn't do it. She was rarely suspicious of him, never questioning what he did with himself all week.

Jack operated by a stringent calendar. He spent certain times with certain people every hour of every day. He saw a few people daily because there was something about them that he needed for his well-being. Most people bored him after a month or two. I rarely heard of anyone being in his life for longer than a few months, at the most. Those few who made it past the six-month mark were important to him.

If a woman demonstrated the tiniest bit of possessiveness, she was out the door. Or more correctly, he was out of her door. Years ago—I think he and Pam had just moved to the beach—he was seeing a showgirl, really a dancer and not bada bing, either. She was a principle in one of the big dance companies. He was nuts about her; evidently she was insatiable, which was right up his alley. One Saturday, he was sitting on the terrace with Pam, drinking morning coffee and chatting. Out of the corner of his eye, he saw this young woman on his stretch of the beach. He told me that he almost pissed himself. He asked Pam if she would make him an omelet, and she got up right away to cook it for him. He quickly walked down the wooden path to apprehend her; it was obvious she was searching for his house. She ran to him and before she could hug him, he took her arm and led her away from the view of the kitchen window.

He told her to go to a certain hotel there on the highway as you came into Babylon, and he would meet her as soon as he could get away from his wife. He asked her to please not make a scene or call the house. Jack was a superb actor, and he called forth all of his talents for this one. He was even able to make her think he was pleased to see her. She left, excited about the prospect of seeing him over a weekend, something they had never done before. He ate his omelet and then told Pam he was going to have a game of golf. She was happy for him, and went off to do whatever it was that Pam did. He was pretty free to live his life and not feel obligated to spend the day with her. Weird, isn't it? I mean, he had this gorgeous wife—have you seen Pam? She is a knockout for a woman her age, and she was beautiful in her youth.

Anyway, as early as I can remember, the adult Jack took incriminating photographs of all his sexual escapades. He kept large, full-color copies of each and every woman he had slept with. If he couldn't get them, he hired private investigators to do it. On this Saturday, he went into his home-office under the guise of getting his wallet, and got his stash of filthy shots of this dancer. I mean, we're talkin' real beaver shots, masturbatory, *grotesque-amentes*. The hotel was on the outskirts of town, but he was still careful not to be caught by anyone he knew. He went to her room and didn't throttle her, as he really wanted to. He simply spread the contents of his photo file across the bed.

"Aren't these lovely? I especially like this shot of you," he said, referring to a particularly graphic pose utilizing a foreign object. "I hope we understand each other. I made it clear in the beginning that what you and I had together was private. You know about my life and what I need, and I know about yours. You almost compromised mine, and I am telling you that I will do the same thing to you if you ever, ever do anything like this again. If you ever come to my house again, or call my wife, or try to see me when we don't have a time set up, your boss will get full-sized copies of all of these shots. Do you understand what I am saying to you?"

She was trembling, on the verge of tears. "Yes. I understand. Please don't show those pictures to any-one, I beg you!"

Jack told me he was sorry it had come to that because he would have loved to bang her right there in that seedy hotel. But he was over it. He didn't want to even think about what his afternoon would be like if Pam had seen him with this woman. He gathered up the photos for effect and left without saying good-bye. He never saw her again. His "dates" didn't have his cell phone number, and although if they dug deeply enough they might get his home or apartment num-bers, he never was too concerned about anyone getting in touch with Pam. He was so arrogant! And when you think about it, he didn't get caught. He lived the life of an infidel and worse for almost thirty years and she never suspected him. As far as we know.

I got off the topic. I was telling you about Jack and me. We've been lovers since we were in our teens. Jack would never be able to live a gay man's life. He wanted a hetero relationship with a home and family and a woman subservient to him. That is a cruel way to put it, and I might be somewhat off base, because Jack would support whatever Pam wanted. It just happened that she didn't want anything more than to take care of him, like a valet. Pam was Jack's dresser. And his personal servant. Jack told me one time that Pam spent an entire week getting his winter suits ready for him to wear. She didn't like driving into the city, so she had him ship them all home in the spring, and she took them and had repairs made. I remember Jack saying that he came home and she had his suits hanging up all over their house, with shirts and ties selected, even socks. She wanted to make sure he had the appropriate accessories to go with each suit. She boxed everything up and shipped it back to the city for him.

He said he came home unexpectedly one Wednesday, and Pam had on a pink Valentino jogging suit with ballet slippers, perfectly coiffed hair, false eyelashes, and full makeup. She was standing on the extension ladder with a dust mop, trying to reach the cobwebs on the vaulted ceilings in their house. She could have hired live-in help if she wanted it, yet she did her own cleaning. Landscaping was another passion of Pam's. She had a trailer hitch put on the back of their utility car and when she wanted trees or mulch, Jack said she drove into town and rented a trailer to haul the stuff back to the beach. She was always perfect for him, even when he wasn't home.

We were sitting at a bar in the Village one night having a drink before he went back up to his apartment. He told me about how she was careful of every word that came out of her mouth because he had teased her once years ago, before they were married. She had grown used to his mother's treatment of her, calling her silly and scattered to her face, and worse behind her back. But she broke down crying when, in frustration over stopped-up plumbing, Jack had once used the term "slob" to describe his pristine wife because she had accidently flushed a tampon down the toilet.

He always spoke of Pam in a soft voice, prefacing the term "wife" with words like sweet, gentle, wonderful, and beautiful. When she had their babies, Jack was mesmerized by them and by Pam. He couldn't fathom how his petite and dainty wife could give birth to such huge babies and then a week later, be walking up to the grocery store in her pre-pregnancy capris and high heels, pushing a baby carriage.

In spite of her amazingness, Jack couldn't stay faithful to her. That she never found any of this out until his death only served to strengthen my belief that you can live in denial and be happy. More people should adopt that philosophy.

I keep getting off the subject about Jack and me. We started out comparing genitals, as little boys will do. But when we got older, we really loved each other, making love whenever we got together. I fell deeply for him. We had to be secretive about our relationship because Mr. Smith would have killed Jack if he knew.

Jack wanted to date women. He loved women. I know it seemed like he was a misogynist, but he wasn't. He just had to have continuous stimulation. The longest he was with anyone after me was Dale. He met Dale in college; she was one of his math professors. Dale was your proverbial old maid. She'd lived in the same Upper East Side apartment since she was twenty-two and when Jack met her, she was in her forties. During his freshman year, Dale was his advisor. He was a math major. He said he was intrigued by so much about her. She was innocent, he said. No matter what someone did or said, Dale would be able to rationalize it. She believed in the goodness of everyone. If a person said something bad, it had to have come from that person's place of pain. Jack didn't believe in it himself, but her entire aesthetic was based on love and forgiveness. She was rather unattractive, I thought. But Jack liked her look. She was plain, with colorless hair and skin. But she wore makeup and her taste in clothes was exceptional.

Jack was an authority on style for as long as I can remember. He claimed it was from reading the paper, but I thought it was an innate gift. He'd critique our classmates and teachers, giving out imaginary prizes for the best outfits, or the worst dresser, or the most outlandish suits. From time to time, you would hear one of the members of our group say, "Pass that one by Jack before you wear it in public." Jack would give it the thumbs up or thumbs down. The kids in our group were known as the snazziest dressers in the school, and it was because of Jack. He confided that he would have liked to be a designer. But his father wouldn't hear of it. "No son of mine is going to be a designer!" he hollered. So Jack got through school and he ended up being a designer of sorts, but of city blocks and neighborhoods.

Getting back to Dale, their relationship began by having coffee together whenever they had a free moment. Jack said he didn't think about sleeping with her initially because she didn't appeal to him. But coffee led to hikes in the park, which led to museum openings and art shows, and segued into nighttime gallery openings, and finally, since they were sort of "seeing" each other, sleeping together. When Jack started to date Pam, he told Dale and she was heartbroken. But since she had over twenty years on him, and she understood that Jack wanted children; their relationship would have to remain casual. Dale waited for Jack for weeks and then he would show up unexpectedly for an afternoon get-together. Even though it wasn't ideal and she often felt like he was using her, eventually she grew used to their arrangement.

They weren't able to meet in public anymore because Pam wouldn't have stood for it, Jack said. He wanted a traditional family with her. Having a girlfriend that his wife knew about was never an option for him. It didn't make any sense. Pam was desirable and very sexual. Jack said that in their youth, he was afraid she would hurt herself she was so wild in bed.

Wild and willing. So why would he want to hurt her, shake up her security, by telling her that he was going to see other women? Jack was an enigma because he was the most immoral, perverted, upper-middle-class, moral man I will ever meet. He had exacting standards for everything else in his life—his finances, honesty (except for where it collided with his sexual appetite), kindness, and generosity.

Money was a big thing with Jack. He was born into it but he was driven, as well. He had ideas that he continuously put into practice. As some were more successful than others, he would phase out the less profitable ones. He often said the good thing about Peter Romney as a partner was that he never questioned Jack and supported every new idea he had. When Jack was sleeping with Peter's Argentine sister-in-law, Peter pretended not to be aware of it. He brother was a reprobate, as well. Peter was as straight as an arrow. They were certainly odd bedfellows, that Jack and Peter. Peter was the male equivalent of Pam, I think. Did you ever notice his clothes? Oh my God, I think that the word dapper was made for Peter. Peter is so impeccably dressed that he makes Jack, who was a walking Armani model, look seedy.

Years ago, Peter's brother got married in a Saturday morning wedding. I was invited because I do design work for their firm all the time. I sat with Jack and Marie, and so help me God, when the groomsmen walked from the nave up to the altar, Jack gasped, "Holy Christ, they are wearing morning coats before lunch!" Peter's suit was complete with cutaways, waistcoat and striped trousers. I almost fell off the pew. It was so Peter! Later, he told us that he'd always wanted one and finally had a reason to buy it. We had no idea where the man would wear it again, but it made him happy. Peter was also an ascot wearer when the function was informal. He wore a bow tie that he tied himself every single day of the week. He had a collection of hand-woven silk bow ties. I had heard he also starched and ironed his own shirts. Why? Even Pam didn't do that.

Dale called me last week, crying. She is having an awful time letting go since Jack died. She's over seventy, but still looks exactly the same as she did when she was forty-five and teaching us math at NYU. I met her for lunch. She is slightly homophobic; that is something I couldn't figure out for years. I wondered if it was my imagination but Jack confirmed it for me. She told him she was accused of being a lesbian because she never dated and didn't get married, so she avoided the appearance of that lifestyle by keeping her distance from other gays. Maybe at age seventy-four, she can finally relax. It's enough that she is willing to see me now, and initiates the meetings. I like having someone like Dale to talk to about Jack. I need to warn her, of course. It hasn't escaped my attention that I know more of the players than almost anyone. I know the long-term ones. Believe it or not, I was the only man, I think. I could be wrong. And I knew he loved me. But that's neither here nor there now. So I have a huge responsibility to Dale.

I wasn't going to talk about it. But the truth is, Jack knew he was sick. We found out together years ago. The women before that time whom he stopped seeing are not safe. Everyone is at risk because he didn't know when he contacted it or from whom. He was getting worse, using his ticker as the excuse for drinking less and trying to eat healthily. But it was too late.

Everything changed dramatically when he met Sandra. You realize I never met her. He wanted Sandra to have a certain illusion of him and the gay man didn't fit the picture. He was madly in love with her. He told me that when she used to come to the office from the Bronx before her transfer, he'd watch her move around the office and have to retreat to his private bathroom for self-abuse. Just looking at her wound him up. He told Peter to get her downtown permanently and he made up some excuse to have her transferred. They were considering closing the Bronx office, anyway; keeping it open was a favor he was doing for his crazy old man who couldn't afford it anymore. Jack didn't want to fire the people, so they divided the staff among Jack and Peter and Jack's old man. The people who were close to retirement stayed with the old man. It wouldn't hurt as much when his company tanked.

Jack didn't hit on Sandra. It was the first time I had ever seen him use restraint. He became her friend. She is very young; not much older than Brent. All through high school and college, she held down a job. A New Yorker through and through, she is the only woman I know who went to Marymount and didn't get married right out of school and leave the city. Jack admired Sandra for who she was. Pam fit an image he wanted to uphold. The other women filled a need. But Sandra, well she only had to be herself and he was crazy about her. When I asked Jack what was so special about her, besides the fact that she was probably the most beautiful woman I had ever seen who wasn't an actress or a model, it took him a few moments to gather his thoughts. "Where do I even begin?" he replied. "For one thing, look at her." We smiled at the memory of her face. "She's smart and funny, she's independent. She's not in awe of me! Give it a break, ladies! I'm flesh and blood, not a god."

"Oh for god's sake," I said to him, "you are so fucking full of yourself!" We could talk like that together, him and me.

But then I had to ask the hard question. "Does she know about you? I mean, are you protecting her?" Jack's eyes glazed over. I really think that he never took full responsibility for what he did. That's why I say he was sick. He didn't see the danger, or he was in such complete denial that he just fucked his way through the city of women and never thought there was anything wrong with it. He never took any medication, either, which is the most bizarre part of it. The drugs they have today will even help to keep your partner safer if you continue to practice safe sex. He wouldn't even wear a rubber.

The thing about Jack that set him apart from your average player was his ability to make each one feel like she was special, that she was the only one. I know he had a few girlfriends who were simple receptacles for his sperm. Those poor women are the ones who I feel especially sorry for. They didn't have any other connection to him, so when he died, they were abandoned. Women like Dale heard from me. I told several of his closest friends. Maryanne sort of slid through the cracks. I'm so sorry about that. However, I could never understand that relationship. He was with her for almost as long as he was with Pam. She wasn't particularly attractive; she had wild red hair, I mean a bushel basket of it. And this odd little girl with a deformed face. I think Jack felt sorry for her so he risked his marriage for years. He slept with her just enough to gain access to the daughter.

During his final days, everything was coming to a head. He didn't have the energy to hide his life from his wife and was starting to slip up. He'd spent the last year trying to make restitution for wrongs done, not by coming clean and being honest with people, but by giving money to those who were the most important to him. He wanted to make sure that they were taken care of. But during those final weeks, the stress with his brother—who is a real asshole—and a few of the women whom he had strung along started to pile up. During this time, he also started to see more of Sandra, staying in the city over the weekends to be close to her, raising suspicion even in his sister-in-law's eyes, although I think Pam was okay with whatever he did. If he had to suddenly start working or be out of town for a few days, it was okay with her.

I keep thinking about one young woman that he saw the winter before last. She was a part-time researcher for another firm in town, a college student. She came into his office, he said, to drop off title work he ordered that had accidently gone to the firm she worked for. He swears she hit on him right away and he went with it. Well, she got pregnant. And she was a wild woman about it. I was afraid he would kill her to shut her up. She was making a spectacle of the situation. Even went up to his mother's place. Oh my lord, I forget to tell you about that house, didn't I? Another time. Anyway, they paid her off in big cash, like a million dollars. He said he forced her to get rid of the baby, but how can you force someone? Unless you do it yourself. The stress of the possibility of this girl showing up on his doorstep got the best of him. I saw a huge downward spiral then. Falling in love with Sandra was in the backlash of crap Jack did before he died. He was in his lawyer's office more last year than he had been in all the years before. I know he did something to his will but he wouldn't tell me anymore than that. Just that he made changes.

Jack gave me money before he died. I don't need it; I am a successful designer. I do all the apartments on the Upper East Side for the big real estate firms. The warehouses I have around town, up in the Bronx and in Queens, are filled with props and furniture. I can tell you right now where the littlest piece of china is, where each piece of furniture is stored. My insurance bill for the contents alone is more than most people make in a lifetime. But Jack was worried about me. I think that if he had just been honest with himself, he would have realized that I was really the one who could make him happy, who could satisfy him in the long run. I used to cry on his shoulder. "We can adopt children!" I would tell him. We could have hired a surrogate. I think he wanted to make a home like the one he didn't have. He'd be the "normal" father. I know he worshiped his children, too. He never spoke of them without reverence. So, yes, Jack gave me money, too. I put most of it into trust for his children; over a million dollars. The rest I am going to use to completely revamp my apartment.

Jack was larger than life. Life is so empty without him. As soon as he got married, I started dating again. But in all of these years, I couldn't make a commitment to anyone else because he still came around. We saw each other as often as he would need me. I mean, we had coffee all the time; he would go up to Columbus Circle and have breakfast at that little dive so he could see Maryanne, then he would come across town to the East Side and we would spend at least half an hour catching up. He called me every day just to say hi. "You need to get out more," he always said, but no one could compare to Jack. He ruined it for me. I'm fifty-six and alone. Of course, now I'm free. He's gone and I fully intend on trying to allow someone else to have a chance at me.

18
Alyssa

I hardly got any sleep last night because Eric has an earache and he kept me up all night. He is such a sweet boy most of the time! It's not his fault that his ears hurt. The only thing that soothes him is being carried around, which is not easy. He weighs at least twenty-five pounds now. I walk him up and down the hallway, which is the only place in the apartment that doesn't have anyone living below. I know it would be annoying to having a continuous squeaking above for hours in the middle of the night.

Being a parent is so lonely. I had no idea. This little guy is such a sweetie pie, I can't imagine not having him. But it doesn't change the fact that caring for him is so much harder than I thought it would be. The nighttime when he was a fussy baby and there was no one to talk to and nothing to watch on television was the worst. That's when I start wondering and thinking that things could have been so different if I hadn't slept with that monster, Jack. I have a plan now, devised in the night hours when I am here alone with a toddler. I am going to find out if my contract with him is still in force with him dead. I want badly to confront his wife; oh my God, I want her to know what a real motherfucker her husband was. His mother already knows; I went to her right away, trying to get at Jack. It didn't work, of course, but I did get money out of it. His friends think that he got screwed giving me a million dollars, but I actually got more. Almost a million and a half. I am frugal to the extreme with the money, so I should never have to work again. I mean, I am miserly. I only go into that office to have something to do and so I can continue getting the gossip about Sandra. My parents can provide for us, but I have to be independent, so it's nice having my own money.

Jack told everyone he made me have an abortion. Ha ha ha! Guess what? In the first place, my parents are Dutch Reformed. Do you think ever in a thousand years that one of their children would have an abortion? It was bad enough having to go to them for protection when he was threatening me, threatening to kill me if I told his wife! Screw you, Jack Smith! Don't believe him for a second. He enjoyed every second he spent with me, trust me. He told someone I work with—went right to my office—that I came on to him and he was upset about his father dying so he succumbed and that it wasn't worth a million dollars. Yeah, right! You've got to be kidding me! I did come on to him because he is ravishing; you know that about Jack, right? He is so handsome; the word "hunk" was made to describe him. It didn't make any difference that he was ten years older than my own father.

I remember the first time I saw him. Not the first time I spoke with him, but the first time I laid on eyes on him. I'll never forget it. He was in his office, talking on the phone. He was pacing. I was leaning on the desk of one of his associates, waiting for her to sign a receipt for the document I had brought, when I looked up, and there he was. Back and forth, back and forth he walked. He was talking loudly, laughing, pointing to the air, gesturing like he was conducting an orchestra. I later found out that that was Jack, through and through. He was animated to the extreme. He was in such good shape for his age—early fifties, I think, when we met. He was fifty-five when he died. By the way, I don't have AIDS or HIV or whichever the hell it is. One of his contacts told the health department about me and they got in touch. I almost fainted. But thank God, the test was negative. I don't know if he ever used a condom. Obviously, he didn't use one at least once. I certainly didn't touch him and couldn't feel the difference if I had. We did it several times a week for a couple of months.

He got away with murder with me. I mean, he never took me for a meal or got a hotel. We did it right in his office. I got completely grossed out because all I could think of was how smooth he was and I probably wasn't the first one he had screwed there. I imagined the DNA on his desk or carpet.

We almost got caught once; it was the last time we did it. A girl who looked like she was a model knocked on his door and called his name out. He pushed me off him so quickly that I almost fell over. In seconds, he zipped up and walked to the door. He touched the top of an air-purifier thing he kept on his desk. I was too naïve to know the meaning of that until later. Any sex smell would be eradicated. He opened the door to the girl he called Sandra, but I was in the bathroom by then, cowering. Although now I feel differently, at the time I didn't want him to get into trouble. He must have been in some kind of relationship with Sandra because she said right off, "What's going on in here?" He didn't get defensive at all and I thought I heard her giggle. He closed the door when their conversation ended and he rushed me out of there like the wind. Of course, when my period didn't come and I took the test, it never occurred to me to go to Sandra. I bet they were involved. Maybe I need to confront her, rather than the wife?

My apartment is in Chelsea. I love this part of the city. When I was at Barnard, I lived with my parents on the Upper East Side. Although I need my parents to be involved with Eric, living in the same neighborhood as they do would be too confining. It took them months to forgive me for having pre-marital sex, not to mention sex with a married man. I had to tell them because, like I said, I was afraid Jack would kill me. I needed someone on my side.

Here's the whole story. When I found out I was pregnant, I went back to his office. I had tried calling and he would never accept my calls. I didn't have his cell phone number, and I didn't even know where he lived. He wouldn't see me at his office, and I have too much pride to make a scene where I had to do business occasionally. To say I was frantic is an understatement. I was stupid enough to think he would sweep me off my feet, divorce his wife, and marry me. He didn't care about me. As a matter of fact, he didn't even like me.

He didn't think of me at all. So I was a childish school-girl who lost her virginity to a creepy, older man, dying of AIDS. Now I have to make up some story about Eric's dad that the kid can be proud of. I guess I'll just leave out the truth.

Anyway, he wouldn't see me and I figured out by going online and searching that his mother lived uptown on the Upper West Side. After work one Friday night, I took the subway uptown and walked ten blocks to her house. It was hotter than hell that night, and the streets were packed. Every restaurant had a line of people waiting to get in. It's not like that on the East Side. At least not in the neighborhood I grew up in. People call ahead for reservations so you don't have all of this human congestion. I got to Jack's mother's house at about eight p.m. and to say I was shocked is an understatement. My parents are well off, I should explain. My great-great-great-grandparents came to Manhattan from the Netherlands and were among the early Dutch settlers. I grew up with a nanny who I realize now was a personal maid. Our house is a lovely single-family home with about seven thousand square feet of living space. Jack's mother's place is twice that size. And the yard! We have a back yard on the East Side, but this place sat on at least an acre of park land and had a six-car carriage house in the back. It was a true New York mansion. I tried to open the front gate without making it squeak but it was impossible. It was a gigantic, black, wrought-iron thing at least six feet tall or higher, so it took all my strength to push it open. I saw lights, so I knew someone was there.

Jack's over-protective little brother was there and he was even more fanatical about the family name than Jack was. He twisted my arm so hard I thought he would break it, and pulled me into the house when I started yelling on the porch that I was pregnant and I needed to see Jack right away. He threw me in a chair in the biggest family room I have ever seen, and told me to shut the hell up, he would call Jack but only if I didn't make a sound. He left the room, closing the doors behind him. I could hear murmuring out in the hallway. Jack was there within the hour. He gave me about two hundred in cash and said there would be more but that I had to promise to have an abortion. Then he pulled out his phone and showed me pictures that I didn't realize he had taken while we were screwing away in his office—really obscene crotch shots. He threatened to publish them on the Internet and send copies to my mom and dad. I didn't say anything about telling his wife. I thought I would save that for when my family was behind me and I had some protection. As it turned out, I never had to threaten him with that because my parents got our lawyers involved right away. Part of the deal they made was that I was never, ever to get into touch with any member of his family, or his associates, or anyone who was remotely involved with him; nor was I to tell any of my friends the baby's paternity. He could do whatever he wanted because Jack was loaded. It seemed so simple for them; they may have had a lot of experience buying off his sexual conquests. I'll never know because I can't investigate. That's why I need to find out if there is a death clause that would make everything null and void. I am chomping at the bit to tell someone in his family about little Eric. He looks exactly like Jack, by the way. There is no mistake who his father is. I could take him to the wife's house and she would know by looking at him, right away.

I wonder who has those pictures?

19

After having coffee with Maryanne at the mansion, Pam thought about trying to see Sandra before she went back to Long Island. Nelda and Bernice were settled in for the evening and didn't seem to notice that she was there. The way things had worked out with the two of them was reason for rejoicing. Nelda's memory seemed better since she had someone to talk to every day and Bernice was definitely on the mend. It meant that Pam was free to grieve, free to contemplate everything she was learning about Jack.

The surprise visit to the beach house from Maryanne was probably the most difficult of Jack's secrets revealed yet. With Sandra, and even Melissa, she could blame midlife crisis for his lapse of character. With Marie, it was the act of a sick mind. But with Maryanne, there was simply no explanation that Pam could come up with that exonerated her husband. Why did he need that affirmation? The child was almost the same age as his own two children. Was he doing it all for charity? She had wracked her brain for days, trying to form a picture of who her husband was that would explain everything. She just couldn't do it.

The face of the Jack she knew was not that of a real person, it couldn't be. It was a fake that he had created that would satisfy her need to know who her husband was. Because she was so shallow, it didn't take much effort on his part. She still couldn't believe that there wasn't one instance that she could think of that shed any suspicion on him. The impulse to start crying was strong; she felt like such a jerk. Gathering up what little strength she had left, Pam pulled herself together and went in to say good-bye to her mother and Bernice. When she got to her car, she called Sandra, who answered on the first ring.

"Hi! I just got in from work. What are you doing in town?" Sandra asked. Pam decided to keep Maryanne private.

"I stopped in to check up on the elders. Can you spare a cup of tea? I thought I'd see you before I head back to the beach," Pam answered.

Sandra didn't want to upset the apple cart; she and Tom were fixing dinner together and recently had had the conversation about how she was going to slowly cut her ties with the Smith family. She thought of all the weekends that summer that the wife of her late lover had entertained her at the beach, treating her like royalty. She couldn't turn Pam away this one time, no matter what Tom wanted.

"I'd love to see you, too. Come on over," she replied. When she hung up, she told Tom that Pam was on her way.

"Okay, do you want me to go downstairs?" He was sincerely trying to stay out of the way so that Sandra and Pam could have some down time.

"Not at all! She would feel like an intruder if I sent you away! Let's get the coffee things out, okay? Besides, you need to keep making my dinner," she teased. In a few moments, the buzzer went off and Pam was at the door. She came in and they embraced. Then Tom yelled out, "Hello!"

"Oh you should have said something! Now I feel terrible about interrupting you two." She winked at Sandra. Tom came out of the kitchen with a towel wrapped around his waist for an apron and embraced Pam.

"Stay for dinner. I'm cooking for Sandra and there is plenty."

"He cooks, too? Wow, you are a keeper!" Pam exclaimed. "Thank you, but no. I don't like driving in the dark and if I time it just right, I will be on the road by seven and home by eight-thirty. I have just enough time to drink my tea and leave."

"Well, I have a surprise for you. I have real coffee now; Tom is a coffee fanatic, so I had to get rid of the instant stuff and buy a pot," she said, holding it up for Pam to see.

Pam had noticed a change the minute she walked into the apartment; it was so subtle as to be almost imperceptible. Sandra was happy. To bring up Jack's name or any of the garbage about AIDS or other women would be to diminish her peace. Pam felt as though even her presence, the knowledge that her husband had fathered the baby, would no longer bring comfort to Sandra. Instead, it would be a reminder of something shameful. However, Sandra wasn't ready to call it quits.

She brought the coffee in and was bending over to place it on the table next to Pam. "I really need to talk," Sandra whispered. "I found out about another woman, maybe even two, that he was sleeping with while we were together." She straightened up and with raised eyebrows, nodded her head at Pam. The gesture said, *See, it's not over yet*.

Pam nodded back to her. It was confirmation that talking about Jack would continue to be okay. But as far as Pam was concerned, the visits from Melissa and Maryanne were too painful to share and she wondered if they were the women to whom Sandra referred. He had rarely slept with Maryanne and Melissa said she stopped sleeping with him when she found out about Maryanne. Not sure if she wanted to know about more women, at that moment she was certain that she wouldn't be sharing. She sipped her coffee and looked at her watch. She had fifteen more minutes.

"How's work? I haven't heard from Peter, but my accountant did request a statement." Although she wasn't directly involved in the running of Jack's business, she was entitled to receive half of the profits. Now that his former mistress was part owner, Pam had expected Sandra to update her more often than she had. No one was keeping her in the loop directly, which she found a little scary.

"We're having a general meeting with the partners and the sales staff Friday morning," Sandra said. "Why don't you come? You can ask questions directly then. I don't know any more than you do, believe it or not. Peter and I butt heads regularly." They chatted about the children and general news, keeping light in case Tom was eavesdropping. Pam finished her coffee and excused herself to go to the ladies room before she started her trip back to Babylon. Although her relationship with Sandra may have run its course as far as its connection to Jack, Pam would go to the meeting to protect her interests. That might be the one thing that would bind Sandra and Pam together. It was something positive and forward moving.

The two women embraced at the door. Pam yelled out "Good-bye" to Tom and he came out and gave her a hug, too. Pam was glad there was nothing final about it; she wasn't going to give up Sandra's friendship completely yet.

The trip back home wasn't bad. She pulled up to her door just as the sun disappeared behind her. The glow on the house and water always took her breath away. The front door was unlocked, so Marie must be back from her adventure with Jeff. She called out her name, but got no answer. Putting her purse and keys down, she went to the veranda; Marie wasn't there. Then she thought she heard a moan coming from the children's wing of the house. "Oh my God! Marie!" She ran to Marie's room, throwing the door open.

"Jesus Christ, Pam! Didn't you ever hear of knocking first?" Marie yelled. Pam turned her back before anymore of the scene could penetrate her brain, but it was too late. An older man was kneeling in between her sister's legs. There was no doubt what they were doing.

"Sorry!" she said and slammed the door. In rare display of humor, Pam started laughing. She muffled it at first, but could feel it rising to the surface so she ran to her room on the other end of the house and closed the door behind her. Poor Marie. Pam didn't know who that man was, but she was pretty certain this encounter was finished. She rocked back and forth on her bed laughing. Why was sex so funny? When you were doing it, it wasn't. But to watch it, well, it was definitely comical. Pam thought she was probably one of the rare people who didn't get turned on by watching porn. Jack had tried to get her involved when they were first married, but she couldn't watch without laughing. It confused him. He thought it would have the same effect on Pam as it did on him.

"Everyone gets turned on by porn!" he told her. "Doesn't it make you want me more?"

"I already want you! Watching two exhibitionists get it on doesn't do it for me, Jack."

He was visibly upset, but went to the TV and turned it off. She made up for it with passionate lovemaking and he never tried to get her to watch again.

Then she had a change of mood. *No,* she told herself as she remembered that time with Jack, *she didn't suspect he was making love with someone else until the very end. Someone? How many?* Suddenly tired and getting angry, she thought it was inconsiderate of her sister to bring a stranger into the house for sex. Who the hell was he, anyway? Pam hoped he wasn't someone she had picked up on the beach. The vision of Marie with her legs wrapped around this man's back brought her to laughter again. It would be awhile before she would forget this evening. Besides, she wasn't going to spend the night locked up in her bedroom. She took her city clothes off and got into her sweats.

Pam was in the kitchen throwing something together for dinner when Marie and her friend finally came out of the bedroom. They had taken the time to dress neatly. If she didn't know better, she'd have thought they had been playing bridge in there.

"Sorry about that, Pam," Marie said. "This is Steve Marks, a friend from work." She didn't mean to add that last part, but it had just slipped out. He looked at Marie and then at Pam, putting his hand out to shake hers. Pam hesitated before she took it, but Marie yelled out, "For God's sake! We bathed!" Pam gave her a dirty look and took his hand.

"I'm sorry, too," Steve Marks said. "If I thought for one second that anyone else would be here, that would have never happened. I actually came here to kill Marie, didn't I, dear?" He looked at her as he spoke.

"Oh shut up, will you? My sister has enough on her mind without worrying about us," Marie added.

"What did I miss? Marie, have you been naughty again?" Pam was in the mood to get even, something she hadn't been able to do lately. She'd had enough of Marie's crap to last a lifetime and she didn't care at this point if she embarrassed Marie, or made her angry, or lost her friendship all together. Why was she even in a relationship with her? "Yes, why were you two in my house, doing that? I don't want to be exposed to your fornicatory activities. Go to your own place. I feel like

I need to burn the bed now." She turned her back to make coffee.

"Well, I hope you can forgive me," Steve Marks said. "Fortunately or unfortunately for me, I like your sister. She is a liar and a con artist, but I used to be, too."

Marie looked at him and smiled. "I don't know if I like you or not, but I'll give it my consideration. Pam, can I help you fix something to eat? I can't believe I'm saying this, but I'm hungry."

Pam turned to her. Wouldn't it be wonderful if she could say, *Sure! Come on! Join in! I don't care that I just saw this older stranger naked. I'd be glad to eat with him!* But she couldn't. She wanted her house to herself tonight. Marie wasn't a teenager anymore. Pam wondered for just a moment how many times Marie had screwed Jack in this very house and then come into the kitchen to help Pam with dinner. No. She had had enough.

"Truly, I don't care if you are hungry. What I would really like now is for the two of you to get your belongings together and get out of my house."

Marie was shocked. She opened her mouth to protest when Pam cut in. "If you say one word, I am going to tell my story. Would you like that?" She stood there waiting for one of them to make a move. Pam started to open her mouth.

"I'm leaving! I'm leaving!" Marie hurried back to her bedroom to get her bag and purse while Steve Marks stood there.

Pam noticed that he had curiosity written all over his face. But she was not going to have any dialogue with him, ever. Marie came out with her things. "I'm sorry!"

Pam let her have the last word. She did lock the door after them, which wouldn't do much good since Marie had a key, so she put the safety chain up, too. Then she went into the mudroom, locked and chained the door to the garage, and set the alarm.

And then for some reason, she thought of Andy. Andy was the local cop with whom she had had coffee and dinner a few times after Jack's death. But he wanted more from her than she was ready to give. She hadn't seen or heard from him since the last time she asked him to leave her alone. It would be one more night that she wouldn't call him; it was just too soon. She couldn't imagine having to rehash all of the horrible junk she had found out about her husband over the past summer. It was better if she let some of the dust settle before she got in touch with him again. Plus there was the AIDS issue; he would probably run when he heard that news.

After she ate, Pam grabbed a shawl and went out onto the veranda. It was a beautiful night. The heat from the sand was reflecting and she could feel the warmth flowing near her feet. Her shoulders were cold, so she wrapped the shawl around herself. Lights were visible way out at sea; it was the mast of a large sailboat with its lighted dinghy trailing behind. She wondered where they were going. They were headed south. Maybe to Virginia Beach, but probably just to New York Harbor. Her house was empty and she would try to keep it that way. Everyone had someone now; Sandra had Tom, Nelda had Bernice, Marie had Steve-what-ever-his-name-was. He was a handsome man but in a used car salesman kind of way. Pam giggled. She would judge every man from now until she died by comparing them to Jack. At least physically. Steve was definitely a loser in other ways. Having sex like that in someone's home was proof of it.

Pam realized that one of the reasons Jack had been able to treat women as he did was because they were isolated. She certainly was. Maryanne was alone with her daughter and no friends or family to help her after her husband died. Jack must have seemed like a savoir to her. Melissa was set apart by her appearance. It didn't sound like she had many friends, either. Sandra was completely alone with that sister who was jealous of her and a few friends whom she rarely saw. And poor Marie, friendless and crazy. She knew there had to be others.

20

Marie and Steve walked together to his car. They were embarrassed about what had just happened and didn't have much to say to each other. He wasn't sure how they had ended up in bed, but he was sure that he was in love with her. Steve accepted Marie's apology for lying to him. He was going to get an HIV test in the morning. She accepted his apology for the damage he did to her car. She insisted on paying for the repairs herself.

Standing beside the driver's door, he turned to her. He wanted to be honest but knew what he had to say might make her angry. "I'm wondering if this isn't an omen that I better run like heck from you." He looked down at her, staring into her eyes. "Lesser men have been brought low by such a woman," he recited from some long-lost sonnet.

She refused to keep eye contact. "Look, you go do whatever you want to do. I never intended on any of this happening! I have to work, and now I've jeopardized my job by getting involved with you. If you don't think I am worth the effort to be with, then go. Leave me alone, for God's sake!"

It was true that he had pursued her, making a pest of himself and even pushing her to the point of thinking about getting the police involved. But when she was with him, she wanted to do better. Something about him made her want to take care of herself physically, to eat and stop drinking, to start taking her medication. The word she was looking for was "hope." He gave her hope.

He grabbed her and put his arms around her. "Do you think I want to leave you alone? I know I'm responsible for us being together. And I would like to scream it from the roof tops! I swear to you, my motives are honorable."

Marie stood there rigid, unyielding.

Steve wasn't letting go of her. "Now I'm almost certain you might destroy me!"

She looked at him, shocked.

"I'm just kidding!" he said. "Look. I'm single; I have no kids, no one to interfere with us. Move in with me, okay? You hate your place. My apartment is in a nicer neighborhood. I don't have your view, but right outside my door is a coffee shop and a Korean grocery. There are restaurants on my block. We have a used bookstore and a vintage clothing shop around the corner. You can hop on the train at Twenty-eighth Street and get to work in ten minutes. What do you say?"

Marie, starting to relax, had fallen against him. She felt safe there.

"What do you think about it?" he asked.

Everything he'd just said appealed to her. She wasn't thinking about what it would be like to live with him. Except for Pam and Jack and her college roommates, she had never lived with anyone. She was thinking about Steve's Chelsea apartment, the grocery next door, the used bookshop. *Oh, she was so ready for a change.*

"Yes, I'll consider living with you," she said. "But we have a lot to work out. For one thing, I don't cook. I won't cook. I may bake when the mood strikes, but that is about it. I need people around me so you'll have to let me invite my family there." That was an outright lie; she had never entertained anyone in her apartment. But there was the dream of it in the back of her mind. "How will we work out finances? Fifty-fifty? Do I keep my place or sell it?"

"You *own* that place?" Steve asked, incredulous that someone who worked where they did could own such a great place, albeit in a crappy location.

"Yes." She didn't add, *Pam and her husband bought it for me twenty years ago*, but it was on the tip of her tongue. She was sorry she had let it slip that she owned it. "What difference does it make?"

"Well, maybe we should move into your place, then. I rent and it goes up every year. I pay over two thousand a month now."

Marie got the creeps thinking about him or any man moving in with her. That was where she had waited for Jack night after night. Plus, she was used to being alone. There was that old escape thing; she could leave his place if she had to but how would she get him out of hers if it didn't work out? No, she wouldn't get rid of her apartment.

"Look, I don't want to decide my fate on the street. Can we go back to the city and discuss this?" Marie asked. "Maybe I spoke too soon. It seems like there are a lot of issues that need to be worked out." She didn't add, *I'm not sure I really want to make a commitment to you.* "Let's get going. I'll meet you at your place, okay? I can look around and see if it suits me," she said smiling at him. They parted ways, she going back to her rental car. He wanted her to follow him but that made her too nervous. She hung back on purpose, letting him go ahead of her. Just the thought of living with him suddenly frightened her.

The next day, Marie went back to work. She wasn't prepared for what Carolyn Zimmerman, her new right hand, had waiting for her. Carolyn was one of the employees who'd arrived with Steve as part of a company merger. Marie had trusted her with a file that came from Jack's office. Marie had procrastinated working on it all summer, so when Carolyn needed something to do, Marie immediately thought of Jack's file.

Carolyn had worked on the file diligently for weeks, and when she was finally finished with it, taking a look through the box that had contained all the documents, she found one last item. It was a thick sheath of paper with a list of names. Mostly women's names. She had intended to give the list to Marie the following day, but Marie didn't come in. The list sat in her top drawer until Marie returned to the office and called her in for a review of what had happened while she was out.

"Oh! I almost forgot. This was in the file box." She produced the pile of papers and handed them to Marie.

"What are they?" She thumbed through the papers and in the next moment, knew. *Oh great. Jack's girl-friends. It had to be.* She felt the heat spreading through her body. "Okay, thanks Carolyn. Let's wrap up this thing and I'll take it over to Lang today," she said, referring to the project that had been Jack's. "They've probably forgotten all about it. This will pay both of our salaries this year."

She stood up and turned her back, reaching for her purse, dismissing Carolyn. What the hell was she going to do with these names? Not wanting to lose her train of thought, she folded the papers up and stuffed them into her purse. She had a lot of work to catch up on after her exodus earlier in the week. She and Steve had decided to do nothing about their relationship until the weekend; they would avoid each other at work but he wanted to see her tonight and she was looking forward to it. Right now, he was on his way to his doctor's office to get a blood test. She prayed it would be negative. He had joked to her that morning, "If it's positive, we don't have to worry about it anymore." She wouldn't be so flip about it, knowing the responsibility she had if his HIV test turned out to be positive.

21

The next morning, Pam decided to forgo the gym and grocery store and putter around her house. She put on capri pants and a sleeveless top that showed off her buff arms and calves. After grabbing a bucket and a pair of gardening gloves, she put her straw hat on and went to the back of the house to pull weeds. She had landscaped the yard herself, deciding where each plant would go, and over the years, selecting them at the garden center in town and hauling them home in the back of her pristine SUV. Every time she went, she imagined Jack coming with her on a Saturday, the two of them wandering around the aisles of plants like other middle-aged couples did.

She never asked him to go, however, because he always planned his weekends to the last second. During the summer months, he golfed and played tennis, or horsed around on the beach with Marie and the kids. During the winter when the garden centers were closed, he would make himself available to her from time to time. What did she do then to engage him? She thought about how year after year he came home to the same silly wife who expected him to enjoy sitting around their house, playing board games and cards with their children. He was probably bored to tears.

But he never said he needed more from her, so how was she to know that change was in order? She thought the same thing she had been thinking for months now: he chose her because she would make it easy for him to continue his bachelor behavior. She wished there was someone who knew the real Jack, someone who could confirm that she hadn't had anything to do with the way he'd acted. She knew it in theory, but needed that validation from someone who could say, *Jack was born like that*.

Soon her bucket was full of weeds and debris that had blown in from the beach. She went around to the front of the house to dump it in the trashcan. Just as she opened the lid, Detective Andrews pulled up in his unmarked car. Her heart did a little flip-flop. He was here to rescue her from an afternoon of depression, of thinking about Jack the Infidel.

"Hello, Mrs. Smith," he said cheerfully as he walked from the car to the sidewalk. "Am I interrupting anything?" He held his hands up, palms out, and said, "I know I am supposed to leave you alone, but I couldn't just drive by and not stop and say hi, could I?" He stopped on the sidewalk, not wanting to infringe on her territory, not sure if she was angry with his decision. She was difficult to read.

Pam stood there for less than a minute, seconds actually, and pictures of Tom and Sandra flew through her mind, and then of Steve Marks humping away on her sister, which brought a giggle to her throat, and then of Nelda and Bernice arguing over a card game. In her imagination, she saw Andy Andrews walking through the local garden center with her, interested in her choices, and then coming back to the house and helping her plant them.

"No you couldn't just drive by. I would have been hurt. I know I'm not the friendliest woman around, but I do have feelings." She walked toward him and held out her hand to take his, and the changed her mind. Right there in front of the whole world, she hugged him. He bent down to kiss her, but she backed away. "Before we do that, you need to come in and listen to something I need to tell you. Do you have time now?"

Pam had made the split-second decision that she was going to tell Andy about the AIDS. Let him decide if he wanted any more involvement with her or not. She was finished denying herself love because it had only been months since Jack died. She had evidently died for him a long time ago.

"I can come in. Are you okay?" He held her at arm's length, looking into her eyes. "What's wrong?"

She took his hand and led him through her garage and he chuckled as he looked around. "I hope you don't expect my garage to look this organized," he said. Hers was as perfect as the inside of the house—everything in its place, no clutter or junk piled up.

"My husband liked it like this, so I tried to make him happy by keeping it neat. Now I find out that no matter what I did, it wouldn't have been enough."

Andy followed her into the house, allowing her to talk without commenting.

"Have a seat," she said, pointing to the stools around the counter. "I'll make coffee. I'm sorry about everything, about shutting you out. It's been a rough summer." She poured the water into the coffee maker and got the filters and ground coffee out of the cupboard. She wanted to explain herself to him without making excuses for Jack. Or making him look like an evil person. But wasn't he? She was tired of her loyalty to him. Or maybe it was foolish pride. She was embarrassed about him because of what his behavior said about her. She slid onto a stool next to Andy and looked at him. What should she say that would give her an edge? She would be so sad if he fled the house.

"I'm going to come right out and say it. I have AIDS. My husband gave it to me. They found out when I was in the hospital; evidently, in New York they can test you without your consent if they have reason." She hadn't said those words aloud since she had told her sister and her mother about having AIDS. It wasn't cathartic at all. Her throat hurt, the way it did when she wanted to cry and held it back. She felt awful. She should have told him right away, weeks ago rather than pushing him away from her. "So! There you have it! My dirty little secret. Wow! I feel so much better! I'm glad I don't have a gun I could put to my head." Pam got up to go through the motions of making coffee for them both. Andy hadn't said a word yet; she didn't know what to expect of him. She stood with her back to him, taking the water pitcher from the fridge and filling the coffee maker with it.

"Pam, I think I'm going to go." Andy Andrews pushed back from the counter and stood up.

Pam turned around to look at him, her eyes big and round. She was stunned. He was going to leave! She'd spilled her guts and he was leaving.

"I need to think about this for a while. I'll call you later." He picked up his keys off the table and walked to her, kissing her on top of her head. "Okay?"

He looked down at her expecting—what? She nodded. Okay.

22

During times of crisis, people often forget their normal routines and leave what is important behind them. When Pam walked in on Marie and Steve after hearing moaning coming from her bedroom, Steve had just ejaculated. But the surprise of Pam catching them having sex made his erection disappear and his condom full of semen fall off in the bed. Neither one of them had thought to dispose of it; they'd had getting dressed on their minds.

After Andy left, Pam got back to work. She was numb from her confession and the cold reception she'd gotten. She had expected it in theory, but she'd put hope out there instead. Why did she expect him to rally the way Tom and Steve had? There were two ways this could go: she could get into bed and never get out again, or she could go on with her life.

Work was what she needed, physical activity. She went into Marie's bedroom to take a four pack of toilet paper into her bathroom and scour the tub. That's when she saw the unmade bed.

"Now that's just nasty," she said aloud to no one. She pulled back the bedspread to strip the sheets off the mattress and saw the condom filled with congealed sperm. "Oh my God!" She even jumped back slightly. "What the heck?" She stomped into her pantry and got rubber gloves and plastic grocery bags and went back for the retrieval. She thought of all the allowances she had made for her sister, one thing after another that she had tolerated and forgiven, over and over and over again. But for some reason, this oversight was in the realm of the unforgivable. It was more than gross; it was disrespectful and disgusting. Marie may have crossed a line; she had placed the straw that broke the camel's back.

Pam was on a rampage. A used condom had pushed her over the edge. Nothing that anyone had done to her so far had made her as angry as this slight. She got rid of the condom, finished stripping the bed, and put clean sheets on it. Not that Marie would be welcomed back. Pam was going to call her after five. With luck, Marie would be home and Pam would have it out with her sister over the phone.

Pam decided to go to the gym to work off some of her aggression so that when she called Marie, the conversation wouldn't deteriorate. While she was running on the treadmill, she planned what she would say. Telling Marie anything positive never worked. She was so self-absorbed that she felt entitled to that sort of stroking. Pam would try to stick to facts and her feelings and not go off the deep end and comment about her sister's character, which was nonexistent as far as she was concerned. The longer Pam ran, the angrier she got. Where did Marie get off having that strange guy in the house, anyway? Did Marie think that since she wasn't screwing Jack in his house, she could do it with other men? This was the kind of talk she would avoid when she confronted Marie.

After she finished at the gym, she went home, had a shower, and got dressed for the evening. She definitely wanted to call Marie and get that off her chest first. She poured herself a glass of wine and went out to the veranda to drink it. She rarely drank anymore, but tonight would be an exception. The sun was just creeping down behind the house. In a few weeks, it would be setting by dinnertime. Time was moving so quickly, and there was nothing anyone could do to slow it down.

Pam finished her wine and went into the house to get her phone. She decided to call Marie from the bedroom. It was cool and shaded in there, and if she sat on her chaise lounge, it would relax her and promote peace. She poured another glass of wine and then did something that she rarely succumbed to; up on the top shelf of the china closet in her dining room, she fished out an ancient pack of Kool menthols. They belonged to Jack, but she was not above sneaking one during times of stress. She was going to light up while she told her sister off. She'd have a good buzz from the smoke and the wine. She took her cigarettes and a vintage plate that she used for an ashtray and went back to her bedroom, locking the door on the remote chance that someone came home. *Who? There is no one,* she reminded herself. *Okay,* she said, *in case her mother made a surprise visit from Manhattan.* She was feeling a little tipsy. It would give her an edge talking to Marie, who could be brutal and hurtful at the drop of a hat. With the cigarette lit and a full wine glass at her side, she dialed her sister's cell phone number. Marie answered on the first ring.

"What's up?" she said. "I was just thinking about you."

"Can you talk now?" Pam asked. "I mean are you alone at home or at work?"

"I'm home. What's going on? You sound stressed." Marie filled her wineglass and took it into the living room.

"I am stressed. I went into your room to put away toilet paper and found a rubber filled with semen." Pam had to put her glass down and cover the phone because she started laughing and didn't want Marie to think she wasn't serious. Maybe it was a mistake to do this while she was drinking.

Marie gasped. "Oh Jesus! Pam! I'm so sorry! How gross! That was awful of us. Please, please forgive me. Jeez, I feel horrible!" Marie went on and on.

It completely defused Pam's anger. She just laughed. "You don't know how lucky you are that you being contrite, young lady. I have been stomping around my house cussing you out all day! I even did eight miles on the treadmill, I was so pissed off." Pam took a drag of her cigarette.

"Are you smoking?" Marie asked. "Look, I am sorry. I have to tell you that the entire week has sucked. First of all, the woman from the health department came to my apartment and made me feel guilty because I have been sleeping with Steve for a week and never told him I have AIDS. So I told him and you can imagine that he was really angry; threatened to kill me, did about two grand worth of damage to my car, was going to tell everyone in the office. Yes, he works with me. So anyway, I made a death run to you and he found out where I was and while you were out, he and I made up and ended up in bed. So that's the whole story. I thought you were in the city for the day. He had his test today and it's negative, thank God. Do you forgive me?" Marie waited for Pam to answer. Suddenly, she heard snoring noises. "Pam!" But Pam was just kidding. Marie wondered what had come over her sister. Smoking? Teasing?

"How am I ever going to look that guy in the eye?" Pam said. "I mean, are you serious about him? He's older than I am! First, I see his naked rear end up in the air and then I find that thing in the bed. I mean, give me a break will you?" They started laughing again. They said good-bye to each other, promising to be in touch later in the week to make plans for the weekend.

Pam decided that in the scheme of things, what Marie had done wasn't so bad after all. It was just something that happened when people were stressed out, and they qualified for being stressed. She was glad she hadn't called her sister when she first found the condom; she would have said unforgiveable things. And then who would she have? Who would be her friend? The wine must have gone right to her head, because the still small Voice said, *That's a friend? Someone who betrays you for years and years? You better reevaluate what a friend is.*

Pam ignored the Voice. If she divorced herself from Marie, the problems it would create would be never-ending.

She would have to make excuses to her mother. Marie would most likely tell Nelda the reason Pam wasn't speaking to her and then all hell would break loose. Marie was Pam's only friend now that she and Sandra were growing apart. It looked like maybe Andy would be history. If her relationship with him survived the AIDS disclosure, she would need to tell the truth about her marriage. *It could wait, couldn't it?* He now knew she had AIDS; he could fill in the blanks.

She got up and went to the bathroom to brush her teeth and wash her hair again. She reeked of smoke and wine. Being presentable had been part of who she was since childhood. When she'd had her gallbladder removed six or seven years ago and refused to take out her bridgework, the head of the anesthesia department had agreed to put her to sleep. He would take responsibility for her dental work and then give it right back to her to put in before she saw her husband. Jack never saw her without at least lipstick on. Her hair was neat when she went to bed and she rarely stayed in bed after he did. She'd be up with full war paint on first thing in the morning. What good did it do? He needed that perfection around him, but it did no good at all. It was superficial.

When Brent and Lisa were born, she did the same thing, looking fabulous while she was in labor, giving him a break and not expecting him to come into the delivery room with her. Instead, she had stayed out in the waiting room with him, chatting and walking the halls until it was time to push, and then she'd kissed him and gone back into the labor room. She didn't know that he bragged about that to the other fathers he knew, the men whose wives insisted that their husbands see them at their worst, with bad breath, shitting on the delivery table.

That family birthing room scene wasn't for Pam. She liked her privacy. At home, she locked the door to the bathroom unless she and Jack made arrangements to bathe together. Her friends made fun of her in high school; it went back that far, because she never, ever was seen without her makeup on and every hair in place. "You're beautiful, and you're nice," her friends would tell her. "No wonder you got that freakin' hunk, Jack Smith!"

Yes, she was so lucky. She had been the dateless queen of the prom; how did that happen? She never dated. She was asked, but always made excuses, and now she realized why. She was afraid. Men were choplicking lechers. The only man who didn't scare her to death was the perfect Jack Smith. It was as though he was made for her. He gave her plenty of space and was there when she needed him. She wanted children, and as soon as he finished his master's degree, he made it his duty to impregnate her. They were the perfect couple. And Jack had ended up being the biggest of the lechers.

She put her head down and started sobbing. The combination of the wine and the anticipation of telling sister off had exhausted her. All of her defenses were down. She was totally exposed. But it wouldn't last long. She put her makeup on and did her hair and prepared for an evening alone.

23

"You're really a pig, you know that?" Marie said to Steve Marks as she hung up the phone after talking to Pam. They were sitting on her couch, looking at the view, and drinking wine. He wasn't thrilled with her drinking, but didn't want to start hounding her about it. The relief of his being HIV-negative was palpable. He would have to go back in six weeks for another test, but the caseworker had said that he probably was safe.

"What did I do now?" he asked, confused.

"You left your rubber full of spunk in my bed at my sister's house and Miss Perfect found it. I thought she was going to explode, she was so angry."

Steve turned bright red.

"I have seen her hear the worst news a woman can hear and nothing made her as mad as your condom did." Marie started laughing hysterically. "Yes, I'd keep my distance if I were you."

"Oh no, that's horrible! I feel awful. That's disgusting! I'll never be able to face her now."

"She saw your bare ass while you were fucking me; I think she'll get over a little sperm." Marie was already sick of talking about it. Pam could be such a prude. After what her husband had done, leaving a rubber behind in a bed shouldn't seem like such a big deal.

"What do you want for dinner?" Steve stood and up and stretched. He had discovered during that first week together that he would be responsible for food preparation. In spite of her food issues, Marie always knew what she wanted or didn't want.

"Not that pasta crap again. Anything else," she replied.

He walked to the kitchen and opened the refrigerator. His feelings were hurt. He'd made her his famous pasta carbonara.

"How about grilled cheese again? Look, if you want me to cook, do you think you could get something in here besides Spaghetti-Os and American cheese? Meet me half way, will you?" Steve decided they were going out; he couldn't stand the thought of another grilled-cheese sandwich.

"There's nowhere to shop here."

He went back into the living room and held out his hand. "Come on, we are getting out of here. I hate this place; you hate it. Why the hell are we staying here? Pack a bag."

She took his hand and let him pull her to a standing position.

"Where's your suitcase?" he asked. He'd help her pack; the routine was slowly developing in which Marie was allowing Steve to take over; she thought, *almost as completely as Jack had*. Only Steve didn't have Jack's money.

And Steve didn't really want the control. This apartment was creepy, with just the single, giant window wall that looked out onto sky only unless you looked down; and the small, airless bedroom. He thought of his second floor walkup with the quaint molding and fireplace, the cool neighborhood and convenient shopping. He might be sixty-plus years old, but he wasn't ready to die in this dead place.

"How much should I pack?" Marie asked. "What day is it?"

"Pack as much as you can; I don't want to have to come back here for a couple of days." He was thinking about the weekend; what would they do? He was broke. That left out most activities in Manhattan. Because of his faux pas, they probably wouldn't be invited to the beach anytime soon. He'd resort to finding free things to do, as a college student had to.

"I'll bring beach stuff. I can't remember what I left there. Should we take the rental car?" Marie seemed unable to make a decision about anything. "If I leave it here, we'll have to come back to get it tomorrow to go to the beach. If we take it, I won't have anywhere to park." She sat on the bed, scratching her head.

"If we need the car, we'll come get it, okay? You don't have to worry about that now." He suspected that her car, the one in the repair shop, thanks to him, was a gift from the previous boyfriend. A car theft may be welcome, if they ever got it back. They would take the car.

Marie went into the bathroom to get her toiletry bag while Steve zipped her suitcase closed and they prepared to leave. "Good-bye, apartment. See you later," he said to the air.

"Let's just get out of here," Marie said. The oppression was palpable. He wondered if she would gradually feel better after being away from such a grim place.

"I need to get rid of this apartment," Marie whined.

"When we get home, I'll pick something up from the Grill Bar down the street. It's getting too late to make a big deal about cooking tonight. Is that okay with you?" Another issue was her weight; she would probably be thrilled to skip dinner. But not on his watch. *What are you doing?* he thought. *An anorexic, twenty years younger than you are, with a ton of baggage.*

They got to Steve's apartment and found parking right in front; Marie could keep an eye on the damn car all night if she wanted. After they got settled, Marie with a stack of menus in her hand, Steve sorted through his mail. The credit card bills were two inches thick. He slipped them into his desk drawer. She didn't need to know all of his garbage this soon, did she? In time, they would learn things about each other that would make them question the wisdom of their relationship, but for now, he would just leave it alone.

24
Alyssa

My mind is made up. I'm going to Babylon to confront Jack's wife. The contract doesn't say that for Eric's lifetime I can't approach anyone who knows Jack. For sure, I am reading between the lines. Sandra is next. I'll see her later. She almost caught us together that time; would she remember that encounter? Jack certainly wouldn't want her to know that he was screwing a college student in his office, now would he?

The thing that has pushed me to make the trip, to jeopardize the money is this: While he was fucking me he whispered to me, "You are my dream lover, do you know that? I have been waiting for you. I'll do anything for you." If he said that to me once, he said it fifty, one hundred times. He told me he liked little girls. Those exact words. "I like young girls. I like you little girls," he said. He was feeling my breasts—well, where my breast should be because I am completely flat-chested—and I said something like, "I'm so flat there," and he just moaned while he was feeling me up. "I like little girls." Of course, in a court of law, an attorney would argue that what Jack meant was "small of stature." That's total bullshit. He liked young girls. He went down on me and came just by looking at me; I'm also hairless, like a child. So guess what? I decided that

I am going to use that information about the famous Jack Smith. There are so many tabloids that would love a story like that.

But that's not all. Another friend, a bartender friend in the Village, saved a paper for me, one of those obscure rags that publishes the poetry of local jerks and runs ads for sex-therapy clinics that people hold in their own apartments. There was an ad looking for people who knew Jack! I might be dumb when it comes to stuff like choosing men, but I read in between the lines, as did my bartender friend. It was an ad looking for Jack's bed partners. I have seen enough of them to know it means: He is on the health department's most-wanted list for spreading AIDS around town. He was a real sicko.

⚝

Well, forget everything I said. It was all hot air. I went to Babylon to confront the wife. And guess what? She was so lovely that I backed right down. I could hardly be cruel to someone who acknowledged me, who validated me. I took the damn train and it was horrible with Eric; I thought he would love it and he ended up hating every second of it. Trying to keep him in his seat was a nightmare; the other passengers were furious with me, but there was nothing I could do. He wouldn't stay put.

When we pulled into Babylon, I almost lost my nerve. But I gave myself a negative pep talk about what she owed me. If she had kept an eye on Jack, none of this would have happened. By the time the cab pulled up to her house, I was back in form, ready for a fight.

She opened the door and looked from my face to Eric's, then back to my face. You could see the recognition in her eyes. And then, shocking the hell out of me, she gave us a huge grin.

"Well! What do you know! Come right in!" she said. "I hope you didn't have trouble finding the place!" She held the door open for us, smiling as we walked in. "I'm Pam Smith, but I guess you already know that. And you and the young man are?"

"I'm Alyssa and this is Eric." He was exhausted from the trip and actually docile. She led us to a beautiful enclosed patio and offered us a seat. She gave me lemonade and Eric a glass of milk, and brought out a plate of cookies. She kept up chatter the entire time she was serving us. I knew as soon as I saw her that my original plan was ridiculous. She wasn't the cause of my stupidity. It wasn't her fault that Jack was a jerk. Although she never badmouthed him, I could tell that she was appalled by his actions.

"Tell me about you," she asked. "Are you finished with school? It must be a handful with a little one." She was interested in me as a person, concerned over the job I had being a single parent. After we had our refreshments, we walked on the beach. She played with Eric, running with him and showing him shells and seaweed that had washed up on the sand.

Then, with some reservation, "Are you healthy?" She looked at me with fear when she asked that question, and I reassured her without divulging too much. I felt like I owed someone so graceful the respect that I hadn't gotten. I just couldn't lower myself to get revenge. She was such a lady that I felt empowered to rise above what Jack had done to me. When I left Pam's house, I thought that I would finally be able to move forward. I believe she made it possible for me to forgive myself.

I wondered how someone as depraved as Jack Smith could have such a nice woman for a wife. I doubt if I will ever see her again. Although Eric is her children's half-brother, it seems unlikely that they will meet. But stranger things have happened. I think I'm ready to date. There is a guy at work who has asked me to dinner several times. I might give him a chance. I have a lot to offer the right guy. For one thing, I am really rich.

25

As September unfolded, the weather went from summer to fall, and Pam fell into a comfortable place once again. Her life wasn't turning out to be as different as she thought it would be without Jack. There were many things to look forward to each day, after all. She absolutely loved autumn. Every morning brought a new change in the weather. There were summerlike days where she would put her shorts on and grab her straw hat and sit on the beach to read for hours like she used to do when the children were home. They would play in the surf with their friends, kids who lived inland and would show up in droves every morning, exhausted looking mothers and fathers dropping them off on their way to work, grateful that Pam was willing to keep an extra half dozen kids all day. The truth was she loved it. She shopped for their lunches and snacks with as much thought as if she were going to entertain royalty. Although she was sad that those days were gone, the peace of sitting on the beach and not having to worry about anyone else's child drowning was lovely. If she got lonely enough, she would ask her sisters Sharon and Susan to visit and that would take care of her desire to have kids around. Those little monsters would drive the impulse to have children from the most saintly of mothers. She thought of

Alyssa and Eric; maybe someday. Maybe after Sandra had the baby she would invite them all for the day.

Brent and Lisa stayed in touch with their mother. When it rained or was too cold to walk or sit on the beach, Pam spent hours packing boxes of homemade cookies and other goodies, books she thought they might like and funny T-shirts she saw, and sending the packages off. They both loved getting things from home.

The day after the kids left to go back to school, Pam went to her favorite garden center and got everything she would need to decorate the yard for fall. She bought giant pumpkins; dried corn stalks; bunches of bittersweet; bales of straw; braided ropes of garlic; giant gourds; huge decorative kale; and the piece de resistance, a scarecrow. She decorated both the front of the house and the back, a titillating surprise for beachcombers to discover. It was a tradition in the neighborhood that the Smith house would be the first one on the block to celebrate the end of the tourist season. Although you rarely heard it spoken aloud, many locals hated having to leave their homes between July 4 and Labor Day to do even the simplest task like getting gas in the car. The crowds and traffic were hard to bear. Didn't people realize that their behavior would have consequences somewhere down the road? Pam didn't mind. She loved everything about living in Babylon, even the tourists. They acted as that important counter-irritant that would make her appreciate it even more when they left town.

On cooler fall days, Pam would put a sweater on, grab a plastic grocery bag, and go out for a beach walk. She would go north first and walk as far as the inlet that led to the canals. Then she would turn and go south, passing her house and going as far as the causeway. She always came home with a bag full of beach finds: shells, beach glass and the ever-present litter. Nelda stayed in the city after all that autumn, choosing to spend her days as Bernice's companion. The two women enjoyed the same things: shopping, playing cards, a good bottle of scotch. Pam was thinking of spending winter there with her mother and mother-in-law but she was keeping her options open.

Definitely a creature of habit, Pam loved her routine. She didn't care for the intrusion into her life that another man would cause. Maybe she and Jack had lasted all those years because she liked to be left alone rather than because she'd had her head stuck in the sand. Andy hadn't called her yet and it was a relief. He would have expected more from her than she was willing to give. And then the final embarrassment; he would walk by her in the hardware store while holding the hand of another woman, a local divorcee Pam recognized from the gym, and make eye contact without acknowledging Pam.

26
Pam

I feel like I am getting stronger every day. My life has been a lie, and I am ready to come clean and start over. The most difficult part of this will be talking to my children. They will be home over Christmas, but I don't want to wait that long. I would rather we be on neutral turf when I turn their world upside down and I do not want to do it over the phone, but how is that possible? The three of us will have to find a way to move on.

I'm healthy as a horse. I know I must avoid stress and watch my diet and I'm even more obsessive about exercise and eating right then I was before. Before Jack died. My doctor is wonderful. I have never felt ostracized by his staff. Having AIDS has been good for me. I know that sounds like a contradiction. What I mean is that it has forced me to take stock of what is important.

My life up until last summer was made up of increments of time spent doing senseless and unnecessary things, going from one task to the next. I know I was wasting time until Jack got home. Day after day, year after year, I prepared for his arrival, and then when he got here, I was lonelier than when I was alone. We could be in the same room and I was lonely.

He wasn't completely with me, and now I know that is exactly what the problem was. He was keeping the biggest part of himself separate from me. What is it about women—me, in particular—who would allow a life to be wasted because of fear? I was afraid to get what I needed, what I deserved, what was rightfully mine. My mother said that to me at one time. Why did I always put myself last? She said I relinquished that which was mine to my sisters. Where Marie had been concerned, that was true. I had turned my head when my suspicions were aroused. My husband was having sex with her. I knew something was wrong, my intuition telling me over and over again that there was something not right about their relationship. Yet I as much as promoted it by sticking my head in the sand. That is my biggest regret!

I cannot deny that my children must have been affected by what was going on. Children know; they are silent observers and they see more than you think they do. The very worst thing that I did was to hide in my bedroom on the other side of the house, which was designed that way so that our bedroom would be away from the children's two bedrooms. And all along, their father was having sex with their aunt in the next room. I wonder how I can come out and ask them if they ever heard anything. I know noise carries from that part of the house. Would it be cruel? If they did hear sounds, they are probably doing their best to stifle the memories, to cover them up. Would I be doing them a favor by allowing them to purge such knowledge? Or making it worse by acknowledging it? It is never too late to be honest. I have to remember that.

Exposing Jack's lies has helped me to understand so much about myself. Of course, I regret the time I wasted. After the children started college, during that first year both were gone, it should have been so obvious that something was amiss. I am still processing how I could have been so blind. If Jack had lived, I'm positive we would be getting a divorce right now because his relationship with Sandra would have been discovered and he probably would have left me to live with her once he found out she was pregnant. That has been a bitter pill to swallow.

Last night I had a dream about my dad. Not exactly a dream, more of a daydream. I was lying in bed thinking about everything that has happened this past summer. I remembered how he once told us at the dinner table—barely able to get the words out because he was so emotional—that having four daughters who were all nice girls had humbled him. He didn't know why he deserved such good fortune. It was a lie, of course. Marie was horrible to him and worse to Nelda, and caused them so much anxiety with the anorexia. She should have directed her misery toward Jack, but it was just the opposite. She worshiped him. That is why I hold her partially responsible. She may have been considered blameless because she was a child, just fifteen years old, but she provoked much of what happened to her, I am certain. She and Jack were made for each other. I wonder how many young people she protected by being the sacrificial lamb.

But to get back to my father, I thought about how he got up at five every single day of the week, sick or not, and went to his job working for the city. He was one of the men who wore that mucky green uniform. My mother spent a good part of her life washing and ironing those uniforms; men who worked in the subway tunnels didn't take their uniforms to the cleaners. I saw her doing that every week and she would hum while she was ironing his clothes. My father had installed a metal bar in our kitchen that fit into a pipe attached to the wall, and as she ironed, she would hang his uniforms on this bar. On ironing day, we would come home from school and there would be a big pot of chicken soup on the stove and my dad's uniforms hanging neatly from the bar. The ritual never varied. He came home from work and lifted the bar out of the pipe, carrying it into their bedroom with my mother following after, and transferred his uniforms to the closet bar. He'd change his clothes and wash up and we would be waiting for them with the table set and the soup ready to be served. He and my mother came out of the bedroom, smiling at us. I often think that is why I made such a big deal out of taking care of Jack's clothes. I mean, it was almost a full-time job. He appreciated it, too. I'm not sorry I did it now. My mother did it as an act of worship, and I took that on myself.

Years ago, in a women's Bible Study on marriage that I attended, the leader said when she ironed her husband's shirts, she would pray over where his heart would be as she ironed the left side of the shirt. I should have prayed over the crotch area. It's clear that

Jack was a walking encyclopedia of sexual aberrations. His earliest memories had to be of violent sexual abuse at the hands of his father. That is no excuse for hurting others. I hope he never killed anyone. I have a fear every single day that someone is going to come to the door with evidence of something worse that he did. I never could have imagined that one day I would open the door to a young girl holding a two-year-old carbon copy of my late husband. It was surreal! I felt the breath get knocked out of me. She looked like she was about twelve years old. I was completely unprepared for it. I wondered if I would feel anything for the little boy outside of sadness, and I didn't. He will never know his real father. That may be a good thing; we will never know.

Fortunately, the boy didn't look anything like Brent. Brent looks more like Bernice. He has light hair and eyes as she does. Jack must have looked like his father. His real father, Albert. Harold was brawny and muscular; Jack was leaner. Brent takes after Jack in that department. He is tall and lanky; he'd make a good male model. But don't tell him that! I find myself more curious than emotional about Sandra's baby. They will be able to tell the sex at her next doctor's appointment this week. I hope it's a girl. This may be a horrible generalization, but I think Tom will have an easier time accepting a little girl than a little boy.

We don't see each other on the weekend anymore. She is busy with Tom now, and that is the way it should be. Last weekend, they started fixing up a corner of her bedroom for the baby. I don't remember the size of the area, but it's big enough for them to put a decorative privacy screen in place to cordon off an area for the crib. Sandra is still so tiny through the belly area that no one at work has even noticed that she is pregnant. I am going to have a shower for her at the mansion. My mother, Bernice, and Marie will be there. I am not inviting my sister-in-law Anne, who I understand is out of jail and plans to divorce Bill. Good for her! She still has a chance for a life. I wonder if I should invite Alyssa. I'll ask Sandra.

I take Bernice to Riker's Island to see her son, Bill, every Wednesday. He is in denial. He won't admit he did anything wrong! Although he would like to blame me for his incarceration, I really didn't have much to do with it. It's true that the original complaint was mine, I guess. The police showed me stills of him from surveillance video taken on the train as he approached Jack, and then rifled his jacket for the wallet and left the train. I did identify him. But holding a knife to my mother's throat? I fail to see how I had anything to do with that! All I did was shoot him in the elbow. It was clearly in defense of my mother. He is an interesting character, that Bill. I'm glad he isn't one of my problems. It's the females to whom I feel that I have an obligation. Those who were hurt by my husband. There is an entire legion of us. I should form a club.

I was so certain that Jack loved me. I made excuses for his behavior, even took the blame myself at first. I was too busy, didn't want to do the things he did, gave him too much space. The truth is that I probably am guilty of all of those things. I hate to golf or play tennis, but he loved them. He played with Marie until the children were big enough to learn. He was an avid theater-goer. The theater and movies bore me to tears. I felt trapped there. Jack liked action movies and heavy stories, depressing stuff like *Schindler's List*. I am sorry, but if I have to be away from my comfortable house and the ocean, it had better be to see something that will bring some joy to my life.

He also loved going to the symphony and the ballet. When we lived in the city, I went with him faithfully, to every single performance. His family was a longtime supporter of the arts in the city and I think he felt responsible for attending. I love music and dancing if I am participating! Take me to any club in the Village for live music and I am a happy camper. Jack would never! Now I know it was probably because we would run into someone down there that he was sleeping with.

So much makes sense to me now; things that were said after he died, for instance. At least three people told me that Jack felt that he was going to die soon. Why? Well, dummy, because he had AIDS! He was sick. And he knew it. I plan to get a copy of his autopsy report before the week is up. I don't think Jack came inside of me most of the times that we made love, or, more appropriately, had sex. The times he did were messier. Sorry for this disgusting confession. I know, what a disjointed way to look at it; why the hell didn't he just own up to it and keep me safe? I will never know. One thing is certain, Jack was a coward.

Oh, it hurts me to say that. I do want to remain loyal to him. There was so much that was good about Jack! I go back and forth like this continuously; he loves me, he loves me not, he loves me, he loves me not.

He was larger than life. Wherever we went, and I mean from the smallest hole-in-the-wall dive to the fanciest restaurant in town, Jack commanded respect, and he gave it back in return. From the president of the Stock Exchange to the driver of a Central Park horse and carriage, he treated everyone the same. I never saw Jack talk down to another human being. He was a softy when it came to animals and children. Jack couldn't watch television except for the Weather Channel because the news upset him to tears most of the time. Now, of course, I wonder if he wasn't just suffering from depression like the rest of us. It's clear to me now that he was mentally ill.

We were treated like royalty wherever we went when we lived in the city. After we moved to Babylon, he made a name for himself here, as well. I will never say this to another soul, but I get very nervous when I think about his involvement in local youth sporting groups. I think something would have come out by now if he had compromised himself in any way. Wouldn't it have? Our kids were involved in all the different teams, and I find it very unlikely that he would do anything to hurt or embarrass our children. I feel very strongly that I am right about this.

His looks got him so much attention. I felt like I had married a movie star the way people looked at him. I bet he and Sandra attracted a lot of stares, too.

That makes me sad. I think it was easier knowing about Sandra when I loved my husband and thought he had once loved me. Knowing that she was just another body in his retinue of bodies is very upsetting to me. Having her in my life now doesn't bring the same comfort it did right after his death. When I first met her, I thought, *It figures that he would love her, look at her. I love her!* Now I realize that he may have loved her more than he loved the others, but she started out as a piece of ass. Having Melissa and Maryanne tell me that he loved Sandra really cheapens it. They weren't much more than prostitutes, in my opinion. He paid them off each month. Did he really care that much about them? Two thousand a month is hardly a fortune. I know there had to be others. Sandra found seven envelopes, each containing one hundred twenty-dollar bills. At first, I thought it was the money for his mother, but now I believe that he was paying seven women. I know of two; there are five more. I don't know how I am going to find out who they are, but I am going to try my darnedest!

27

On Friday, Marie and Carolyn boxed up the files to be shipped back to Lang, Smith and Romney. Marie would be taking the presentation downtown. She made an appointment with Sandra for one o'clock and left the office at twelve-thirty. Of course, she couldn't get a cab, so she ended up taking the train. Her purse, containing the list of women's names, kept bumping against her leg with each shake of the train. She hadn't yet made her mind up what she would do with it. Would she give it to Pam? Burn it? Or would it be wiser to give it to Sandra? Marie couldn't help the teensiest flutter of glee; it would serve Sandra right to know what Marie suspected, that they were but two of a large group of women that Jack had been with.

The visits to the beach by Jack's former lovers had not yet been divulged to Marie. Pam held on to some information out of respect for her children. *The entire world didn't need to know everything, did it?* Marie had never heard of Melissa or Maryanne or Alyssa. She was in the dark about Cindy Thomasini, too. So unbeknownst to Marie, Jack's women had slowly started to come out of the shadows. The list wouldn't be a big surprise to Pam or Sandra except for its length.

The subway stopped at the Wall Street Station and Marie was pushed out of the train with the rest of the riders, clutching her purse with the list of names to her chest while she held the precious presentation file carelessly under her arm. The jostling continued as the mass of people moved as one unit up the stairs and out onto the street.

"Goddamnit!" Marie yelled to no one. She hated this part of the city more than the one she lived and worked in; it looked like a vibrant, dynamic place, but it was just as boring as Hell's Kitchen. She fought the lunch-hour crowds to make her way to Jack's building, up the steps, and into the foyer, and didn't relax until she was on the elevator going up. When it stopped on Jack's floor and the door opened, she breathed a sigh of relief. The receptionist told her to have a seat while she called Sandra, but Marie was too antsy to sit.

"You can go back," she told Marie. Walking to Sandra's office didn't excite her as it once had; would she ever forget the implications of this office, or would it be part of her thought process forever? It was part of the wages of sin, she decided. *You make a mistake and it tortures you the rest of your life*. Sandra opened the door and stood aside to allow Marie to enter. Marie's eyes went right to Sandra's midsection. *I wonder if she is even pregnant?* Marie thought.

"I guess traffic was bad?" Sandra asked with a frown.

"I couldn't get a cab. The train was awful, as usual. I don't know how people can stand being down here. The sun has been shining all day and it's as dark as a cave here." *The bitch had better not complain about me being ten minutes late*, Marie thought. "Where do you want me to lay this out?" She looked around the room for a place to put the file folder.

"It should be fairly self-explanatory. There is really no need to go into an in-depth presentation." Sandra wasn't in the mood to have her afternoon taken over by Marie and her theatrics.

"It really isn't. Self-explanatory, that is. I won't take up much of your time, but I do want to show you what we did. It meant something to Jack, and I want the last thing he gave me to do to be honored in some way." Marie was shocked at her own patience with Sandra, when punching her face in with a fist was really what she desired to do.

"It's not necessary, Marie." Sandra was not going to be pushed around. She was in a foul mood as it was. "I've had a rough morning and don't think that we need to make more of this project than it was meant to be. Peter didn't even know anything about it," Sandra lied.

"It's a wonderful development. You'll see. Just give me a few minutes. I mean, what did you think I was coming down here for anyway?" She shoved some papers over on Sandra's desk and started to pull graphs and charts out, and some photos.

Sandra wanted to jump forward and tear the paper out of Marie's hand, but she controlled herself. "Don't mess up my piles! Those papers are in order!" Sandra took the paper Marie just moved and put it back where it had been. "Here, give me the file," she said loudly, putting out her hand toward to Marie. "If you are going to make such a big deal out of this, let's go into the conference room." She stomped out of her office without looking back after she grabbed the file.

Marie just shrugged, baffled as to what Sandra thought the purpose of the trip was if not to make a presentation. *Why hadn't she offered the use of the conference room in the first place?*

Sandra opened the door and threw the file folder on the table. Marie calmly walked to the table, opened the folder, and began placing the charts and photos in an order that made sense. Then she began her speech, highlighting the benefits of the development to the community, what the advantages would be for the tenants who lived there, and ultimately, the financial gain the developers would realize by following the advice set forth in the proposal. When she was finished with the statistical information, Marie added what she thought would be the most important feature of the plan: Jack's original goal to preserve the history and origins of the neighborhood while improving the services to the area. He had been criticized in the past for gentrifying an area, and avoiding ill will had been important to him this time around. She felt satisfied that she would have made Jack proud. She began sorting through the charts and photos to get them back in some kind of order before she put them away when she looked up at Sandra. She was sitting back in the chair, hands folded across her stomach. It was evident that she was moved by something, probably the references to Jack, Marie thought.

"Well, what do you think?" she asked Sandra.

"Very nice. Let me ask you something, though. Why'd you think that after all the time that has passed, we would even be interested in this? It doesn't make any sense to me. Jack gave you the job six months ago, and now, over three months after he dies, you show up with it. What do you think my responsibility to you is?" Sandra had a hard look on her face, one Marie had seen before.

"You have no responsibility to me at all. But Lang owes the company I work for about four hundred hours of employee time. You'll be billed. I have the invoices from the messenger company Jack used to ship the file cabinet of crap over to us back in March, and copies of all the communication between him and me regarding his expectations. All we did was collate the information Lang gathered." Marie picked up the file. "The cabinet is on its way back here, by the way. This is your copy of the presentation; I have one at my office," she said, handing the file to Sandra. She walked out without saying good-bye, fairly certain that she wouldn't be seeing Miss Benson again, Jack's baby notwithstanding. The sheath of papers folded in her purse continued to taunt her with their names, but she made the decision that Sandra Benson wouldn't be getting her hands on it. The names belonged to her sister, Jack's wife. Marie walked out into the reception area with her head up, happy for the first time in a while. She thought that maybe she would be okay after all in spite of all the pain she had caused others and her own broken heart. All summer she had felt awful about the way she had betrayed her sister, and although what she did would always be an issue that would lurk under the surface, she was moving on. The knowledge of Sandra and of other women in Jack's life would only be stumbling blocks to her well-being if she allowed it. Sandra was really only one of the names. Pam had given her an importance she didn't deserve. Marie would try to follow Pam's example, however. Pam had been nothing but gracious and forgiving to everyone who had hurt her.

Marie was walking along, looking up at buildings and half-heartedly looking for a cab when she heard her name being called. "Oh fuck," she said. She turned around and there was Sandra, jogging along to catch up with her. She waited, thinking Sandra might want to pick a fight out here in public and Marie was ready. She even flexed her fists for effect.

"Marie, thanks. Whew! I'm out of shape. Thanks for waiting." Sandra was out breath. They stepped aside, out of the way of the other pedestrians. Marie didn't say anything. She waited for Sandra to get on with it, resisting the urge to look at her phone to check the time.

"I'm sorry for what I said back there. Chalk it up to bad manners, or pregnancy. I'm not trying to make excuses, honestly. Of course, you'll be paid. It was awful of me to insinuate otherwise. Shake?" She held out her hand to Marie. Marie took it and gently shook her hand.

"I was ready to box, but you do have a disadvantage," Marie said.

"And why is that?" Sandra retorted.

"You're sane," Marie replied, and walked away from her. She looked back and smiled warmly at Sandra, who was standing on the corner of Broadway and Wall Street, clearly confused.

"I don't get it," Sandra said. Marie looked up at Trinity Church and thought, *What a lovely building*. The ancient brownstone was stained almost black, its ornate medieval Gothic Revival ornamentation out of place in the hodgepodge of midcentury architecture downtown. She closed her eyes for just a second, taking a deep breath. *I'm sorry I said I hated it down here*. Marie didn't turn around to see if Sandra was still standing there. She let her have the last word. It felt good.

28

The weather was forecast to be beautiful for the weekend; real fall weather, not too hot, with clear, sunny skies. Nelda was staying in the city and Pam planned on a peaceful, private time alone. Friday morning she started her weekend odyssey by stopping at Organic Bonanza on her way home from the gym. She would prepare her meals as though she were a lone honored guest. With Nelda away and some of her sadness lifted, she was enjoying old favorites from her life with Jack, including cooking. It seemed right to do for herself that which she had formerly done for Jack. She chose a nice looking steak and fresh flounder for the grill. The deli had fabulous potato salad. It didn't make any sense to make it from scratch when you could get it here fresh and made from organic ingredients. She approached the counter, and although there were only three women in line waiting, Pam took a number. The two deli clerks got through the orders quickly and then it was Pam's turn.

"Hi Jean!" Pam said to the girl closest to her. "I'll take a half pound of potato salad." The young woman looked right at Pam, but didn't acknowledge her. She opened the deli case and straightened the serving spoons, turning her back on Pam. She walked away and started to fuss with some paper supplies. Pam was confused for a second; Jean had looked right at her. "Jean, could I have a half-pound of potato salad, please?" *Maybe because she didn't say "please"?* Pam thought. Again, she was ignored. The other clerk, a surly young woman Pam remembered as Marion from Lisa's softball team, stood off to the side with a smirk on her face. Pam was baffled. She remembered being ignored by the two clerks last summer and that memory made her angry. She was tempted to walk away as she had that time weeks ago, but she really want that damn potato salad.

"Jean. Marion. Would one of you please wait on me?" Neither girl responded. So Pam did something so out of character that she shocked even herself. She picked up her purse and, leaving her cart in front of the deli case, walked around through the "employees only" area to get her own order.

Marion yelled out, "Get out of here! What are you doing?" She came over to Pam and made a motion to grab her arm. "Get out of here! I don't even want to touch you without gloves, you skank!"

Not quite getting it yet, not thinking about her health or that anyone could know anything about her private life, Pam immediately thought that maybe Marion knew something about Jack. Maybe she had heard about him. It made her ill. She suddenly lost her taste for Organic Bonanza's potato salad. She turned to walk back to her cart when the store manager appeared.

"What's going on here?" he asked. Mrs. Smith was a longtime customer, a faithful big spender. That she was behind the deli counter was strange enough, but if she wanted to get her own order, he'd see to it that she could. There seemed to be more going on than just dishing up salad however; the two clerks stood apart and one of them had assumed an aggressive stance toward Pam.

"Can I help you with anything Mrs. Smith? What's going on Marion?" He said her name slowly, elongating the vowels, narrowing his eyes.

"You can see what's going on," the young woman said. "She came around back here to dish up her own salad, touching the spoons without gloves on. It's enough to make me sick."

"Marion, go to the office right now. Jean," he said, looking at the other clerk, "go with her. Mrs. Smith, do you want to tell me what's happening?" He softly spoke to Pam, his body language saying that he was eager to help her. He glared at the clerks. "Go, now!" he said to them.

It took her awhile, but Pam finally got what it was all about. Somehow, they knew she had AIDS. Two young women, contemporaries of her children, knew what Pam thought was a well-kept secret. If she didn't act quickly, someone might tell Lisa and Brent that their mother was infected with the AIDS virus, and she didn't want that.

Then she remembered that Jean, the older of the two deli clerks, had a sister who was a nurse in the Emergency Room at the hospital. Would she have discovered Pam's health condition and told her family? The store manager was standing there, and although

Pam wanted to just shake it off and walk away, something told her that now was the time to take a stand.

"Those young women are very rude, I am so sorry to say. Every time I have come into the store for the past several months, since my husband died to be exact, they have ignored my requests for service. I am about ready to shop elsewhere." Pam couldn't help herself; she started laughing. "That's a lie. I love it here. But I do miss getting things from the deli."

The manager went right behind the counter and got her order for her, yammering the whole time. "I am so sorry, Mrs. Smith, it won't happen again. If it does, I'll personally wait on you myself every time you come into the store." He gave Pam her packages and she continued shopping, planning how she was going to tell her children the truth. And when she was done with that nightmare, she was going to get an attorney to find out who had divulged her personal health information. She was in a litigious mood. She would take out her anger at Jack on the nurse who had opened her big mouth. Feeling a deep sense of satisfaction, Pam smiled. She was about to go public.

29

Sandra Benson walked back to her office, wondering what had just happened between her and Marie. She thought that some line had been crossed; where she had been the levelheaded one in the past, able to justify looking down her nose at the frenzied Marie, Marie was now the "normal" one, and Sandra was the unstable one. The smell of the roasting fat and spices from a hotdog cart made her mouth water. As much as she hated to put anything unhealthy into her body, she put her soul-searching on hold and ordered a dog with all the fixings and enough acid to send her into early labor, along with an order of French fries. She walked half a block south to the triangle, a place furnished with picnic tables and trash barrels. It was after lunchtime, and the place was deserted. Spreading a paper napkin down for a placemat, she arranged her food and began to eat. The first bite of the hot dog sent boiling juices squirting everywhere, including down the front of her perfectly tailored, beige silk suit. She cleaned up the mess as best she could with the flimsy paper napkin, rubbing the grease deeper into the fabric. *Oh great.*

As hard as she tried, she could not get Marie Fabian out of her mind. She felt anxious, as though she had lost some footing, some self-respect. Was she just as badly behaved as Marie was? She had rationalized her behavior with Jack by lying to herself; telling herself that because she didn't know Pam, it was okay. They were destined to be together in spite of his marriage. Although Sandra always felt like the relationship was short lived, because of the pregnancy she had fantasized that it was a love affair that would have transcended its shady origins if Jack hadn't died. Marie was more at fault because she had betrayed her own sister. She'd probably come on to Jack, and he, being a highly sexual human being, had succumbed in a moment of weakness. She then remembered Cindy Thomasini. Where did she fit into the picture? *Give it a rest*, she said to herself. *Stick to the issue.*

The issue was why was she always so mean to Marie? *You are jealous of her, that's obvious.* And the truth was that Sandra's relationship with Jack was nothing more than a momentary lapse in judgment and that theirs probably was but one of many, many illicit romances. She looked around the park, noticing for the first time that some of the trees had been vandalized; the bark sliced with deep, machete like cuts. Some of the lower branches of the trees were broken off, leaving jagged ends. There was a small sparrow sitting on the remains of one of the branches, grooming itself with a small, delicate wing poised over its head. The gesture was so innocent that Sandra gave out an involuntary gasp and began to cry. The juxtaposition of the little bird on the destroyed tree in that pathetic little park, empty of anyone but Sandra, magnified her sense of loneliness. And then she thought of Tom. *What future was there with him, really?* she thought.

Eventually, she was afraid that the very company Jack had left her might become anathema to Tom. He had made a few remarks under his breath about the hours she had been putting in lately, preparing for maternity leave. Thankfully, he didn't know that her share of the profits from the company was going to Pam. Sandra's draw was substantial however, and she wasn't about to divulge that yet. There was a twist to his mouth whenever she tried to share something interesting from her day at work. She didn't do anything else, didn't have any hobbies, or go out with friends, so her conversation about herself was limited to what she did at her job. And she didn't really want to be forced to change that. Soon, she'd have a baby to occupy the rest of her thoughts.

Flattered almost desperately that he was interested in her, at first it had seemed like enough. But as the weeks passed and she was getting to know him better, she formed a deeper concern that possibly he wasn't smart enough for her. She never would have breathed that fact to a soul. But the truth was that one of the things that had attracted her to Jack was his brilliance. It was the most positive thing about him. He was an enigma in the business world, internationally known for his demographic acumen, but that wasn't all. Jack was a voracious reader. There wasn't a topic he couldn't discuss. And he was interested in everyone and everything. No matter where they went together, people knew Jack. He was forever being stopped by friends, or recognizing old acquaintances and stopping to greet them. He always introduced her as well, seemly unconcerned that someone might tell his wife about seeing Jack with another woman. She couldn't recall ever taking a walk with him that was not an adventure. He couldn't pass a street musician without speaking to him, finding out how long he had played his instrument, if he played in a group anywhere, anything the musician cared to share about his life with a stranger. He loved to talk politics and never let an opportunity pass to get someone else's opinion on a topic.

In the middle of the week, there was a farmer's market north of Wall Street and once, shortly before he died, Jack invited her to wander around the stalls with him. He spoke to every vendor, finding out something about his life. He truly wanted to know. It was almost as if he was planning to run for political office, but that was ridiculous. Jack just didn't want to waste a second of time.

Sandra realized that comparing Tom, an honest, hardworking, twenty-nine-year-old Brooklyn boy to a worldly man twice his age was unfair. She also made the discovery that she was grieving still, and it was a mistake to interrupt the process. It didn't mean that they could never be in a relationship but rather, that now may not be the best time to start one. She was using Tom. The fear that no one else would want her was a big concern. Maybe she was underestimating Tom, however. He'd broken it off once and then returned on his own, understanding that she had a lot of work to do to recover from losing Jack. But did he really know her deepest feelings? Probably not, since it appeared she wasn't in touch with them herself.

"Oh what a mess," she said aloud. She stood up and gathered up her trash, her stomach rebelling from the hot dog. She'd carry her stained jacket back to the office and get it to the cleaners as soon as possible. That would be the only decision she would make, leaving her sadness about Jack and her questions about Tom behind in the triangle park. She wasn't really up to doing anything life-changing at the moment.

⌖

As soon as she got back to her office, Marie called Pam. She wanted to get the list of women's names to her sister even though she knew that Pam might interpret it as a hurtful action. Somehow, she had to get it across to Pam that she was not purposefully trying to upset her. It was information that belonged to Pam and Pam alone, and she would never mention it again if need be. She locked her office door and went right to the phone. Pam picked up on the first ring.

"Oh! I was just going to call you! When we do this, it always catches me off guard," she confessed. "Someday I will get used to our ESP. What's up?"

"What were you going to call me about?" Marie asked. She was losing nerve and maybe if she allowed Pam to talk first, revealing the list wouldn't seem so aggressive on her part.

"Are you in a rush? This might take some time," Pam said, prepared to tell her sister about her grocery store encounter, and that she was going to call her children and tell them the truth about her health and their father's role in it, if it came up. Marie encouraged Pam to go ahead and begin, more than glad to delay what she had to say. Pam told her what happened, and Marie was furious.

"You know, I hate that store. It seems like such a wholesome, friendly place and it's really just a haven for snobs. How can a goddamned deli clerk get away with talking to you like that?" Marie asked.

"Well, I don't think I'm going to allow her to," Pam confided. "On Monday I am going to talk to my lawyer about her sister, the nurse. I'm sure she broke some law by gossiping about me to her sister. I have never felt vindictive before, but I do today. Isn't it strange? Why now? I've certainly had the opportunity to do so this summer."

"Maybe you've just had your fill of rude behavior," Marie said, embarrassed, since she had given her the most reason, outside of Jack. "Besides, you don't need an excuse. That's why the laws are written, why every time you enter a doctor's office now you have to sign that HIPAA form. I'm glad I wasn't with you this time. Can you imagine?" The sisters laughed, the vision of Marie getting involved in the confrontation horrible and hysterical at the same time.

"What were you calling me about?" Pam asked.

"I'll cut right to the chase. Jack gave my company a project last spring. It was mine to complete, and I put it aside for the obvious reasons until the merger. It contained an entire file cabinet of information, and when the writer was finished with it and cleaning up the last files, she found a list of women's names. I don't want to hurt you anymore, but I think this belongs to you. I could have thrown it in the trash, but it really wasn't an option. You may toss it, but it wasn't mine to destroy."

There was silence. Finally, Pam replied. "I have his cell phone. There are hundreds of women's names on it. I didn't know a phone could store so much, to tell you the truth. So I am not surprised. I wonder why he made a list?" Pam was beginning to feel anxious. *What was he thinking when he wrote down the names?*

"He started out typing names on an old type-writer. The first pages are on different types of paper, all typewritten. When he started to use a computer, he began printing the lists; there are even a couple of sheets of paper that have the holes along the edge, like computer paper used to be—the long, continuous sheets that could be separated by perforations." Marie paused. "I guess we will never know what Jack was thinking. Or why he did the things he did. I wish I had some answers. Maybe he was keeping track of his conquests."

"Hang on to it, okay? You can give it to me when we are together next. Thank you, though. I know it wasn't easy for you to see the names, to recognize the implication." Pam was purposely being cagy; she want-ed Marie to ask questions, to start probing into the murky possibility that she was but a drop in a bucket of women with whom Jack had had sex.

Marie did get it; she wasn't stupid. But she was not going there with her sister. "It wasn't hard seeing them at all. It means nothing to me." *How odd!* She thought. *Why is my sister baiting me?* Marie had had an intense relationship with Jack that spanned thirty-five years, thirty of them sexual. She not only saw him during the week for lunches, the theater, the ballet, and the symphony, but she was with him all weekend, golfing, playing tennis, and swimming in the summer, and skiing and snowboarding in the winter. When she really thought about it, what she'd had with Jack was more exciting and involved that what her sister had had. *Would challenging Pam with this information be worth what such a confrontation would do to their relationship? Probably not.*

"So when will I see you again?" Pam asked, secretly hoping she wouldn't say, "Tomorrow."

"I'm not sure. Are you coming into the city to see Mom this weekend? I'd like you to see where Steve lives. I'm thinking about moving in with him and now's as good a time as any." Oddly, Pam had never visited Marie's apartment before—Jack and Marie's love nest.

"I don't think so. I'm decorating outside for fall already. I'd like to do the 'fall weekend' thing we used to do. Do you remember it? I want to get cider and doughnuts, bake apple pie, and buy mums for the veranda. It will be strange doing it alone, but I think I need to try it. I loved doing it with you and the children, and when Jack was here, although I'm not sure he noticed. Most men don't care about that sort of thing, do they?" Pam asked.

"Why are you asking me? I've no experience with men. Besides, I think Jack did notice what you did," Marie said. "He talked about how the house reflected every season and holiday. Last fall, when you put lit pumpkins all over the place, I think his actual words were, 'I thought I walked into the wrong house last night.'" Pam had bought dozens of ceramic jack-o-lanterns and put battery-operated candles in each one, lining the front of the house with them, and leaving a trail of them through the entryway, and out to the veranda. "He said it was spooky and beautiful at the same time."

"So he actually noticed!" Pam remarked, pleased.

"If your traditions bring you pleasure, you should keep doing them for yourself. I remember when leaf-burning was still legal. Daddy raked a huge pile out into the street in front of our house and lit a match. We roasted marshmallows over the fire and they would be covered with leaf ash. Any kind of burning wood reminds me of fall now. Sick."

"Why's that sick? I feel the same way," Pam replied.

"Homeless people burning trash in my neighborhood shouldn't remind me of our father, that's why," Marie said. "There's a farmer's market near Steve's place, and I noticed piles of gourds and corn stalks tied together at one of the stands. Maybe I'll buy one for his stoop." She thought about it for a second. "Nix that." She wasn't beginning any domestic traditions with Steve Marks. At least not yet.

"So I guess I'll see you next weekend?" Marie felt sad; she was going to miss another weekend at the beach. *How would spending an entire weekend with Steve measure up?* Just the thought of it was making her depressed.

Determined to allow Steve to make the first moves so his routine would become evident to her, Marie wasn't going to say a word to him. Was he a slug who wanted to laze around, reading the paper all weekend, or did he jam activities into every second that he was awake, getting up at the crack of dawn and going to bed in the middle of the night? She didn't know which one would appeal to her. Jack was always moving, always on the go. She was exhausted by the time the workweek was due to begin after they spent the weekend together. But she loved it.

The past summer had been long and boring and then Steve Marks came along to rescue her. She would be happy going in whatever direction he would lead her. Boring and lazy might be preferable to crazy and driven. She would try it on for size.

Pam hung up the phone and went out to look at the water. *Why did she still care whether Jack had noticed her life?* She was angry with herself, both for the pleasure Marie's comments about him brought her, and because she continued to look for information that would validate her marriage. It was so over. Even if he had lived, it would have been over. She allowed herself to imagine what the scenario would have been had Jack lived. Sandra would have gone to him with the announcement of their pregnancy. *What would Jack have done? Would he have asked her to abort the baby?*

Pam didn't think so. He would have mustered up the courage to take the train home to Babylon that same day. She pictured him pulling into the garage as he always did. Only this time he wouldn't kiss her on the mouth. He would ask her to sit down in the kitchen. He would come right out and say he wanted a divorce. He was cagy. He wouldn't tell her the truth: that he had gotten someone pregnant. Jack would never admit to making a mistake. He would lie to her. He'd say that he wanted to try living alone, that he didn't love her, and that he was dying. He'd make up some catastrophic lie. But it wasn't a lie. He would go to their bedroom and pack his clothes right away, never to spend another night in bed with her again.

She'd felt the difference in him before he had died, hadn't she? He wasn't initiating lovemaking; he didn't even say good-bye to her that last morning when he left for the city. He was so over his life at the beach.

But back to her daydream. Jack knew Pam wouldn't make a scene. She wouldn't even try to reason with him, to ask him to stay. She would be shocked, for sure, but she would let him go. She might not answer the phone for a few days, finally calling her sister Marie and confessing to her that the marriage was over. *Would Marie have come clean then, too? Confess that she was in love with Jack and had been sleeping with him for years? Or would she call Jack and rail against him, threaten him with exposure if he left her, too?*

It was easier in the long run for the children to have lost their father to death rather than divorce. Knowing Jack, knowing about his fickle behavior now, would he have stayed in touch with the children if he had left her? Finally succeeding in making herself physically ill, Pam cleared her head. She went back into the house and said aloud, "Enough! No more fantasy."

Jack was gone. It was impossible to second guess what he would have done if he had lived. She had to allow herself to face the truth about him and stop trying to cover for him. *What would that do to her children?* She needed professional help to guide her now. She didn't have the skills or the strength to know what was best. Her instincts told her that the truth was vital. The possibility that she would get sicker was real. That thought, that she would die before her children were established in their lives, scared the hell out of her. It was the only thing about AIDS that frightened her. She didn't care about anything else anymore. Once her children knew the truth, the whole town could know about her.

30

Sandra Benson left her office in a daze. After her messy lunch, she tried to do something useful, to accomplish something at work. But it was impossible. The train of thought that had started in the triangle—that she needed to break it off with Tom—monopolized her thought life. Once she recognized that she was with him for just two reasons (he was good looking and he gave her the time of day), she realized that those reasons were not enough. She didn't know him well enough, which was the big problem. They'd had an instant physical response to each other, intense chemistry and sexual attraction. He was kind, he was interesting, but he was also provincial, if that could be said about a Brooklyn cop. His ideas came from a place that no longer existed. How could he be so accepting of her condition on one hand, and so rigid in his thinking on the other? Tom was conservative in the extreme. She feared that down the road, he would suddenly come to his senses and realize that she was a mess after all.

She was sort of stumbling along in the direction of the subway station when a car pulled up alongside of her. She looked over, distracted by her thoughts, and saw that it was Tom. He rolled the window down.

"Hey beautiful! Hop in!"

She stood on the sidewalk paralyzed, looking at him vacantly.

"What's wrong? Come on, I'll take you home." He was concerned suddenly. *What the hell was wrong with Sandra?*

She looked up and down the street to see if it was clear, and stepped off the curb. Tom reached over to open the door for her. "Are you okay?" he asked.

Sandra slid across the seat, looking ahead. "I'm okay. I need to get home," she told him. "Lucky you dropped by. I ate a hot dog for lunch and it didn't agree with me."

"What happened to your jacket?"

Sandra looked down at her silk shell; she had forgotten about her hot dog mishap.

"I got grease on it. The cleaners picked it up. You're observant!" She smiled at him, making the first eye contact.

"Are you okay?" Tom repeated. "You seem a little discombobulated." He pulled away from the curb.

"Actually, I don't feel well; like I said, street cart syndrome, probably." Sandra couldn't wait to get home and lock her door. She needed to think about what her next step would be.

31

Pam decided to call the children and tell them that evening. Tell them that she had AIDS. She would make sure that she had a therapist's names available for them. Although the weather was beautiful, seventy degrees with blue skies, the waves crashing on the beach mirrored what was going on in her head. Pam could feel the salt spray on her face as she stood on the veranda. There must be a storm out at sea. She stood there with her arms wrapped across her body, formulating the narrative that she would speak to her son and daughter.

Jack's name would only be mentioned if the children brought him up, but she had to be prepared for whatever they asked. *Wouldn't it be easier to just come out and say, "Your dad gave me AIDS."?* She felt that was too negative, too accusatory. So Jack gave her AIDS, big deal. She didn't know what the source was and that was the truth. He could have gotten stuck by a needle somewhere. She was not going to go into details regarding his sexual misconduct unless expressly asked, and then she would try to get them to look beyond that, for her sake.

Going back into the house to get a shawl and a cup of coffee, Pam was suddenly tired. She knew it was due to the stress this was putting on her, but it had to be faced. She imagined the hateful deli clerk calling Lisa on the phone that morning and telling her the news. There was really no way in hell she could take the chance that that might happen. Having to call a lawyer about the breech of confidence at the hospital was adding to her worry, so she decided to postpone that until after she made the calls to the children.

That thought had barely left her mind when the phone rang; it was Lisa. "Shit," Pam said, but answered it. Breathing a sigh of relief, her daughter was up early and just wanted to chat with her mother. Pam wasn't ready to divulge her news yet; waiting until later in the day would be okay. Lisa had classes to go to and Pam didn't want her to miss any so early in the semester. Pam took the phone back out to the veranda and sat down, putting her feet up in preparation for a long talk. Lisa liked her classes this semester. As a sophomore, she couldn't yet see the light at the end of the tunnel, but she was enjoying the process. After about ten minutes of catching up, just as Pam was ready to say good-bye, Lisa dropped a bomb.

"Mom, I heard something today that is bothering me and I need you to put my mind at ease." Pam's heart started beating wildly in her chest. She quickly tried to gather herself together before opening her mouth. She wanted her voice to sound normal, unsuspecting. But she wasn't able to pull it off. The tremor was obvious.

"What's going on?" Pam asked, knowing what was wrong, dreading to hear it from Lisa. She closed her eyes, silently praying.

"Do you remember Paulette Vargas?" Lisa asked. "She was in my Brownie Troop and then they moved to Smithtown in third grade." Pam wracked her brain trying to remember how Paulette Vargas was related to either Jean or Marion.

"I think I remember her. She had brown braids, didn't she?" Pam was stalling, trying to drag out this preliminary discussion as long as she could. She felt faint; the previous warmth that had spread through her body had gone, replaced with icy cold.

"She was blonde, but that doesn't matter. Anyway, her aunt lives on West End, near Ninetieth. She knows Bubby. She told me her aunt swears she saw Bubby and Grandma in Zabar's and they had been drinking, and it was first thing in the morning."

Pam did her best to stifle the gasp that involuntarily escaped her mouth.

"Her aunt said that Bubby was a known lush for years. Could this be true, Mom?" Lisa asked, clearly concerned. Pam had lowered her head in relief. Now was the time to start being truthful.

"Lisa, I can honestly say that I never saw Bubby intoxicated, and Daddy never told me she drank excessively, but I have heard that she drank when Uncle Bill and Daddy were boys," Pam admitted. "I wonder what Paulette's aunt hoped to accomplish by passing that tale along to her niece? It seems sort of cruel, don't you think?"

"Yes, it does. I told her that Bubby just lost my dad and her husband. But what about Grandma? It concerns me that the two of them are wandering around the city, drunk."

"Okay, Lisa, I'll look into it later. I don't want you to worry about it though. Bubby has lived in the city all of her life. She knows her way around. As far as my mother goes, that's another story. I know I shouldn't laugh, but the thought of those two women calling attention to themselves in that way is totally out of character. When we hang up, I'll call the house and talk to Ben. He should be driving them everywhere for the money I am paying him."

Mother and daughter chatted for another fifteen minutes and finally when Lisa was laughing, Pam felt it was okay to end the conversation.

"I'll call you later, after I've had a chance to find out what is going on in high-society New York." Pam said good-bye to Lisa. She got up from her chair and walked back into the house to hang up the phone. Her relief that she wasn't caught without her AIDS speech ready was enormous. Immediately, she went into the den to get some paper from Jack's desk.

She thought she was past any further discoveries, but she was wrong.

She sat down in his chair and opened the top, middle drawer, expecting to find some blank paper. However, the drawer held only pens and stamps. She opened each drawer without luck, thinking, *Didn't I do this once already? Or did I stop at the first drawer I came to, the drawer that held the cryptic notes from Marie?* Months before, shortly after Jack's death, Pam had found a folder full of scraps of paper Marie had written on, some of the notes threatening him with exposure and others apologizing for some unknown misdeed. Pam promptly burned the notes. She couldn't remember if she had gone through the entire desk. When she came to a locked door on the bottom left, she was certain she hadn't tried to open it before. She went through the desk again, looking for a key. Nothing. She got up and went out to the mudroom to the key rack where she hung the keys to all the cars, and to Jack's Lexus. She searched on the key ring; his keys to the Columbus Circle mansion, the key to his Madison Avenue apartment, the house key, the key to his locker at the club (she'd better empty that), and finally, a lone key that looked like it would work in a desk drawer. She took the bunch of keys back to the den and, bending over, slipped the key into the lock. It didn't go in. "Humph," she said aloud.

She went into their bedroom and stood in the center of it, slowly turning around. She eyed his nightstand. She hadn't gone through it, or his clothes, or the garage. She sat on the edge of the bed and slowly opened the drawer. There was nothing private in her own nightstand drawer. Other women talked about their drawer like it held the key to their sexuality. She had whatever current book she was reading in bed, some earplugs, a small bottle of hand lotion, and a nail clipper. Jack's held similar items, along with this favorite dental floss. She took everything out, having decided that she might as well be done with it and throw it all away. Keeping his intimate things would not bring him back, or change history. She went back into the kitchen and got a large trash bag. As she bent over to close the drawer where the bags were stored, she saw the light from the den.

Slowly standing up, she opened the cutlery drawer and took out a steak knife. *Why would that desk drawer be locked?* She walked back to the den. When she got to the desk, she sat down in Jack's chair. *Should I? Should I risk my well-being for the day?* "What the hell is in there?" she asked aloud. She stuck the tip of the knife in the lock and jimmied it around, bending it back and forth, trying with all her strength to turn it. Nothing.

She stood, now more determined to get the lock open just for the sake of it and not because she was even thinking of the contents. Putting the knife down, she went out to the garage. Jack's tool chest was to the right of the workbench. She went to open the top drawer, hoping to find a tool that would allow her to pick the desk lock and discovered that the tool chest was locked, too.

Now frustrated, she ran back to the mudroom and retrieved the unknown key. It slid easily into the lock of the red metal chest. The drawer popped open without her touching it. The tools were lined up perfectly, the bottoms of the handles precisely aligned, the sizes graduated from largest to smallest. So like Jack to insist on his tools being perfectly lined up like a surgeon's instruments. She was reaching for an awl when she saw it. The crisp, white edge of paper peeking out from under the red rubber drawer liner.

Pam pushed the tools aside and lifted the drawer liner. She saw what she thought was a leg, and then realized she was looking at the back of Jack's thigh with his small, brown birthmark visible, and as she pulled the photo out further, the inside of a woman's leg and her crotch. Pam's heart beat wildly, yet again. *How often could you raise your heart rate like this and survive?* Intense heat flooding her body, she shoved the tools to the back of the drawer and exposed the photo. It was a stack of them. Pam wrenched them out of the tool chest and then opened each succeeding drawer, discovered more of the same thing. She methodically removed all of the pictures from the chest and turned to go back into the house as she picked the stack up. A large sledgehammer caught her eye on the way out of the garage; she grabbed that as well, surprised but not hampered by its weight. She didn't notice she was stomping her feet with each step back into the house. She threw the photos into the kitchen pantry and locked the door, stomping back to the den. Without thinking, without a wasted second, she brought the sludge hammer up over her head and down on the desk with a crack. The report was so loud that beachgoers walking in front of her house looked up, wondering if it was gunfire.

Over and over again, tiny Pam Smith brought the heavy sledgehammer up over her head and smashed it down on what had once been the beautiful, hand-crafted desk of her late husband, Jack. Once the top was destroyed, she was able to reach into the offending locked drawer and pulled out its contents. Seeing what could be more photos, she took the entire drawer into the kitchen, unlocked the pantry, put the drawer inside with the porn, and locked the door again, putting the key down the front of her bra. Going back out to the garage with the sledgehammer dragging alongside her, she put it back on the hooks in the pegboard and walked to the other side of the garage where the recycling was kept. She found a large, cardboard box, flattened, and a roll of packing tape. She struggled with it to get it into the house, not because of its weight, but because it was so awkward in size. Back in the den, she taped the box back together and started picking up the shattered wood that had once been the desk at which her husband sat to do whatever it was he did when he was home. At that moment, she couldn't honestly say she knew what he did. Now it looked like he might have been cataloging his photography collection.

The pieces of wood that were too large to manage in the box where broken over Pam's knee. She knew she might suffer the consequences of this madness later, but for now, it was serving its purpose. Her mind was crystal clear. Any doubts, muddled thoughts, or sadness had been banished. After the destruction was completed, she boxed up the rest of the impersonal contents of the desk and hauled them and the desk remains out to the curb. What was left of the top was cumbersome and she struggled to get it through the doorway and down the path to the street. A neighbor raking leaves heard the ruckus and yelled to Pam, "Need a hand?"

"No Ed! But thanks, anyway!" She brushed her hands off, admiring her pile of junk, turned her back on it, and returned to the house.

She dragged out the vacuum and ran it over the entire den. Her hand on her hip, she looked at his desk chair. She'd take it to Bernice. Whenever there had been a family get-together, Bernice ended up in that damn chair. Pam wanted to annihilate it along with the desk, but she decided the bigger thing to do would be to haul it into the city. It would bring Bernice happiness. Once again, she went through the steps of struggling to get something that weighed almost as much as she did out of the house, into the garage, and into the back of her SUV. Back in the den, she looked around with satisfaction. The bookcases were a little too sterile for her liking. Jack's books so neat and organized that they looked like a law library. She would tackle that another time.

Suddenly lighthearted and carefree, the last thing she wanted to do was to talk to her kids about AIDS. But then she thought it might be the best time. It would take a lot to get her down. She tried to remember why she had gone into that damn den in the first place; it was to get paper to write a script. No longer needing the support, she would just come out and tell them.

Making herself a cup of coffee, she took it and the phone out to the veranda. She'd call Brent first; he was often the quieter of the two children. He may need more from her than Lisa would. Brent answered on the first ring. He was alone; studying for a quiz, chillin' out.

"Brent, I want to say something to you, so just hear me out, will you dear? I'll give you plenty of opportunity to ask questions."

"Jeez Mom, are you getting married again?" he asked with just a hint of teasing in his voice. "Sorry," he said when she didn't respond right away.

"Brent, I was ill a few weeks ago and the tests came back positive for AIDS. It sounds worse than it is. The stigma is the most unfortunate part of it." There was the slightest tremor to her voice, barely noticeable to anyone but those who knew her well. Her son picked up on it immediately. Brent didn't say anything. Pam allowed the silence, not knowing what to say to break it. Finally, he spoke.

"I heard you, Mom. But I'm speechless. I need to think for a minute." He wanted her to know he was listening, but he had nothing to say because it didn't mean anything to him yet. He almost wished he were appalled, that he could start screaming and hang up on her. But that wasn't where he was being taken. He thought of AIDS and what it meant. Certain death? He'd just lost his father. What would it be like to be an orphan at the age of twenty-two? The first question that occurred to him was how had his gentle mother gotten AIDS? But he wouldn't do that to her. His lovely, perfect mother. His brain finally clicked into gear.

"Mom, how awful for you! How can I help you?" Brent asked, head bowed, just hopeful she wasn't all that sick.

A wave of relief flowed over Pam. "Thank you Brent. I'm doing well, better than I thought. Redoubling all my efforts in the fitness and health routine. It seems to be paying off." She wanted to move on now, call Lisa, and get that over with, but she knew he had to have questions that he may not know how to ask. "Do you need any information about AIDS? You can still hug me. I can cook for you when you're home and you will be safe." Pam struggled to get those last words out. Would he ever want to come home again?

"I know about AIDS, Mom. You'd better be planning Thanksgiving dinner since you are talking about cooking for me!" They laughed. She was relieved he was planning to spend the day with her. "I'm worried about you, though. Are you sure you are okay?" He didn't add, *because my dad gave you AIDS. There was no other way, was there?* he thought.

"I'm fine, Brent. Telling you and Lisa has been my biggest concern. Thank you for being so gracious. If you don't have any questions for me now, I am going to say good-bye because I have to call Lisa." *I hope she takes it as well as you did*, she thought. "I love you, Son. Thank you again." That tremor. They said good-bye and Pam hung up the phone. She was emotionally spent, the lump in her thought making breathing difficult. She put her head down on her arm and started to cry.

Brent had been her talisman, her touchstone, all of his life. She had heard other mothers talking about their sons as if they were gods, and although she didn't quite look at him like that, she understood where they were coming from. Brent had a charm about him that was honest and kind. She believed him when he complimented her. Unlike his father, Brent had no reason to lie to her. Pam remembered her own father weeping at the dinner table one night, telling his daughters that their presence on earth validated him as a man. That is what Brent's birth did for Pam. Confessing her health problems to him was the most grievous thing she could imagine doing to him. What a way to reward her son after all he had given to her. It just made her sick. Her anger at Jack renewed yet again, she wished she could destroy another piece of furniture before she called Lisa. And then she thought of something better, more satisfying. She visualized taking that wonderful sledgehammer to Jack's beloved Lexus. It brought a smile to her face, seeing the windshield smashed in her mind's eye, the roof collapsed in, the doors and hood bashed in. Never one to concentrate on the negative, this meditation was having a powerful effect on her.

Pam took a deep breath and felt like she was ready to make that second, difficult call. She picked up the phone again and dialed. Lisa picked up on the first ring, surprised to hear from her mother already. "How's everything at the beach?" Lisa asked. "Did you talk to Ben yet?"

"Lisa, I'm calling back because I have something to tell you that I didn't feel ready to share when you called earlier," she began. "This sounds much worse than it is. I found out I have AIDS. I was sick with the flu and the doctor ran some tests." Pam, out of breath, stopped talking, waited for a response. She heard a sniffle, but there was no screaming, yet.

"Oh, God Mother, I don't even know what to say to you," Lisa responded. "How do you feel?" That caught Pam off guard. It wasn't like her daughter to think about someone else right off the bat. Maybe she was growing up!

"Amazingly, I feel great! And I'm not just saying that, Lisa. I redoubled my efforts at fitness and nutrition and think it is paying off. The doctor is certainly happy," Pam related, leaving out the details about decreased viral loads. Some things just didn't need to be said.

"I'm so glad!" Lisa said. "I'm still numb, but at least you feel good." Pam talked more about loving her and being grateful for her daughter's understanding. There was a few seconds of silence and Pam decided to get out while the getting was good. They proclaimed their love for each other and said their good-byes. Pam hung up the phone. She remained sitting on the veranda for the next hour as the sun went down and she was left in the dark. She finished what was left of her cold coffee, and looked out over the water, the reflection of the setting sun behind the house throwing a bright orange glow on the water. Soon, the only lights she would see would be the landscaping lights that led down the wooden path to the beach, and the lights on boats yet out on the water.

She imagined fishermen returning home from a day of fishing, the smell of brine, the catch on ice in the holds. And a cruise ship or two, headed toward New

York Harbor. She and Jack had never taken a cruise, or even gone on a vacation aside from seeing Brent in California. When he was home for a week or two or three during the summer, he wanted to stay right there. She would fantasize that he wanted to stay with the family because he had missed them so much. But now she wondered if he needed to regroup; his hectic, confusing life getting the best of him and the only way he could manage was to step away from it for a while. It didn't make any difference to her. She loved her home and when the family was all there, she was happiest. It made no difference to her what he was doing while he was in town, because it didn't affect her at all. Pam snickered to herself. They were a perfect match, she and Jack. He wanted to play, and she wanted to be left alone. *Oh well,* she thought. *I asked for it.* Pushing herself away from the table, she got up to go into the house. She was hungry for a change, and would prepare a real meal. It was the least she could do. She owed it to her children to continue taking care of herself.

32
Brent

Well, I just got some shitty news. I don't even know how to react or what to think. Your life goes in one direction for a while and then suddenly, without warning, it swerves in another direction, or out of control.

My dad died five months ago. He was healthy, vital, young for his age, and he just up and croaked on me. I barely saw him all year except for the holidays. He surprised me by coming out to California for my birthday. I should have known something was wrong, because he talked to me like he had never talked before, intimately and at times, with tears. My dad was the type of guy who didn't talk about his feelings much. He spent every second that he was home from work with me and my sister and I always felt like that was evidence enough of his love for us and told him that when he flew out. I never, ever felt like he was ignoring me, or neglecting me. I know Lisa feels the same way.

Evidently, there had been some issue that I wasn't aware of, because about three hours ago, my mother called here and told me she has AIDS. I know my mother, and unless she shot up, the only place she could have gotten it was from my father. She says she just found out that she was sick. You have to know my mother to appreciate this contradiction. My mother is perfect. I'm not just saying this because she is mine. Ask anyone. Our friends, the neighbors, the guy who cuts our grass. My mother and AIDS just don't make sense. It's not possible.

Back to my father. I wonder if he knew and told her and she didn't want to disrupt our lives further by telling us about it too soon after his death. Ha! I can imagine my sister. We haven't talked yet. She did try to call me, but I didn't answer. I have to straighten out my own screwed up feelings before I can address hers. My mother said not to worry, that she was healthy. Again, you have to know my mother. She's never missed a day at the gym except for when my dad died. She had her gall bladder out not too long ago and went back to the gym the next day, just to walk on the treadmill, she said. She could have walked on the beach, but there was something about the momentum of getting to the gym daily that was important to her. I drove her because she wasn't supposed to drive yet. I never begrudged doing anything for my parents.

Healthy eating is a big issue with my mother. My aunt had anorexia; yeah, we kids weren't supposed to know, but neither Lisa nor I is stupid. We could see her not eating and getting thinner and thinner and then one weekend, she didn't come for her visit. My mother has always been a stickler about nutrition, especially for us kids. She would eat like a bird, but it was healthy stuff. We never had fast food when we were small. I remember crying for a chicken nugget when I was about five. She tried making them for us, but it wasn't the same.

Some of my earliest memories are of my mother, running behind our stroller. She had one that both of us kids could ride in. She'd run across town from the west side to the east and back. She was attractive and always commanded a lot of looks. My dad didn't hide the fact that her looks were a big selling point with him. "The first time I laid eyes on your mother," he'd say, "I knew I would try to get to know her better." Or, "I am lucky your mom would look my way." Her response was always the same: a laugh and "Oh yeah, right." She thought he was being smart, but he meant it. He always told Lisa and me how much he loved our mother. Do all fathers do that? Now I wonder if he wasn't trying to convince us of it, afraid that maybe we saw something that would lead us to believe otherwise.

I grew up never worried, never forced to hear or see things that would make me wonder how safe I was. I know other kids didn't have that luxury. I remember hearing stories from my friends and I would think, *How can they sleep at night?* One kid's dad got hauled off to jail by the police, and another had a mother who drank too much. On one of the rare nights that I slept at a friend's house, his parents got into a fight while I was there, screaming at each other with the children all crying. I got so scared I called my mom and she came right over to get me. I never asked to sleep over again and she wouldn't have allowed it anyway.

She wasn't over protective, either. Lisa and I were allowed to do a lot of things that other kids couldn't do because my mother said she "wanted us to have that experience." My parents didn't bat an eye when I told them I wanted to go to UCLA and then Lisa wanted to go to Oahu. My mother was a little concerned about getting us home from so far away if we ever got sick, but as it turned out, in four years, I have never had to leave school because I didn't feel well. With Lisa, so far so good.

Every year, my parents rented a house in San Diego during Thanksgiving and they and Lisa met me there. It was the only time I have ever known my parents to leave New York. Why the hell am I doing this to myself? During the summer, my mother mentioned coming here for the holidays, but now I am sure that idea is kaput. Here she is, sick and alone in Babylon without her husband or kids and I'm whining about having to go home so she can cook a turkey for me. I don't allow myself to think about my dad too much; trying to hold back the tears never works and I share a room with three other guys. Now there is the real possibility that I could lose my mother, as well. That is truly the only issue I have; the loss of my mother. I am not ready to be an orphan! I don't want her to die. I'm sure that later on, the question of my father's contribution to this will be something I am going to have to deal with, but right now, I don't care. I had the two best parents a kid could have and nothing they can ever do will change the way I feel about them.

33
Lisa

Oh God! I don't know if I want to talk about this yet! How can this be happening to my family? First my dad, now my mother? No friggin' way! I can't lose her. There is no one in my family who could ever take her place, even as a stand-in. I can't believe there is the remotest possibility that she won't always be at the beach, waiting for me and Brent. It was horrible learning that my dad had died. It's only been five months since he's been gone. I'm not used to it yet by a long shot. I just told her during the Fourth of July that I didn't want to come home so often, that it was too difficult with dad not being there! How could I have said that to her! I apologized and she immediately said it was no problem, she hadn't given it a thought. It was her usual, gracious way of handling any slight Brent and I have given to her; complete forgiveness. She has been such an unbelievable role model, but I could never live up to her standard.

She and I have a great relationship. Even when I was a teenager in high school, I knew that my mom would always hear me out about any topic. A big one in my house was whom I could date. My mom liked keeping that to a small circle of boys she knew from my school. They had to be in my grade, from Babylon, going to Babylon High. If she was feeling generous, she'd let me go out with someone from Saint Benedict's. But only if the kid lived in the neighborhood and only if he was in the same grade. I wasn't allowed to date anyone older, not even if he was still in high school.

My mom is about as perfect as you can get for a parent. She must have never slept at night to accomplish all she did every day, the way she took care of us kids and my dad. My mom served a home-cooked meal every single night of my life, with a set table and fresh flowers in the center. She used to laugh when we asked what was for dinner; her reply was always the same. She'd say, "a starch, a protein, a vegetable, and a dessert." And it was! My mother never served hot dogs for dinner unless they were done on the grill. And then she would serve homemade potato salad and baked beans with them.

I know my mom dotes on me. My friends were all jealous of the treatment I got at home. Since I was a little girl, my mother helped me with my bath, washing my hair, massaging my feet, giving me facials and pedicures. It's what we did. Beauty night, she called it. My mom talked to me about growing up, menstruation, and that sort of thing, when I was just eight. She was so worried I wouldn't be prepared. I had my own stash of personal products, too. Everything I would ever need, I had, and then some. I saw my mom spend extra time on my clothes, making sure I had plenty of underwear and socks, and when I started to develop, I was the first one in my class to have a wardrobe of bras. Overindulged? Probably. I knew that it was from her own childhood; she told me once that when she was about six, her mother complained that she smelled in front of an aunt whom she really liked, and the adults laughed at her. She went to her room and changed her underwear, not aware that she should have been doing that daily because no one had taught her. After that, she made it her business to know everything there was to know about hygiene and to put into practice the measures she used all of her life: continuous bathing, primping, caring for herself. I am not quite as bad as Mom is, but almost. My brother is the quintessential metrosexual...trust me when I say he is Pam Junior, but in a nice way.

This is why I cannot believe that my mother has AIDS. It just can't be. In the first place, I refuse to believe that my father, someone who was always referred to teasingly as Mr. Perfect, would ever, ever have something so disgusting. So where did she get it? I don't see my mother being unfaithful to my dad. In the first place, she wouldn't have had time! She was too busy running around taking care of everyone. I have three aunts and two grandmothers and my mother alone prepared every holiday meal I have eaten, in my recollection. As a matter of fact, I have never been to my aunts' homes or eaten a meal they prepared. Everyone wanted to come to the beach, even in the winter. And my mom never complained. I have never heard her say she was tired, or that she dreaded a holiday. She would start preparing for Thanksgiving in September, decorating the house and yard right after Labor Day. On Black Friday, she would call the handyman to get the Christmas decorations down from the rafters in the garage. He'd string the lights all over the outside of the house. My mom never forgot anyone on Christmas. People didn't just come to our house to eat; she bought gifts for everyone, too—thoughtful gifts, not just token presents. She sent cards, and this past year, we reached a new all-time high of cards received: over a thousand. My dad teased her unmercifully, said he would cut off her postage allowance if she sent out a thousand cards in return. She winked at me; I think she had surpassed that years ago. The extended family spent all three summer holidays at the beach. The Memorial Day party was an annual event from the first year they moved to Babylon. My parents didn't spare any expense, getting a lavish fireworks display out over the ocean, renting out the entire bed and breakfast down the beach from our house, and my mother preparing everything that would be served. Well, almost. My grandmother made potato salad. That was the sole contribution to a spread for a hundred people.

When my dad was home on the weekends, every meal was a celebration. She planned what we would eat down to the last crumb. Nothing was left to chance. She dealt with the house, all the repairs, improvements, and maintenance; she paid the bills and did the banking. All my dad had to do on Friday was show up. She made that place an oasis for him. I don't know how my dad started out in life, but at the end of it, he loved the way my mother took care of him. He told Brent and me every time we were together that he loved our mother, that the way she took care of her family was a testimony of her love for us and that he knew how lucky he was. I don't see how he could have been to blame for the AIDS. I took it for granted that what my dad said about his marriage was the truth. That it was information he shared with his wife. If he was unfaithful, well, I just don't get it. Maybe he was infected when they got married and it took that long to incubate. Is that possible?

34

The weekend started out dicey for Marie. She left the office with Steve Marks but forgot she was staying with him, and started walking toward her apartment.

"Whoa! Where are you going?" he exclaimed. "You're coming with me tonight, remember?"

Marie looked confused, and then memory fell into place. Right. "Habit," she answered. "How are we getting home?"

"Subway," he said. "The stop is four blocks from my house."

She turned around with resignation, not thrilled that she had a trek ahead of her. *Bingo! Another reason to stay at her own place!* she thought.

He glanced at her as they walked side by side. She was obviously exhausted. Her head was hanging down, and if her arms were long enough, she would have been dragging her briefcase along the pavement. "Here, let me take that," he said, reaching for the handle. She gave it up willingly, but with a long sigh.

"I'm so tired today. Are we staying in tonight?" she asked, hoping that he hadn't planned anything extravagant.

"We are. I do have something planned, but you don't have to leave the apartment or lift a finger." He smiled at her.

Marie, suddenly energized at the thought of a surprise, picked up her step a little. He noticed the impact his words had had on her. That small revelation would carry a lot of weight in their relationship. They walked to the station in silence, but she had a smile on her face.

When they arrived at his apartment, she was happy to see that he had made an effort to clean it up a little bit over the past few days—not that she was a neatnik or anything.

"I'm going to prepare your bath, Madam," he told her, after he had thrown their briefcases into the hall closet. Her heart sank; she wasn't in the mood for a sex marathon tonight. He saw her countenance change and quickly said with a laugh, "Don't worry, you won't have to do a thing." She looked at him with suspicion, but let it go. "Sit down here," he shoved her into his ratty recliner and pulled the mechanism that raised the footrest. She immediately closed her eyes. Steve Marks went into the bathroom and got the basket of feminine goodies out of the linen closet. The clerk at the store had told him to place the candles around the tub and light them after the bathtub was full. He put some smelly stuff into the bath water, and it bubbled up, but not too much. Clean towels and a new, terrycloth bathrobe, and the first part of the surprise was ready.

"Come on, Sleeping Beauty," he said to her. "Time for your bath."

She was clearly amused, and a little embarrassed by all the attention. But she allowed him to lead her into the bathroom. When she saw the transformation—the candles and the bubble bath, the flowers on the back of the toilet, she gasped. "How lovely!" Then she frowned. "Are you sure you don't have an ulterior motive?"

"I swear to God, no," Steve said. "You have so much going on right now, and I just wanted to do something to help you relax..." He smiled broadly. "I'm going to leave now, although I would love to stay, humph, and watch." They laughed, and Steve leaned over to kiss Marie. "I'll be right out here if you need anything." He left Marie, closing the door behind him.

She looked around the tiny bathroom with one motive: to find the hidden camera. She went over every inch of the room and didn't see anything that set off any alarm bells. She knew all about spy cameras; Jack had been a pro at it. He had videotaped almost every one of their sexual liaisons in her apartment. Her heart jumped in her chest thinking about it. *Where are those damn tapes?* She hadn't thought of them in months. *Oh well, there is nothing I can do about it now, and if they are in the house and Pam finds them, at least she knows the truth.* Deciding the comfort of the bath overshadowed the worry that her privacy might be invaded, she did a striptease to the invisible lens and got into the water. For the first five minutes, she overacted bathing, making sure to accentuate the washing of her breasts, standing up and scrubbing her crotch seductively and then finally, giving up with a laugh and sitting down in the water. It was so warm and the candlelight, comforting. She relaxed completely. Lying back, she closed her eyes. A man had never done something like this for her before. *Jack* had never done anything like this. Steve was really wooing her. Making an imaginary pro and con list, Marie thought of all the bad things about Steve first. He had behaved badly when she first met him, harassing her and stalking her. He was obviously broke, although he hadn't come out and said it. There must be a reason a man his age who had worked all his life didn't have much to show for it. She was determined to find out what it was; or was she? She didn't even know if that was important. And why hadn't he ever married? That was creepy. She suddenly thought of her own marital history and had a laugh. *She* was creepy, too! She thought of her own failures, how she had betrayed her own sister for most of her life and now had AIDS, and the anorexia; she was a real prize, too.

So at the top of his pro list was that he was willing to overlook her diseased state. He was really interested in her. He wanted to protect her. The superficial stuff was that he was hot looking, no Jack by any stretch of the imagination, but she didn't want that. She was thrilled that she didn't feel overwhelmed by his appearance. Jack was too good to be true. Steve dressed nicely, had great teeth and breath and good hygiene. He was smart. Maybe he didn't have the greatest common sense, but he had brains, alright. He had a good sense of humor, didn't take himself too seriously, and the most important thing to her right at that moment was that he wanted her. He lusted after her. He thought she was great looking and told her so all the time. So the pros definitely outnumbered the cons. She'd give it whatever she had, she'd be honest with him, and loyal. She'd try to take better care of herself for his sake. Stop drinking so much, take her medication, and eat. She finished her bath and was getting out when there was a knock on the door. She told Steve to come in.

"Are you finished? Am I too late to wash your hair?" he asked.

"What are you talking about?" Marie responded. "You think you're Robert Redford?" she said, referring to the scene in *Out of Africa* in which Redford washed Meryl Streep's hair while they camped in the African bush. Steve was embarrassed, and she caught that and back-pedaled.

"Hmm, maybe that would be nice." She got back in the water, smiling at him. He came over and sat at the edge of the tub.

"I'm not sure how to do this," Steve confessed. "Do you want to dunk your head?" It was disarming that he thought washing her hair would be something that would bring her pleasure. She thought she would probably have to rewash it, but was willing to go along with it just to keep from shooting him down. She didn't want to be responsible for any damaged egos so early in the weekend.

"I'll dunk down and you just take the shampoo and put it in your hand and then on my head. You don't have to use too much." She slipped down in the tub, wet her hair, and then came back up, water streaming down her face. Steve started massaging the shampoo through Marie's hair. He had such a peaceful look on his face; she imagined he must have planned for this evening for days. When she'd had enough, she said she thought her hair was probably clean, and slid back down into the tub. For a second, she imagined Steve reaching down and putting his hands around her neck, squeezing the life out of her. She popped back up, sputtering, water spraying from her lips. Steve backed off a little to prevent his clothes from getting wet.

"Are you okay?" he asked.

She nodded yes. "I think I'll get under the shower for a bit, get some of the suds off, okay? I'll be right out." She reached forward to pull the plug on the drain and Steve moved toward the door.

"Dinner will be ready in fifteen minutes," he said, smiling at her.

She dried off and put the terry robe on. Revived, she didn't bother putting underpants on; she was ready for the night now. She left the bathroom and smelled beef cooking; he had set the table and lit tapers; the lights were off and the candles provided the only illumination.

"Wow! All this for me?" she asked, walking into the kitchen and going over to Steve as he tossed a salad. She reached her arms around him from behind, pressing her body up against his back. "I'll have to think of something special to repay you with," she teased. Steve put the salad tongs down and turned around to Marie, looking down at her in the robe.

"You look wonderful! Robe is a little big, though." He kissed her neck, slipping his hands under the ter-rycloth. "Your skin is so soft. I like everything about you." He ran his hands over her back. Marie fell against him, enjoying the sensation of having someone want her for the right reasons, whatever those were.

"Will dinner keep if we wait to eat?" Marie asked.

"I'll run out and buy more steak if it doesn't," Steve answered. "Allow me," he said as he swept her up in his arms. She yelped.

"Yikes! You're lucky I haven't been eating lately." She wrapped her arms around his neck as he navigated the narrow hallway back to his bedroom.

"You are light as a feather," he replied. "Perfect, no matter what." He nuzzled her neck. On the tip of his tongue were the words, *I love you*, but he swallowed them, not willing to put that pressure on either one of them yet. *Give it some time, jerk. There will be plenty of time.*

35

Tom Adams pulled up to Sandra's Eighty-second Street apartment in the patrol car. He was unbuckling his seatbelt as she reached for the door handle.

"You don't have to come in," Sandra said, hoping he would get the hint. She was so exhausted, both mentally and physically, that she didn't think she would be able to deal with even the most perfunctory interaction. Nothing good could come from their being together tonight.

He was taken aback. "I know I don't *have to* come in!" He laughed. "I'd have put you in a cab if the point was just to get you home." But he wasn't slow and he got it a few seconds later. "Unless, that is, you don't *want* me to come in." He stopped on the sidewalk and grabbed her arm as she walked toward the apartment. He pulled her around to look at her face. She was white and drawn and there were dark circles under her eyes. It was the first time Tom had seen her look unkempt.

"What's going on, Sandra? Are you okay?" He looked down into her eyes. She was unable to open her mouth, fear that a scream would escape that she'd be powerless to stop. Her face was set, lips quivering, and eyes glassy. "Oh boy, I completely missed this on the ride uptown. You really aren't doing too well, are you?"

She shook her head no.

"How about if we just go inside? You won't have to say a word. I'll fix your dinner for you and get you settled, and then you can be alone for the night. Does that sound like a plan?"

Sandra didn't really want him there, but how could she say no to the kindness he was offering her? It might help her to pull out of this despair and uncertainty. So, against her better judgment, she nodded yes. Digging through her bag, she got her keys out and handed them to Tom. If he wanted to help out, she would allow him to do everything. She wished he'd read her mind and sweep her up and carry her to the door. She mustered the strength to walk toward her apartment.

Tom sensed that something beyond the normal was at play here, not just food cart syndrome. Something greater than mourning for the dead boyfriend. She was struggling to stay ahead of the game. *How long had she been in this condition?* he wondered. He opened the door to her building and placed his hand on the small of her back to guide her through the door. His touch energized her, propelling her along the hallway toward her apartment. They got inside and she went right to her bedroom, closing the door. He went into the kitchen to get her some tea and to see what was available for dinner. Sandra wasn't one to keep a lot of food around. He didn't feel safe leaving her to go out; if she wanted something he couldn't fix, they could have it delivered. *I'm like an Italian mother*, he thought. He got her tea things together and put them on the tray she had used to serve him numerous times. He went through the motions of preparing it as though it were an old ritual between them. It was the first thing she had done for him; prepare tea.

He knocked on her door with the tea tray in hand and opened it when she didn't respond. She was lying on the bed in her suit skirt and shell, with her shoes still on, her back to the door. He took the tray to the bedside table and put it down. She got up on her elbow and saw that he had made tea. The act was so simple, but so important to her, that she started to weep. He wasn't used to seeing strong Sandra cry, and it scared him. He reached around her to pull the pillows up behind her back, as a nurse would do.

"Here's your tea, honey." He didn't want to pump her for information like a cop, or tell her not to cry. He just wanted to be there for her. Tom took her shoes off and pulled the sheet and blanket up over her legs. There was a box of tissue on her nightstand and he gave it to her. She pulled one out and blew her nose, got another to wipe her eyes. Tom turned to the tea and took the bag out of her cup, adding one teaspoon of sugar to it, as she liked. She took the mug from him and held it in her hands, taking its warmth into her body. She blew on it and then took a sip.

"Oh, that is good. Thank you so much. You have no idea how badly I needed this." Tom got a low stool and brought it to her bedside to sit on. They didn't say anything, but he could see that she was relaxing, that whatever it was that had distressed her so much that afternoon was dissipating, and she was feeling better.

She drank more tea and leaned back against the pillows.

"I'm going to fix dinner now, okay? Do you want a refill?" Tom asked.

"I'm good for now. Thank you, Tom." She kept her hands wrapped around the mug, but she closed her eyes. There was a hint of a smile on her lips. Taking the tea tray with him, Tom went back into the kitchen and opened cupboards and the refrigerator. She had some chicken broth and rice; he would make soup for her. She had a few stalks of wizened celery, but he thought he could revive them in some cold water. He laughed a little; it was a desperate meal, at the very most. It would stave off starvation until he could order something more for her if she wanted that.

Sandra could hear Tom moving around her little kitchen. It was comforting to have him there, after all. She thought maybe her state of mind couldn't be trusted, that maybe it would be smart not to make any rash decisions now, decisions she would later regret. He was a nice, gentle guy; not perfect, but kind and diligent. She felt safe, protected, and loved. He wasn't going to leave shortly to get home to his wife and kids. He could answer her phone if it rang and not hide that he was there with her. If she wanted, he would probably stay the weekend with her in Manhattan. But suddenly, she didn't want to stay there. She needed to get out of her apartment. She called for him, and he came to her room, a questioning look on his face.

"Do you feel like showing me your apartment to-night? I feel like I could benefit from getting out of the city. And, I could finally see your place."

"If that's what you want, pack a bag and let's go!" he replied cheerfully. "I'm not having much luck with dinner preparation, by the way. You are getting chicken and rice soup."

She made a face. "Let's get Brooklyn pizza for dinner, okay?" She swung her legs over the side of the bed. When she stood up, he saw it. Blood.

"Oh boy," he said, going to her. "You're bleeding."

She swung around and when she saw the blood on the bed and cried out, "The baby!"

"Do you have any cramps?" he asked, reaching for the phone.

"No, well I thought it was the hot dog. I do have discomfort."

"What's your doctor's number?" She pointed toward her purse. He got it for her and she dug through it for the appointment card they'd given to her the last time she was there. She spoke the number and he dialed it and when it began to ring, handed the phone over to her.

"Get back in the bed, why don't you?"

She did as she was told. When the answering service picked up, she explained the situation. "I'm about twenty-two weeks along and am bleeding. How much?" She looked at Tom and then turned over so he could see the back of her skirt and the bedding. He took the phone from her.

"This is her boyfriend. The back of her skirt and the sheets on her bed are saturated," he told the operator. Listening for second, he put his hand over the receiver. "She asked me to hold on; she's going to call the doctor while we hold."

After a few minutes, the doctor was on the phone. She told Tom to take Sandra to the hospital.

"Come on, my dear, you are going for a ride in a police car." Tom was trying to keep things light, but he didn't feel good about this situation. Sandra pulled her clothes off without modesty and cried out when she saw the clots in her underpants.

"Oh my God! Am I losing the baby?"

Tom put his arm around her shoulders. "Get something on and I'll take you right now."

Sandra pulled on her pajama bottoms and then went into the bathroom to find a pad to wear so she wouldn't bleed all over Tom's patrol car. Just to be safe, she grabbed a couple of towels, too. There was an air of surrealism about the scene. She felt almost disconnected from her real emotions. *Am I losing Jack's baby? Just like that?*

Tom felt like the reluctant observer. *Why did this have to happen now? How much can this young woman handle without falling apart?* When she came out of the bathroom, Tom asked her if she was ready to go. He was holding her purse and her keys. He said a prayer for the baby in his mind, repeating it over and over again, *Protect the baby, Lord. Protect the baby, Lord.* His police training told him it was too late. But he wasn't going to be a naysayer. Think positive! And then, *Pro-*

tect Sandra, Lord. Protect Sandra. He became frightened
at that, and started thinking it as a chant. *Protect Sandra, Lord. Protect Sandra.*

36

Saturday morning brought the end of Indian summer. It was dark and rainy and there was a chill in the air. Pam took her morning coffee out to the veranda and lit the fire pit. It threw off enough heat to keep her comfortable, but she thought that maybe this was the end of veranda season for her, after all. She turned the fire off and went back into the house. In the den, she opened the curtains so she could see the water. The fireplace was gas, and with the flick of a switch, she had a roaring fire going. With Jack's desk gone, it felt like a new room. She looked around, imagining what she could do to it to make it even more comfortable. The room reminded her of a ship. A huge mullioned window covered the entire exterior wall. Afghans and pillows, most of which she had made, covered the overstuffed leather furniture. Each family member had his or her own afghan. Brent's was a large circle that looked like a Spiderman cape. Lisa's was in a faux plaid that looked very Native American. Jack's had gone to Bernice at her request. Pam's was pink and fluffy. When she'd finished it and brought it out for the family to admire, Jack had said right away, "I should have known." Everyone had laughed. They knew exactly what he meant.

Pam sat in a leather armchair positioned so she could see the ocean. She and Jack used to sit there on winter nights, he with a pair of night vision binoculars and she with a cup of tea. He would talk about what he was looking at and she would listen. Did she ever contribute to their conversations? She had been a sounding board for him, but more than that, she just realized, she had been his audience. Jack could say just about anything to Pam and she would smile and agree, or rarely, frown and give him "a look."

"Oh, Jesus Christ, there's that 'look,'" he would say. "What's wrong now? What don't you agree with?" For some reason, Jack had to have her approval. They would stay up all night with him trying to convince her that he was right, or his opinion was correct. He would listen to her earnestly and take what she said under consideration and in the end, if she couldn't change his mind, or he couldn't change hers, they would call a truce. Jack never, ever allowed Pam to go to bed thinking he was angry. "Let's agree to disagree, okay? Are you okay with that?" he'd say.

She would laugh. "Jack, get over it! It's no big deal," she'd tell him. But on the nights that they sat together while Jack spied on the world, Pam would think to herself, *How lucky am I! My God, why do I deserve this? Thank you, thank you.*

She snickered. Yes, how lucky am I! And that instant, she decided to do what her sister and Sandra had done the day before and make a mental list of sorts. She would eliminate the cons because she felt like she had concentrated too much lately on the negatives in her life and not enough on the good things: her children, her wonderful children. Her family. Her health! Yes, her health, in spite of having AIDS, she was healthy right now and that was a thing to enjoy and not take for granted. This lovely home. She looked out over the dark sea and the rain hitting the water and the window glass. She loved weather. Being at the beach meant seeing the entire gamut of weather. She had never shied from it before and wasn't going to now that she was alone. She might spend a night or two in Manhattan this winter, but she would not move there for any length of time. No. She was embarrassed to add, even silently to herself, that she was grateful for the wealth that Jack had left her. It was nothing to be ashamed of. He had worked like a machine for years to build his business, and he did it for her and their children. It was something to be proud of. They had always been generous to a fault with others. It was okay to be rich. She startled herself by thinking that word. It wasn't one she had ever used in conversation. Polite people didn't talk about money.

Getting up to pour another cup of coffee, Pam heard the phone ring out in the hallway. It was the manager of Organic Bonanza. Pam was surprised to hear his voice.

"Mrs. Smith, this is Dave. I was thinking about you this morning and wanted to give you a call to see how you are. The incident last week was awful and I want you to know how badly I feel," he said.

"Thank you, Dave. I really appreciate you calling. It was sort of...creepy, for lack of a better word.

Anyway, I love the store regardless! I need to come in today and pick up a few things, although I hate going out in this weather." She looked out at the rain lashing the waves.

"What do you need? I live about two blocks from you; I can drop it off on my way home for lunch," he offered.

"You eat lunch at home?" she asked, incredulous. She couldn't help herself and started laughing. "I'd never eat at home again if I worked at that store."

"Sometimes it helps to get out for a little while. Since I live so close, I can get away for a bit and take my dogs for a walk," he explained. "So what's your order? I'm ready with pencil and paper." They laughed together, and Pam told him what she needed: just coffee creamer and bread. "You'd come all the way into the store for that?" he asked. They arranged that he would be there later that afternoon.

After they hung up, Pam fell to thinking about Dave from Organic Bonanza. He was about her age, maybe a little younger, and nice looking in a rugged, non-Long Island way. She wondered how a grocery store manager could afford to live in her neighborhood. And it crossed her mind that maybe he was single because he came home to walk the dogs. Unless his wife was out working all day. She grew annoyed with herself for thinking about him, feeling like a snob because the house thing came up in her thoughts. Then the phone rang again.

"Pam, it's Sandra. I'm in the hospital." And then she started crying.

Pam knew right away. She didn't even have to be told.

"I lost the baby!" Fresh tears. "I have to have a D&C in a few minutes, but I wanted to tell you, I wanted you to know before I went into surgery."

Pam forced herself to speak words of comfort to her grieving friend. Words that she didn't feel. "Sandra, I am so sorry. How awful for you!"

"I can't believe it happened! I didn't feel right this afternoon and Tom was in the apartment with me when everything started," Sandra cried.

"I'm so sorry!" Pam repeated. "What an awful thing to happen!"

Sandra talked a little longer and then said good-bye; the nurse needed to draw some blood.

"Good-bye Sandra, I'm so sorry!" Pam said for the third time. She was shocked with herself. The second she had realized in her heart that the baby was gone, all feeling for Sandra left. The change was swift and brutal. Standing up to retrieve her coffee, Pam was shocked and angered with herself. *What just happened?* she asked herself.

Outside, the storm escalated. Pam imagined it was windy and raining in the city, as well. Rain would be beating against the windows of Sandra's hospital room. It would be gray and depressing. Pam's last connection to Jack through Sandra would be flushed down the toilet, or tossed into the garbage. Sandra would be alone now, no mother or family to comfort her. Pam couldn't bring herself to assume that role. Sandra's young man—the policeman, Tom—would have to do it. Losing the baby was so sad. Pam imagined another part of Jack, gone. But Sandra would have no more power over Pam and her family. She was reduced to what she had formerly been: the immoral, careless young woman who had had an affair with a married man without thinking of the consequences. That Sandra was one of many made no difference to Pam at that moment. She would go through the motions of being a decent human being, but her "friendship" with Sandra had ended with the death of the baby.

Pam picked up the phone and dialed the number for the local florist. She would send flowers, cards, even meet her for coffee. But the hold Sandra had had on her, the demands to tell her innocent children the truth about their father, no longer existed. A long, slow breath escaped Pam, like a balloon deflating over time because it was old and worn out. How long had she been on edge because of Sandra? Time would tell.

She checked the clock. It was almost time for Dave from Organic Bonanza to arrive. She got up to freshen her makeup. She primped a little bit, giving herself the once-over in the mirror. Jack had been gone for five months. Enough time had passed. She was going to have fun again.

Marie woke up Saturday morning to the smell of bacon frying. She swore she still had steak and baked potato in her stomach. Although she hadn't seen any evidence up to this point in their relationship, she prayed that Steve wasn't a foodie like Jeff Babcock was. She rolled over and closed her eyes. Steve would come and get her when he was ready and as long as he didn't care, she was staying in bed. Memories of their lovemaking filtered through her mind. Except for the "safe" part, it had been wonderful. Steve had put so much feeling into it and Marie felt that it was genuine. Blessedly, she had never thought of Jack once.

Sandra lay in her hospital bed, staring out the window. She asked Tom if he wouldn't mind going back to her apartment and getting her makeup bag and clean clothes. The pajama bottoms were in the trash can in the bathroom, covered in baby. The horrible emptiness couldn't be described. It wasn't simply uterine. She felt it in her throat. Her chest was hollow; the ache around her heart brutal. Even her feet were suffering.

Sandra was guilt-ridden. But the loss couldn't be attributed to any one factor, the doctor had said, her kindness overshadowed by her need to look at her watch every thirty seconds. Finally unable to tolerate it another second, Sandra released her. "Please, go! If you look at your watch one more time, I am going to lose it," she said. The doctor turned red and apologized, but she left. Sandra was alone with her thoughts. Life would go on as it had before she'd ever met the flamboyant Jack Smith. She would go to work every day with no plans beyond the immediate needs of her job. She would minimally feed her body. Add the retinue of antiviral drugs, and there was nothing else she needed. At that moment, she was without any emotional feeling for Tom Adams. She wished he would end it as he had before, swiftly and without a look backward. She knew enough about human nature to understand that she shouldn't make any decisions in this state of mind, so she wouldn't do it now, she wouldn't ask him to leave her alone. She had compared him unfairly to Jack. Tom was a fine man, an honorable, faithful man. Jack was a reprobate, apparently a sexual deviate. His interest in her had appealed to her pride, her need for attention. Sandra turned over and put her face in the pillow to cry. *How the hell had it come to this?*

She thought of the little baby. Her pregnancy was over twenty weeks, so the hospital treated the baby like a full-term stillborn. It was a girl. After she was born, the nurses cleaned her up and wrapped her in a tiny blanket. The nurses gave Sandra the choice of whether to see her or not. Sandra hesitated but knew that no matter how sad it would be, she might regret it if she didn't see her, and then it would be too late.

After Sandra left the Recovery Room, the sedation from the procedure barely worn off, they brought the baby in to her. She was confused at first, not understanding what they expected her to do. Was she supposed to just look? Or could she touch her? If she took her from the nurses to unwrap, to examine, how was she going to find the courage to give her back? She had no husband by her side with whom to share her grief. She had never felt so alone.

"What should I do?" she cried.

The nurse grasped her shoulder and squeezed. "You don't have to do anything, dear. This is your baby. That's all." She held her up for Sandra to see. "You may hold her if you want to, but it's not necessary. It's enough to just look at her." Afraid to touch the baby, Sandra lay there and looked, tears streaming down her face. The nursery nurses would take the baby's photo and her footprints, and give Sandra the blanket and little stockinet hat she had on. Those reminders would be all she would have of the five months of pregnancy and of a short, foolish romance. Sandra had never been so despondent.

"Do you want us to take her back to the nursery now?" the nurse asked. Sandra didn't want to give in to her fears, so she shook her head no and reached out to take the baby. She was so small. The nurse kept her hand under the baby's head until Sandra felt sure of herself. The tiny body was still warm in the blanket. Sandra, looking through her tears, carefully lifted the blanket away from the baby's face so she could see her ears. There was a little blood around her earlobe; *my blood,* Sandra thought. *This is my baby. She grew inside of me for five months. Why? Why did this happen?* Sandra began to cry again.

The nurse never left her side. If there had been a father or a support person available, she would have stepped out of the room and allowed the parent to have privacy. *But this young woman is no more than a child,* the nurse thought. She was in her mid-twenties. The nurse wasn't going to leave a patient alone when she was so vulnerable.

Sandra unwrapped the baby with the nurse's help. Her tiny body was so sweet and so sad at the same time. She was no bigger than Sandra's hand. Sandra peeked under the cap and the nurse nodded in approval. She already had hair, and it appeared to be red. Sandra's mother's hair had been red.

"Would you like to name her?" the nurse asked.

"Ellin. It was my mother's name," Sandra said. Tom walked in at that moment, as Sandra broke down crying at the thought of her dead mother and now, her dead baby. His police work had not prepared him for this. He went to her side and peered down at the tiny frame in her lap.

"Oh, my God!" he exclaimed, and then he started crying, as well. He knelt down beside Sandra with his arm around her shoulder. "She's so tiny! Oh, she is so beautiful. Sandra I'm so sorry!" He was so touching, offering his support and showing his concern, that even the nurse was moved. Sandra would never forget how he had offered her exactly what she needed at that moment; validation that her daughter had been important, that she was going to be missed. Sandra reached around with her free arm and hugged Tom. They held each other for a brief minute, the threesome heartbreaking to the onlooker. The nurse left to allow the young couple some time alone.

"Look at her tiny feet," Sandra said, exposing her body. Tom touched the tiny toes, no bigger than grains of rice.

"How are we going to recover from this?" Tom asked, crying unabashedly. "How are *you* going to?" His vulnerability strengthened her.

"We'll just take it one day at time. I don't want to give her up now, but I have to keep telling myself that she is gone. She's not alive." Sandra cried again, but this time, she attempted to pull herself together. She pressed her buzzer and the nurse came in immediately.

"I'll never forget how nice you were to me," Sandra said to her. The nurse bent over and embraced her patient. "I'm ready for you to take her now." Sandra started to sob, but she lifted the bundle up for the nurse. "Thank you! Good-bye, little Ellin!"

The nurse left and Tom and Sandra held each other.

"I've had enough of this damn place. Let's get out of her," Sandra said. She slipped her legs out of the bed. Tom took her clothes out of the Zabar's bag he had put them in. She immodestly pulled her underpants on over the huge pad she had wedged in between her legs. Tom held her spandex pants open for her to put on; she held on to his shoulder and stepped into the legs. He helped her pull the T-shirt over her head. She put some lipstick on, "just so I don't scare anyone," and some blush, combed her hair into a ponytail, grabbed her purse, and motioned to Tom to follow her. She was leaving. They stopped at the nursery for the baby's belongings and at the nurse's desk to thank them once again. Whether her doctor was discharging her or not, she was going home.

37

Dave from Organic Bonanza showed up at the Smith residence with three overflowing bags of deli items for Pam. He remembered to get what she had asked for, but he took the time to check her past deli purchases and brought her containers of all her favorites. He also had sandwiches made for lunch. If she would agree to eat with him, he'd stay; if she were put off by his forwardness, he'd leave. From the moment she opened the door for him, they were friends. Pam couldn't remember him being so attractive. He was tall and lanky, but he had a firm jaw, an impressive hairline, and he was neat and clean. Dave had always admired Pam, thinking she was striking.

She greeted him at the door and could not hide her pleasure that he had thought of her enough to bring lunch. It was still crappy out, the rain beating down and the sky dark and foreboding, but in Pam's den, it was warm and welcoming, even with the curtains open wide to the vista of the choppy, black sea. They unpacked the bags together and made up plates of food to take into the den. Pam dragged a table over to the chairs that afforded the ocean view. She made fresh coffee and brought in a tray with cream and sugar. They ate their lunch, talking like old friends. He said "yes" to coffee afterwards, and they sat and talked, drinking coffee for over an hour. The only uncomfortable moment came when Pam went to the pantry to get napkins and realized that the door was locked. On the floor was a pile of porn and the destroyed drawer full of who knew what. She had forgotten about the travesty of the photos. But she circumvented the awkwardness with her usual grace by saying she'd locked the door because she had tossed her tax papers in there when workmen were in the house the day before. Conversation came so easily for them. She was interested in his dogs—English bulldogs, two of them.

"Couldn't you guess?" Dave teased. "Look at my jaw!"

Pam started laughing, unable to hide her recognition that he had a deep overbite and did sort of look like a bulldog in the jaw! He smiled at her in a way that accentuated his prominent jaw and she just laughed and laughed.

"On a scale of one to ten, I definitely rate this lunch a ten," he told her.

"Well, the food rates a twelve! Thank you so much. I really can't remember when I had more fun at lunch in my own house," Pam said. She picked up her coffee cup, watching him. He was looking around the den, out the window, and finally, at her.

"Can I see you again?" Dave asked. He didn't see any point in beating around the bush. Either she wanted to see him or she didn't. Her husband was gone now for almost five months.

She looked him right in the eyes. "Yes," and she smiled at him.

When she was alone, the afternoon stretched out ahead of her. The contraband in the pantry needed to be dealt with. *But what to do with it?* It was horrible, a chronicle of madness, some of it surely documented right in this very house. She didn't want to see images of her sister being fucked by her own husband. Was there any reason on earth to save the photos? She just didn't know. She certainly wasn't going to look through them; he had to have taken hundreds of pictures. *Just burn them.*

Locking the front door, she turned around and saw the fire pit through the glass sliders that led to the veranda. The motorized canvas roof had been pulled over, so at least it was dry there. She put a jacket on and went out to fire up the pit. Once it was going, she went back into the kitchen and unlocked the pantry door. She turned her eyes away from the photos, suddenly frightened of them, of the knowledge they would force her to have. They needed to be burned as fast as possible. She felt urgent enough about it now, and hoped that someone like Jeff Babcock wouldn't wander over. The weather would work in her favor. She carried one bundle of photos at a time, turning the image upside down. Tearing them in half to facilitate their destruction, she burned each one until it was gone; fine ash that would blow away in the wind. Finally, the task was completed.

Going out to the garage to go through his tools took a few more minutes, but she wanted to make sure nothing else was there that might mortify her children if they happened across it. It seemed that any locked vessel was a potential problem. She took the lone desk drawer with her, as well. She would toss it out on the next trash day. She thought of the apartment in Manhattan. *Why hadn't he stashed his photos there? Why keep them in the house?* She remembered her shock the first time she went into the apartment after Jack's death. The total lack of him there. *Or why not store the photos in his desk at work?* She thought maybe he wanted her to see them. Wanted her to get the full brunt of it. Seeing them ensured that she would get over his death swiftly, not hesitate to move on. They were worse than the AIDS diagnosis. She truly didn't know him at all.

She looked around the garage and decided there was nothing else she could do out there. She had allowed his clothing to sit in the closet because she thought Brent or Lisa might want something of their father's. She'd wait a few more weeks until Thanksgiving, but that was the deadline. After that, his stuff would be out of there.

Dave's visit had been a fine diversion for her. She was looking forward to seeing him again. If a relationship developed, she'd keep it low key so health-related issues wouldn't have to be discussed right away. If he started reaching for her hand, or kissing her, she'd tell him then. Or maybe that wasn't fair. Maybe she should tell him right away, explain why Marion and Jean's treatment of her was so upsetting. Then he could decide if he really wanted to see her again. That settled it. She would tell him the next time they were together, if he called her.

What a hell of a start to the weekend it had been so far. She thought of Sandra. A pang of sadness passed over her for the little baby, the little sibling of her own children. She hoped Sandra wasn't alone, that her friend, Tom, was with her. As tragic as the loss of the baby was, it would make life between the two of them a little easier. It just didn't make any sense why it happened, but she felt certain that Sandra would get through it.

She went in to pour herself yet another cup of coffee; it had to have been her sixth that day. She took a pastry Dave brought and the coffee and went back to the den to gaze out the window. When she was finished, she'd putter for a while and then go to the gym. It would continue to be her way of life. Peaceful, simple, empty.

38

Sandra didn't want Tom to pull the cruiser around to pick her up at the door. They would walk out together. He had one arm around her shoulder and with the other, held an umbrella over them.

"Can we go to my apartment to pick up some things? I still want to go to Brooklyn, if you are okay with it." She looked down at the ground as they walked.

"Yes, I want that," Tom said. Sandra couldn't bear the thought of having to be in the apartment. She made a split-second, spur-of-the-moment decision.

"Can I move in with you?" she asked, trying in vain to keep the desperation out of her voice.

He turned to look at her. "Yes, I want that," he repeated. They laughed. That she could laugh despite the way she felt gave her reason to add one more item to her pro list for Tom Adams; he made her happy.

Steve Marks tiptoed into his bedroom with a cup of coffee for Marie. She opened her eyes as he brought it around to her side of the bed.

"Good morning, sleepy head. How about some coffee?" He sat down on the edge of the bed. Marie rolled over from her stomach to her side and looked up at him.

"How'd I make it this far in life without you? Can you tell me?" She struggled to sit up, the sheets wrapped around her body. She took the coffee from him and took a sip. "Oh, this is good. Coffee brought to me. I smell bacon cooking. A great-looking guy in bed with me. It doesn't get better than this." She looked at him as she drank the coffee and saw the smile.

"You did okay without me. I hope you like it better with me, though," he said.

"Yeah, well there is a lot you don't know. I didn't do okay without you; I can tell you that right off the bat." She looked around the room, at its simple, clean decorating. "Did you fix up this apartment yourself?" she asked.

"Yes, why? Too froufrou for you?"

"No, not at all. It has personality. My place, as you have seen, has none. My sister's is 'decorated,' but devoid of any personality. My mother's is even worse. When we cleaned out her house, we didn't save one stick of furniture. There was no art, no mementos. Nelda wasn't a saver, that's for sure. Pam let her bring her old bedroom furniture so she'd know where she was, but the rest of it was worn-out junk that was junk when it was new."

"Your apartment just looks like you weren't planning on staying long. How long have you been there, anyway?" Steve asked.

"I moved into the building almost twenty years ago but I've been in that apartment for eight. It still feels like I'm not staying long. Oops!" Marie said, laughing. "Guess I blew that one!"

"Do you want to talk about it? About him?" Steve asked gently.

"Not really. No. In the first place, I don't know you well enough. We've already made some big mistakes. For one thing, if this backfires—if we don't make it—how are we going to deal with each other at work? I've been there since college so it's not me who's going anywhere," Marie exclaimed. She knew she was making excuses, changing the subject. How could she tell Steve about Jack? No one would understand and she didn't feel like being put in the position of defending him. It was bad enough that Steve knew someone had given her AIDS without revealing the family connection.

"How'd you know about him?" she asked. "I've never mentioned his name at work and that is the only place you know me from, correct?"

"The story in the office is that your brother-in-law bought your apartment for you. I guess I made an assumption. If I was wrong, I'm sorry," Steve said contritely. Marie sat up in bed, wrapping the sheet tightly around her chest.

"But how'd you know about him and...he and I?" she asked. "No one knew, no one ever even suspected it, as far as I know; not even my sister and we were together right under her nose."

Steve got up from the edge of the bed and went to his desk, opening a small, hidden drawer and taking out a pack of cigarettes.

"Want one?" he asked, knowing that he shouldn't be enabling bad behavior. She nodded and reached out for a cigarette. The act of lighting up and trying not to faint with the first drag took another a few minutes while she processed what Steve had just said to her. He figured it out. How many others had and never said anything?

"I mean, come on, Marie, it's not rocket science. He bought your apartment, your car, and got you this job, and you don't seem to have dated at all. Did you really think you could work somewhere for twenty years and not have your co-workers make observations?" Steve laughed. "You're smarter than that. You didn't *want* anyone to find out, so you just pretended that what was happening was in secret." He sat back down on the bed, hoping he wasn't making her angry.

"What all of this boils down to for me, right this very second, is that I don't want you to know all of the garbage in my life yet. It's not fair. What's the point of us being together now?" Marie said, distraught. "I can't make a good impression on you because you know that I slept with my sister's husband. You know all there is to know about me. Not only do I have AIDS, but I am an adulterer of the worst kind. I betrayed my own sister. I was hoping you could find out something good about me before I had to unveil all the seamy crap."

To her surprise, Steve laughed.

"You are as fresh as the driven snow compared to me. No worries, okay? I am not going to unveil my skeletons yet because some of them are still waiting for *me* to discover them. I don't want you involved, if possible. I wasn't going to say this yet, but the truth is, I love you, Marie. I love you like a man loves a woman he wants to marry, who he'd like to be there in his bed when he wakes up each morning. It's a little early to talk love, I know. But I am getting older by the second and have nothing to lose but you." Steve smiled his disarming smile at her and managed to pull off looking sincere.

"Are you drunk?" Marie asked.

"Jeez! I pour my heart out to you and you accuse me of being drunk? You are a bitch," he said, swatting her on the thigh. "Get up and get some clothes on; breakfast is ready."

Marie snickered. They had narrowly missed what could have been maudlin and therefore regretful.

"Get out then, will you please? I'd like to get dressed without an audience. If this is the amount of privacy I will get here, I'm going back to my own apartment," Marie said.

Steve got up off the bed and left to set the table. He held his breath until the door was closed after him, choking down a sigh of relief. He had wanted her to know how he felt, that he would risk his heart for her. He was mildly angry with himself for allowing it to happen. He wasn't in a position to take care of anyone else, barely being able to do it for himself. Afraid he was being carried along on a wave and had no control over what was happening to him, Steve decided to just let destiny guide him. It had already proved to be better than what he had been able to achieve by himself.

39
Ashton

This week was not to be believed. If it could go wrong, it did. I am lonely, miserable, tired. Finally, I've come to the conclusion that I am too old to have a serious relationship, but my testosterone level is too low to have a fling. The interest just isn't there. Am I the only man in New York who doesn't take sexual performance-enhancing drugs? Ugh! If I'm not in the mood, I'm not in the mood, for God's sake, and a hard-on isn't going to make it happen for me.

I miss Jack so much. The void his absence has made is impossible to fill. I don't care how busy I am at work, or how many parties I go to or have here, I just am unable to shake off the emptiness. My mother reminded me yesterday that he has only been gone for five months. The pain is still intense. Does that ever lessen?

I'd made the decision to contact his wife, Pam. Melissa told me that Pam knew some of the players; she should know about me. Not just for the truth of it, but because I need her. I need someone who knew all about Jack, who can commiserate with me about missing that certain flare he had. I end up comparing every date I've had with Jack. No one ever measures up! It's not fair that I do it, but it's inevitable.

I wondered if she did the same thing. So I called her. Thinking that just going to her door out of the blue would be unkind, I picked up the phone. She answered on the second ring, a soft "Hello."

"Mrs. Smith," I said, "You probably don't remember me, although we danced together at your wedding. I'm Ashton Hageman. Jack and I were childhood friends." There was silence on the other end of the phone. "I attended the funeral, but didn't get to talk to you that day." The truth was that she wouldn't even make eye contact, let alone acknowledge me. I wonder if she knew all along. I waited, the silence uncomfortable, but if she wanted to drag it out, I could drag it out, too.

"What can I do for you, Mr. Hageman?"

Oh Lord, she was playing my game! I'm telling you, I am a male Pam.

"Nothing. I am just calling because I miss Jack and thought that maybe you and I could share some stories. That's all. I know you know about him. There is nothing to hide anymore. I don't want to hurt you. But I was willing to risk it to connect." I barely got the word out before my voice broke. I don't think she noticed. She didn't say anything more and at the count of ten, I was going to say good-bye and hang up. Then she spoke.

"Yes, another surprise. Jack had a childhood friend whom I don't remember. How is that possible? Were you in touch throughout his life or did you lose contact?" Her voice was neutral. I didn't know Pam, had never spoken with her because Jack forbade it, but I do remember him saying she was as cool as a cucumber and you could never tell her mood by talking to her over the phone. He said that in person, Pam was just as unsettling; she would have her poker face on so he never knew if she was on to him or not.

"No, we didn't lose contact. Right about now, I wish we had. Maybe it would be easier then, having lost him." I wanted her to fish; I willed her to ask me the big question. Were we lovers?

"I doubt it. I doubt it would be easier. If Jack was in your life, you are going to suffer one way or the other," she replied. Was there the tiniest note of bitterness? I couldn't tell. "Oh, what the hell," she finally said. "Do you want to meet me? Why are you calling now? Why not five months ago?"

My heart was thumping in my chest. "I wanted the dust to settle. I heard you met Sandra and I didn't want to interfere. She didn't know about me, but I knew about her." I waited for her response, holding my breath. She ignored the hint.

"If you want to come here, to Babylon, you can. I am not going into the city for one of Jack's 'friend's' again. I'll be home all day today and for the rest of the weekend."

The ball was in my court. I seldom left the city for any reason. Jack's funeral was the first time I'd left Manhattan in years. But to see Pam, I would brave the wilds.

"I can come this afternoon. Thank you, thank you very much."

We said good-bye and I hung up. I called a car to come around and get me at one. It would give her a chance to recover from our chat and to decide for sure if she wanted to see me. I called her back to tell her when I'd arrive and the answering machine picked up.

I spent a half an hour primping for my audience with Pamela Smith. Jack said that she never was without makeup and proper clothing, no matter the time of day. He could pop in without warning and she would be ready to go out. I'm the same way. Very rarely, I will wear gym clothes if I feel like cleaning the house myself, but that is unusual. For this visit, I spent extra care on my hair. I wore Marc Jacobs. Would she notice? I'd heard that even her athletic suits were designer.

The ride wasn't bad. I was surprised, as I always am when I go to Long Island, by the horrible slums you have to go through to get there. You'd think the governor would do something about it. Jack used to say that as long as there were people starving in the world, he couldn't really enjoy eating. He said it was one of the ways he kept his weight down, which was always an issue with him. His brother was on the chubby side. I knew their dad was a stickler about their fitness and hygiene. The first thing Jack had to do when he came in from school every day was shower. I'd been at their dinner table enough times when Mr. Smith asked the boys if they had showered. I thought it was very strange. My dad never cared if I smelled, but my mother, she didn't miss a trick. I think old lady Smith was too drunk to notice if her boys were dressed properly or went to the dentist or bathed. The dad oversaw that.

When the car pulled up to the front of Jack's house, I couldn't control the tears from coming. So this is where he lived. I could see him there. It was quaint, for lack of a better word. When I finally got out, Pam had opened the door and was waiting for me. The illusion of the small cottage was immediately forgotten when I saw her diminutive frame standing in the vast doorway. The "cottage" was huge.

I walked down the slate path that narrowed to the door. I wasn't absolutely sure, but I thought I detected a slight pink around her eyes and nose. Had she been crying? I couldn't help myself; I grabbed her and she returned the grab and we embraced and were both crying up a storm. I felt like, finally, someone else who had loved the man. She was clearly brokenhearted, however. She took me by the hand, led me through the door, reached around me to close it, and then locked it. The gesture was protective and gentle at the same time, as though she wanted me to be safe in her house.

"Come with me," she said. She led me through a dramatic entryway with a high, vaulted ceiling. Straight ahead, I saw the water. Jack had told me about this, I remembered. He always went right to that view when he arrived home each weekend. I imagined him pushing the sliding doors aside and walking through the opening as we were doing. Pam had lit a fire in a large, circular fire pit, so it was warm and cozy in what was an outdoor space, open to the sea and the elements. "I wanted you to see this, to feel what Jack did when he was home. If it gets too cold, we will go inside. Here is an afghan from our bedroom; it's one he often covered up with when he was sitting here, reading, and looking out over the water." She carefully laid the blanket over my shoulders.

I couldn't help myself; the tears kept coming. She had recovered but was continuing the narrative about Jack.

"I believed he loved being out here. We sat here every Friday night for the past, oh, at least twenty years. We'd have cocktails and then I would prepare dinner for him while he showered. Now I realize that he must have been bored to tears. But at the time, I thought he lived for those moments together, as I had." She looked at me, pleading for my understanding. "I based my life on a lie. What I believed to be true didn't exist. Do you understand the impact that would have on a person?" She looked carefully at me. I thought I saw recognition in her eyes. "Oh! Boy, I am really thick! You were his lover, weren't you? I mean one of his many lovers."

She began to laugh. "I never would have guessed it in a million years if it weren't for my wonderful brother-in-law Bill, who told Jack's girlfriend, Sandra, that he and Jack were lovers. Announced that fact to a woman, who, for all intents and purposes, was a complete stranger. Sandra lost the baby, did you know that?"

I was shocked. For a moment, I thought that Pam might be just saying that. But then, it wasn't like Pam. She wouldn't stoop to that for effect, would she?

"No. I didn't know that," I said. I felt sick.

"But you knew she was pregnant."

"No! I didn't know. I don't believe it," I cried. "How convenient that she lost it! And I didn't know about his brother. I don't believe that, either!" I put my head in my hands. Pam left the room and came back shortly with a tray. She had prepared coffee and cake for us. She patted me on the shoulder as she walked around to her seat. I suddenly realized what she had just told me: Jack was going to be a father. Did he know it? I found it difficult to believe. But I didn't want to upset her by questioning her. She poured coffee and set a cup in front of me. She pointed to the sugar and cream and I shook my head. "Did he know?" I snorted, trying to hold back the tears.

"I don't know. I don't think so. She claims she found out the week after he died," Pam said quietly. "Truthfully, it is so low on my priority list that I haven't thought of it in a while, except for how I was going to avoid having our children find out about it. Of course, that isn't an issue now." She crossed her legs and held her coffee cup in her hands, blowing across the surface.

She gazed out at the ocean and the wild waves crashing on the shore and then she turned to me. "You were in love with him, that's clear to me. Was he in love with you?" The look on her face told me that it would be one more thing to add to her list of Jack's misdeeds.

"I've been in love with him since I was a kid. He said he loved me. But he wanted a wife and family. He wanted a normal life." When I said it aloud, knowing that she was aware of the truth about it him, it sounded trite. I was sorry to be the one to repeat it. "I know he was crazy. He was truly crazy. He had to be. But it was what made him Jack." I looked over at her and she was smirking, a strangely beautiful twist to her mouth. And then she laughed.

"No offense, Ashton, but you are so full of shit. Thank you for making excuses for him." She turned from me and looked out to sea again. "It's what I have been doing most of my life."

We didn't say anything again for a while, but it wasn't awkward. "I feel as though I have known you for a very long time. How is that possible? It must be because we are somewhat alike, you and I." She looked at me again. "I'm sorry we weren't friends, Ashton Hageman."

We sat in silence for a while longer, looking at the water, and then I began talking about Jack and me when we were kids, a time that wouldn't have affected her, so I did not think I was being disrespectful. She asked me questions about Jack's father that I answered truthfully, but I felt like she might have been fishing for more. I was honest with her and didn't hold anything back.

Weekend traffic into the city would be starting soon, but I wasn't worried about it until I looked closely at her. I could see she was getting tired. It occurred to me that she might not be well, but I certainly didn't ask and she didn't share that information with me. Having lived with him for thirty years, she had to be infected. We stood up and she walked me to the front door.

"Good-bye, Ashton Hageman. Thank you for coming to see me today." She leaned in and embraced me and I returned the hug. I wanted to see her again soon, and told her so. As I was walking toward the car, she called out to me. "Ashton, be well."

I waved to her and she waved back to me. She had a kind look on her face, but I knew when she spoke my name that I would never see her again.